A DAUGHTER'S DUTY

SAMANTHA GROSSER

SAM GROSSER
BOOKS

A DAUGHTER'S DUTY

For Steve, the very best of romantic heroes.

CHAPTER 1

The news came unexpectedly, on an apparently ordinary day. Susannah was breakfasting with her family in the hall before a warm fire in the hearth, and the younger Archer sisters were bickering as always. She was laughing at something her father had said when her mother's voice cut across the chatter.

"Susannah. Your father and I have decided you're going out to live with your aunt as her lady's maid at Hafton Hall."

Silence billowed around the table, and even the smallest daughter stopped eating and looked up from her plate. It was like her mother to blurt out such news, never one to coat anything in sugar. She saw her father wince at the bluntness.

The words took her breath away, unlooked for, and unwelcome. A thread of panic thrilled through her blood – she would have to leave Abbey Leigh, her family, her home.

"I am?" she managed to murmur in reply, turning her eyes to her father for an explanation, hoping for more kindness from him than her mother.

"Indeed." He nodded. "To your Aunt Elizabeth."

"Aunt Elizabeth?" the youngest sister, Charity, breathed. "Isn't she married to a lord?"

"She's married to a viscount. She has a great house in Somerset and is in need of a new lady to wait on her."

"What happened to her old one?" Charity asked.

Susannah caught her father's eye and saw the smile behind them. Lifting her hand to her mouth, she covered her own answering smile. Without her mother to keep order, they would have made up some outrageous end for the previous maid; a long lurid tale that would have had the younger girls on the edge of their seats, wide-eyed and breathless, but her mother's presence and the news she had just delivered forbade such levity, and so they held their tongues.

"She got married."

"Lucky her," the next sister, Olivia, sighed.

"Hush!" Susannah tapped her arm in rebuke. Then, turning again to her father, "Can you tell me any more?"

Her father lifted his eyes briefly to his wife, who nodded her agreement. Then he said, "Your Aunt Elizabeth is my older sister. She is many years my senior and was married when I was still but a boy. My father, that is *your* grandfather, settled a large portion of his wealth on her so that she might marry Lord Hafton."

"Is that all one needs to marry a lord?" Charity said, turning to her father. "Can you settle a large portion on me? Can I marry a lord? Please?"

"Perhaps, my love," her father said, with an indulgent smile. "When the time comes."

"Father?" Susannah turned to her father again. "Perhaps we could talk in your study when we have done taking breakfast?"

"Yes, of course."

"He's going to be very handsome ..." Charity was saying. "And ride a big black horse ..."

"That's quite enough of that, Charity," her mother chided, and Susannah flashed her father a smile.

In Master Archer's office, she sat on one side of the great oak desk that was strewn with papers. It was a comfortable room, dimly lit by the fire that spat and crackled in the hearth. Large oak chests stood about the walls, holding the papers of a hundred years of history. She had loved to peer inside as a child, fascinated by the age of the documents written by hands that were long since dead, their seals dating back to the first Tudor king. Now, her mind was on other things. She made herself comfortable in the hard wooden chair, arranging her skirts as her father took his place across from her. Rolled documents, held with ribbons and sealing wax, tumbled in piles over the great desk that stood between them, and in the centre lay the great ledger that told the story of all the affairs of the estate.

Her father leaned forward on his elbows, looking into her as he had always done.

"I am sorry for the way your mother chose to tell you," he began. "I had planned to tell you myself, and perhaps in a more gentle fashion."

She smiled. "I am used to her ways, sir," she replied. "Though that was especially blunt, even for her."

Her father returned the smile, good natured wrinkles creasing the ageing face, eyes still clear and bright. "We both know she'll never change, but she is a good and honest woman, and has ever been a good wife and mother."

Susannah had never heard her father say a bad word against anyone. She said, "A good wife who has given you four daughters that are the bane of your life."

"I would not be without a single one of you."

"You are very kind. But I'm sure in the deepest hours of the night you must wish that one or two of us had been boys?"

He smiled. "Well, perhaps, one or two."

She let the moment rest a while, enjoying the shared sense of humour while she still could. She would miss these conversations with her father – of all his daughters she was sure he would have wished for her most of all to be a boy, for they shared the same outlook on life, and she was quick and eager to learn. She would have made a good son to him, and an able heir for the estate: Abbey Leigh would have been safe in her hands. But God had chosen to make her a girl and on her father's death the estate would pass to her husband; another man's son, another man's bloodline.

She felt her father's eyes upon her and saw the sadness they contained. He had let his forefathers down. She had seen that look many times before and had long ago vowed to do her duty. She would marry without question whatever man her father chose for her; honouring his choice of heir was her only way to atone for being born the wrong sex.

"Why must I go?"

"The Haftons are a great family with connections at Court – it is a chance for advancement, and perhaps a marriage. Do you see?"

Reluctantly, she nodded. She had no desire to advance in the world, utterly content with her present lot at Abbey Leigh. Letting the mention of marriage slide to the back of her thoughts, and to mask her feelings, she brought the conversation once more to business. "When must I be ready to leave?"

"On Friday."

"But that's only a few days away. Why so soon?"

"Your aunt is sending servants to collect you – it is a two-day ride from here."

Susannah nodded, swallowing down the rising sense of panic. She had thought she would have more time to prepare herself, more time to become accustomed to the idea. But perhaps it was better this way, she decided, with no time for misgivings or regrets. She squeezed her hands against each other in her lap, and set her shoulders.

"Then I must go and make myself ready," she said, and stood abruptly, needing movement to distract her from her emotions. Dropping a slight curtsey to her father, who nodded his head in return, she hurried across the room, her slippered feet silent on the woven rush mats, hands held tightly together in front of her, as if her poise was contained between them. She would not have her father know how upset she really was. At the door, she turned back towards him. He sat with his head lowered, face resting in his hands, shoulders hunched, grey hair thin now across his pate. When had he got so old? she wondered. And why had she never noticed before?

"I will miss you, father," she said.

Startled by her words, he lifted his head and gazed at her a moment before he spoke. "And I will miss you too, Susannah. I surely shall."

She forced a sad little smile, then she slipped out of the door and upstairs to begin packing her belongings.

CHAPTER 2

The ride was beautiful. Long spring days and a warm sun, the season's gifts abundant in the May-trees that were white with flowers among the hedgerows. It was Susannah's favourite time of year, filled with the promise of new beginnings. But as the road led them further from her beloved home, the countryside became less familiar, and she was reminded more often of the purpose of the ride.

For the most part she rode beside the man her aunt had sent to escort her – Francis Aston, Lord Hafton's Gentleman of the Horse. He looked very fine in the deep blue livery doublet that was the uniform of his master, and his face bore an open ruddy countenance. The ruddiness came, she suspected, from a life spent chiefly outdoors, but the openness seemed to come from a gentle honesty of character.

"How long have you served with the Haftons?" she asked when Abbey Leigh was far enough behind her that she could find the strength to set her mind towards the future.

He turned his blue eyes towards her. "Since I was a boy, madam."

"And have you been happy there?"

He looked back towards the road. "I have no complaints."

"Tell me about the family," she asked. She was consumed with curiosity: her father had been able to tell her very little of his sister's life as a viscount's wife, so her imagination had filled the gaps and her new life at Hafton Hall was hard to picture. A smile played about Aston's lips as though he might dismiss her question, but after a moment of thought he turned towards her again.

"Lord Hafton is hard but fair. I doubt you will see him often – the estate takes up much of his time, and for the rest he is seldom indoors, preferring to hunt or hawk or ride as the impulse takes him. And Lady Hafton ..."

"What manner of woman is she?"

"Like her husband – strict but fair, I believe. The house seems to run well under her direction, though it is a quiet life. They seldom entertain, seldom go to Court."

She nodded, encouraging him to say more, and he obliged: it was in his nature to be willing to please.

"Their children, Edward and Eleanor, are about your age, or perhaps a little older. Edward goes to London sometimes, to Court, to see and be seen with other nobles' sons, to make his face known amongst those that hold power in the land. I suspect when he becomes viscount, he'll spend less time in Hafton than his father does, and that he'll want to make his life at Court."

She was fascinated, the world before her opening up, and she wondered if Edward might be the marriage her father had mentioned. "He is ambitious then?"

"Undoubtedly."

She nodded, storing away all he had told her, ready to make her own judgements in due course. But it was a relief to know she was unlikely to go to Court. The thought of it held nothing to attract her. A place where young and pretty girls like herself made progress by alliances or fell away by befriending poorly, it was not a world she sought to belong to, preferring the less whimsical challenge of running a country estate – practical problems to solve and relationships that were born from work done together and shared hopes for success. She had been her parents' willing pupil for as long as she could remember, as adept at helping her father as at running her mother's household.

They travelled mostly in comfortable silence after that,

exchanging odd comments now and then, pointing out landmarks or passing remarks on the landscape. Aston proved an easy companion, and she found the quietness suited her mood, listening to the thud of the horses' hooves on the road and the songs of the blackbirds and chaffinches, whose cheerful calling gave a music to her journey.

They came to Hafton Valley in the mid-afternoon of the second day, the sun still high and bright in a cloudless sky. It boded well, she thought, that the journey had been so pleasant, and as they passed through the village, she turned to her companion.

"I'd like to stop at the church, if I may."

He smiled, nodding in reply, and at the lych-gate to the church, he drew up his horse and took the reins of her mare as she slid lightly from the saddle.

"I shan't be long," she said. Then, stepping lightly through the gate, she trod along the path, pushed open the heavy oak door and stepped into the coolness of the church. Once inside, she stood by the door for a moment, breathing deeply to steady the nerves that were rising with the nearness of her journey's end. When she'd regained her calm, she wandered along the nave towards the chancel, looking around her. It was a pretty church, small but well kept, with ancient stained glass in the windows that cast a kaleidoscope of colour across the flagstones in the chancel. A heavy bible lay open on a table near the steps, and though she had come in to pray for strength in her new life, she found herself drawn to look over to its pages. The page was open at the Psalms, and running a finger lightly over the words, automatically she began to read, her voice carrying clear and sweet in the hush.

"Trust in the LORD, and do good … and he shall give thee the desires of thine heart …"

A sudden movement in the nave caught her eye and she stopped abruptly, her former nerves returning in the quickness of her pulse, eyes searching till they lit on the figure whose movement had so startled her. A man's form was standing in the shadows by the door, and in the dim light of the church she could make out barely more than his shape. She watched, waiting to see what he would do, senses keen and wary.

The man moved closer, into the light, and she saw straight away that he was a gentleman, dressed for the road in dark wool breeches and riding boots with spurs that carried the marks of many miles. A frayed and mud-spattered travelling cloak was tossed carelessly back across his shoulders.

"You read very well," he said. His tone carried a hint of surprise, but his voice was soft and low. "Who taught you?" he asked.

"My father," she answered. "He taught me many things."

Looking up at her from beneath dark brows, his lips curved into a smile. Brown eyes flickered with a glint of humour, but it seemed to Susannah that there was a hardness in them also, an intensity that shadowed a private pain. He was older than her by ten years or more, and the gauntness of his cheeks spoke of a weariness that went beyond a few hard days on the road. His beard was fashionably short, but the rest of his face was unshaven too, lending his skin a dark and handsome roughness. A recent narrow scar cut vividly across the corner of his lower lip, leading down through the beard on his chin. But the smile that touched his mouth lit his eyes also and was infectious. She found herself returning it.

"Forgive me," he said then. "I should have introduced myself. Daniel Gifford, at your service." He bowed lightly, and she curtseyed in return.

"Susannah Archer," she replied, but when she rose, she was less eager to meet his eyes than before, disconcerted by unfamiliar feelings his smile had begun to stir in her. A slight sense of unease rippled through her body: she had never been afraid to meet a man's eyes before, and the realisation brought a heat to her skin, warmth flushing across the whiteness of her neck. She forced herself to breathe slowly and prayed he would not notice.

There was a moment of silence. He paused, and in the silence, she forced her eyes back to his, unwilling to let the feelings beat her. He was still watching her, the smile still playing at the corners of his mouth until, finally, he slid his eyes away from hers and the charge that ran between them ebbed a little. Her breathing slowed and she felt the flush retreat from her skin.

Gifford broke the silence. "So, madam, may I ask what brings you to Hafton?"

She was grateful for the ordinariness of the question, a mundane conversation to cover her agitation, but still it took time to find her voice. She said, "I was on my way to Hafton Hall and I saw the church …" She faltered. Her voice sounded loud in the church's hush, and her words seemed to stumble over one another. He smiled and picked up the sentence where she had dropped it.

"And you came in to pray before your journey's end."

"Yes. That is exactly so." She met his eyes again, relieved he seemed to understand her so well. The smile in his gaze had faded, replaced by something else she could not name, but its intensity disturbed her, and she looked away and down at her hand as it smoothed against the pages of the bible. She could still sense his scrutiny and she felt exposed beneath it. Heat and colour threatened to rise again, and she drew herself up, tautened her body against such treachery.

She forced herself to face him. "You have travelled a long way, sir?"

"Aye. From the Netherlands," he replied.

She looked up sharply. "You were in the war against the Spanish?"

He nodded, and her gaze passed across his face to light on the scar that sliced his lip and chin. He ran his tongue across his lower lip and over the wound, as if he were self-conscious of it.

"You were hurt," she said softly.

"It was nothing but a scratch," he replied, which she could see for herself was a lie.

"I'm glad," she murmured. But her eyes slid across him, wondering if his body bore other scars, if he were hiding other hurts.

He said, "Will you be staying long at the Hall, madam?"

"Indeed. I will be living there. I am come to wait upon Lady Hafton," she replied.

He smiled, making no attempt to hide his pleasure at the news. "Then no doubt we shall meet again."

"I hope so," she heard herself saying.

He laughed. "As do I, Miss Archer," he replied. "As do I." Then he bid her good day and took his leave with a practised bow, turning away from her to go back the way he had come. She watched him walk away, observing the decisive stride along the aisle, the mud-spattered cloak swinging with each step until he reached the door and disappeared.

When the door had scraped shut behind him, she closed her eyes in mortification, the heat of embarrassment blooming on her neck, across her cheeks. She fanned herself with a hand. *I hope so?* Dear God in Heaven! What on earth had she been thinking to say such a thing? She stood for a moment, shaking her head in a vain effort to rid herself of the sense of shame. Whatever must he think of her now?

She took a deep breath. And another, trying to calm herself, to retrieve the sense of rightness and of pleasure that had brought her into the church in the first place. But it had left her and instead she felt only the loneliness of leaving her family behind.

Her eyes fell to the open page of the bible by her hand. "Trust in the LORD," she repeated to herself. "And do good." So saying, she gathered her skirts, took her resolve in hand, and stepped briskly out to where Aston stood waiting with the horses, looking bored.

CHAPTER 3

They came upon Hafton Hall from the ridge of a wide shallow valley that swept away before them, the house at the foot of the opposite bank. The hall was even bigger than she'd imagined; a great sprawling manor in light-coloured stone set amid vast rolling acres of grass and woodland. Mullioned windows winked at the afternoon sun, peeping from behind a covering of ivy. It looked as though it would be a wonderful place for hide and seek, and she wished her sisters were with her to explore it.

Deer bounded away as Aston led the way across the parklands, their tufty tails bobbing in the darkening afternoon, and for a moment she forgot she had embarrassed herself in the church, delighted by the deers' shy elegance. She turned in her saddle to watch them go, and as she did so, she saw that clouds had begun to slide in from the east, light and gauzy now, but threatening to thicken, a greying blanket that would soon cover the brightness of the day. Then she thought of Daniel Gifford and the effect of his smile and hoped she would make a better impression on her aunt.

At the main entrance, a servant opened the great oak door. Aston remained outside on the path. "I must tend to the horses," he said, then bowed his farewell.

She thanked him and stood a moment to watch him go, his back growing smaller as he strode the length of the house away from her.

When he had turned the corner out of sight, she drew her attention back to the door before her. Casting a last quick glance behind her towards the darkening sky, she braced her shoulders, nodded to the servant that she was ready, and followed him into the gloom of the doorway.

Inside, the servant hurried away to find Lady Hafton, leaving her to wait in the vast and draughty entrance hall. She gazed about in awe, taking in the gently curving oak of the staircase that led to an upper floor, the ceiling beams high above her. Exquisite tapestries of medieval hunting scenes hung against the walls, and deer heads had been mounted at intervals as trophies. She felt dwarfed by the grandeur, and a rush of sadness for the modest manor house at Abbey Leigh threatened tears. Blinking them back and breathing deeply to steady herself, she trailed her gaze across the hall, searching for some distraction, until her eyes lit on a bible on a table near the base of the stairs; for guests and servants to use, she supposed. But the sight of it took her mind back to Master Gifford in the church, and a warmth suffused her skin at the memory. Had his smile been in pleasure at her words or had she simply made him laugh with her forwardness? It was impossible to say, and a sense of anger with herself served to chase away any nerves that were lingering. She vowed not to embarrass herself a second time, and to make a good impression from now on.

Footsteps on the wooden boards of the floor above drew her thoughts back to the present and she looked up as a statuesque woman in a gorgeous gown of deep amber silk began to descend the stairs. Her own wool dress, with its skirts that were dusty from the road, seemed positively drab in comparison. The full skirts shimmered as they moved in to the half-light of the hall, the golden embroidery on her kirtle flashing underneath, the same pattern adorning the velvet sleeves. Susannah had never seen such finery up close: at home they wore the finest quality wool, skilfully sewn, soft to the touch and pleasing to the eye, but nothing in comparison to the gown before her now. She thought of her own best gown packed away in her trunk, her favourite shades of blue in a rich brocade: until this moment it had seemed so fine, and her spirit dropped again. But she stopped herself from staring, eyes downcast, waiting instead until the woman almost reached the bottom step. Then she dropped into her deepest curtsey.

"Susannah." The lady approached and stood before her. "Welcome to Hafton Hall. I trust the journey was not too arduous?"

"It was very pleasant, my lady."

The lady laughed. "Get up, girl. Let me look at you. And you may call me Aunt Elizabeth."

Susannah rose and let herself be inspected while she stole fleeting glances at Lady Hafton, trying to gain her first impression. Her aunt was older than her father, by some years it seemed; deeper lines at the corners of her eyes and her lips, a furrow on her brow, but there was the same high forehead and the same long nose.

"Goodness, girl, but you look like your father did at your age."

"Many people have said I have his eyes, Aunt Elizabeth."

"I can see nothing of your mother, though."

"You have met my mother?" She was surprised; there had been little contact between the families since the success of her aunt's grand marriage. There had been no visits between them in her own lifetime that she knew of.

"Of course." Her aunt spoke as though such surprise were foolish. "Though it was many years ago now," she conceded. "You would have been just a babe in arms."

"I didn't know."

"I'm sure there is much you don't know, but we shall do our best to overcome it." She lifted her lips in a smile, but the eyes continued their assessment. Susannah gave a small respectful smile in return and wondered what her aunt's verdict would be.

"I hope I shall serve you well, Aunt Elizabeth."

"I'm sure you will. A willing heart is a good beginning." She looked around. "Now what has Aston done with your things?"

"I'm afraid I don't know, Aunt Elizabeth."

"Do you not? Well, I'm sure they will find their way upstairs in good time. Come, I'll show you to the ladies' quarters, where you'll spend most of your hours."

Susannah followed her new mistress up the stairs, her hand

brushing against the warm smooth wood of the banister, still gazing round her in awe of her new home. She was shown first to Lady Hafton's rooms, a suite that seemed to Susannah to occupy almost half the house, although she knew it could not be so. The main sitting room was an oak-panelled chamber with mullioned windows that looked south across the park she had so recently ridden across. A broad stone hearth took up most of one wall, colourful velvet cushions scattered invitingly before it, and a door beside the fireplace led off to a spacious chamber where a bed that was hung with red damask occupied the farthest wall. Her own narrow bed occupied a small inner chamber that lay between her aunt's room and that of Eleanor's.

Standing in the doorway, looking round at the linen presses, the fine oak chests that lined the walls, and the gorgeous hangings on the walls, she felt as though she had strayed into a different world. It was living quarters such as she imagined the ladies owned at Court – her own mother was far too down-to-earth to be bothered with such things: she shared a simple chamber and a bed with her husband. Susannah wondered if the Haftons had always slept apart.

With a pang of regret, she recalled the bedchamber at home she had shared with her sister, the big bed they had slept in and the childhood dolls propped up at one end. It had been a place of comfort and company, sisterly tears and laughter, a true home. In comparison, the inner chamber seemed like a desolate place to sleep.

She lifted her eyes to the window, her gaze following the fine view across the parkland as it swept southwards to the woods on the crest of the hill. Away to the east, Hafton village nestled in the valley, the tip of the church steeple just in sight above the trees. With the view of the church, a memory of the heat of her shame brushed over her and she shook it off, irritated with herself. She was not going to let one foolish comment to a man she barely knew ruin the beginning of a new life.

"Ah," her aunt said, as she directed her niece through the apartments. "Your things have been brought up already."

The sight of her trunk by the bed, lovingly packed with her mother's help in what seemed to have been another lifetime, fortified her spirit. A young maid appeared in the doorway with a large bowl of warm water, which she set atop one of the oaken chests with great and attentive care. Then she dropped a neat curtsey, her head lowered so that Susannah couldn't see her face.

"This is Lettice," her aunt said. "She has been with us a while, but I think she has the making of a lady's maid. She will share your room and assist you with everything you need. When you're ready, you will find us in the dining chamber for supper."

"Thank you, Aunt Elizabeth," Susannah said, lowering into a curtsey of her own as her aunt swished from the room and left her alone with the maid.

Lettice lifted her face and smiled, a ready open smile that promised friendship.

"Hello, Lettice," Susannah greeted her.

"Madam." Lettice nodded. Then, "Shall I help you undress?"

"Yes. Thank you." She let her new maid untie her sleeves and the outer skirts, the kirtle and the petticoats, the light bodice that hugged her torso, until she was down to the last linen shift. She washed her own face, scrubbing away the remnants of the day's journey with her fingers, but stood quietly to allow Lettice to wipe down her arms, legs, and her body with a cloth, and the girl's gentle touch was comforting.

Then together they dressed her in her favourite blue brocade gown. She turned to see herself in the glass when she was ready, and though she was aware it was but a poor dress compared to her aunt's, she knew that it became her.

"It's a pretty dress, madam." Lettice smiled, standing back to admire it. "You look very fine in it."

"Thank you." Susannah smiled. Then with one last touch of her fingers to her hair, a final glance in the glass, and a deep breath to steady herself, she said, "Time for supper, I believe."

~

The great hall was a high-ceilinged chamber that ran the length of the house. The hearth stood against the southern wall, with wide high windows either side, and oak panelling around them. Above the fireplace the Hafton coat-of-arms stood out in fresh bright paint, a knight's helmet above a shield that bore a white hart on one side of it, and a boar on the other. In the centre of the room a long banquet table held a line of fine silver candlesticks. But unlike Abbey Leigh, where the great hall still served both as dining hall and living chambers, at Hafton the family took their supper in a private dining parlour off to one side of it.

The usher knocked as Susannah smoothed her skirts and lifted her fingers to check her hair. Then, pushing open the doors, he announced her, and stood back to let her enter. She stepped inside and dropped into an immediate curtsey, head bowed, so that she had no idea of the room that lay before her, waiting for permission to rise.

"Come in, girl," Lady Hafton's voice came from the other side of the room. Susannah rose and moved forward, trying to take in the room without seeming to.

Though smaller than the great hall, it was still spacious. To her left, a low fire was burning against the cool of the April evening. The flames beckoned, warm and lively in a room that seemed to be otherwise cheerless. Curtains of a heavy red damask hung at windows too high to see out of, and a table with places set for five stood in the centre. Servants in the blue Hafton livery stood ready to serve supper by a sideboard, awaiting his lordship's command.

Beyond the fire, a young man and a woman of about her own age were seated at a small table, playing cards. She guessed they must be her cousins but neither interrupted their game at her entrance. She stepped forward as Lady Hafton rose from a stool at the edge of the hearth, laid her sewing aside, and came to greet her niece.

"Come in, Susannah," Lady Hafton said. "Come and meet your cousins."

She stepped across rugs that looked too fine to walk on and approached the fire as the card players got up from their game and turned to face her. They were obviously brother and sister, their colouring the same, and such a similarity of manner that she could have picked them from a crowd and known they were related. Both were tall and ash-blonde, big-boned and lean with strong, heavy features and deep-hooded eyes. Dressed richly in velvets and silks, they exuded an easy confidence. Handsome, her mother would have called them, and against them Susannah felt very small and unimpressive.

Lady Hafton motioned her son forward with an impatient twirl of her wrist, and he took an obedient step towards her. "This is my son, Edward. He is a little older than you, I believe." She turned to her son. "How old are you now, Edward? Twenty-four, is it? Twenty-five?"

Edward bit his lip to hide his irritation. "I am twenty-three, Mother."

"Susannah is eighteen, I believe. Is that correct?"

"Yes, Aunt Elizabeth."

Edward gave a small bow; as small, it seemed to her, as he could get away with without actually giving offence. His lips lifted in some semblance of a smile, but his overall expression was one of appraisal, such as he might use to look at a horse he was thinking to buy. Resentful of such a welcome, and missing her family more by the minute, she dropped her head as she curtseyed. *And perhaps a marriage,* she remembered her father saying, and her heart skipped a beat. She knew at once she would never want to be the wife of such a man.

"And this is my daughter, Eleanor."

Eleanor stepped out from her brother's side and took Susannah's hands in her own. "Cousin." She smiled. "I am glad to meet you at last. I hope we shall be great friends."

"It's my wish also," Susannah replied, encouraged, her cousin's hands warm around her own cold fingers.

"You're cold," Eleanor said, still holding her hands. "Come nearer to the fire and warm yourself. Do you play cards?"

"A little," Susannah replied, stretching out her hands towards the hearth. She had played only with her family and was uncertain of the standard expected in such a great house.

Her cousin took her hand again and drew her in towards the

table, ushering her to one of the stools before she resumed her own place opposite.

"We can play trumps if you like. Edward only likes betting games, but we shall be ladies and play for pleasure." She looked up at her brother, leaning now against the side of the hearth, looking bored. "Will you play, Ed?"

"No. You play. I'm sure you *ladies* will have more fun without me. I'll watch and adjudicate if it turns ugly."

Eleanor looked up from the deck of cards in her hand and spoke in a low voice. "Pay him no mind. He's just in a bad humour because his favourite horse went lame today and he had to lead her home." She turned to him. "How far did you say you had to walk, Ed? Three miles?"

"Thereabouts."

Eleanor giggled. "He hates walking. He thinks that a gentleman should always ride."

Edward scowled and shifted his attention away from them, gazing into the flickering embers.

"I like walking," Susannah said, to make conversation. "I used to walk often through the grounds at Abbey Leigh. It's very pretty there."

"There are good walks here at Hafton too," her cousin said. "There are tracks all over the estate. And the woods can be pleasant if you know where you're going, especially at this time of year, with all the bluebells coming out. But it's easy to lose your way in the trees so you should take someone with you the first few times until you're sure of your way."

"I shall. Thank you for the warning," she replied. "Perhaps we could walk together one day?"

"Perhaps." Eleanor nodded, but her interest seemed to have waned, turning instead to deal out the cards. They played trumps as Eleanor had suggested, and Susannah was relieved to find that she was good if not better at the game than her cousin, who laughed as she lost, and told her brother he had better watch out in the future or their cousin would fleece him.

They had just finished their game when a man Susannah assumed was Lord Hafton strode into the room. Grey-haired and bewhiskered, he was tall and rangy, power still latent in the sinewy limbs. He shared his children's hooded eyes and heavy features: in his youth he too would have been a handsome man.

"Damn foxes!" he exclaimed, pacing across the room to the fire, the presence of Susannah unnoticed. His face was florid with his anger and there was a steel in his eyes she would not like to cross. "Another one got into the chickens last night," he raged, "killed far more than it could eat. I've set men to watch with dogs tonight. And every night until we catch him. We'll see who's the sly one now."

No one answered him nor seemed to pay him any attention. But with his presence a tension descended. He stood at the fireplace warming himself while the others waited on his pleasure.

"William," Lady Hafton said after a while, her voice cutting through the hush. "Susannah is here."

"What?" He snapped his thoughts away from the fox, irritated by the interruption. His clear pale eyes narrowed as they slid to focus on his niece. "Oh," he said. "Susannah Archer, is it?"

"Yes, my Lord." She rose from the card table to curtsey and received a curt nod in return.

"Welcome to Hafton," he said, then he turned to one of the servants and signalled he was ready to sup.

The servant's voice rang down the room. "Gentlemen and yeoman, wait upon the carver for my Lord."

The door opened and more servants filed in as the family took their places at the table. Susannah sat beside Eleanor and opposite Edward, but he seemed to pay her no notice, his attention taken by the platters being delivered, examining each dish with care before assenting to be served from it.

She had never seen so much food at a family table. There was enough for a banquet, a choice of meat that bewildered her. Eleanor, noticing, guided her towards the trout pie and the capon in lemon sauce. Susannah smiled her thanks. The food was delicious, her appetite sharpened by the journey and the excitement of her surroundings. She took small sips of the wine from a pewter goblet, a claret that was heavier than she was used to.

There was little talk: Lord Hafton spoke briefly to his wife on matters Susannah knew nothing of, but it was a very different table from the lively conversations that attended meal times at Abbey Leigh, the only time the whole family came together, and all of them vying for Master Archer's attention.

"The meal is to your liking?" Lady Hafton enquired, watching her niece with attentive eyes. "A little different from the fare you're used to, no doubt?"

"It's wonderful," Susannah replied with a smile. She was starting to feel light-headed from the unaccustomed wine, but the sensation was not unwelcome, and she thought that perhaps she might be happy here after all.

After supper, the women retired to Aunt Elizabeth's chambers. Candles blazed through the room, and the last light of the evening beyond the windows offered hints of red behind the thickening clouds.

"Come sit close to me, child," her aunt commanded, so she sat on the floor amongst the rich cushions at Lady Hafton's feet as Eleanor sat close by. The waiting maids sat a little further off from the fire, their eyes lowered attentively to their needle-work, silent but observing all. Susannah would have preferred to sit with her cousin, but there was nothing she could do but obey.

Eleanor strummed idly at a lute on which she had little skill, but the simple tunes made a pleasant accompaniment to the evening. Susannah herself was given a linen shirt of Edward's to mend a tear in the seam on the sleeve. Though the light was poor by the fire, she plied her needle with care, aware her work would be scrutinised as her skills were appraised.

"You have some skill with a needle," her aunt said at last, when the seam was almost done. "Your mother has taught you well."

"Thank you, Aunt Elizabeth. My mother is a fine seamstress." An unexpected ripple of affection for her mother moved through her body, a new appreciation for her mother's many qualities.

"No doubt with four daughters she's had ample chance to practise."

Susannah smiled, though she felt the hurt of the implication. "Indeed."

"And what of your gowns?" She nodded towards Susannah's dress. "Is that your best?"

"Yes, Aunt Elizabeth. Do you not like it?"

"It may suffice at Abbey Leigh, but here at Hafton Hall we keep a higher standard. You will need to have new gowns made. I shall make arrangements for a trip to Bristol. There's a fine selection of fabric to be had there, and I've been recommended a seamstress I would like to try. In the meantime, we may alter some of Eleanor's to fit you – there's a girl in the village who is very good. I shall send someone to fetch her here in the morning."

"'Tis Sunday tomorrow," Eleanor said.

"So it is. Monday, then. Until then you will just have to make do." She stood up. "And now, you must be tired after your journey. We will all of us retire."

Eleanor stopped strumming her lute. "But it's still very early, Mother. Must we go to bed so soon?"

"Yes, we must." Aunt Elizabeth's answer was firm.

Sighing, Eleanor rose and bid her mother good night. Susannah laid her sewing aside, and stood also, taking a single candle and following her cousin from Lady Hafton's chamber into her own narrow room. The two girls embraced and wished each other good night. Then, exhausted by the excitement of the day, Susannah stood to let Lettice undress her, whispering lest she should disturb her aunt in the room next door. By the time the gown and all its pieces were neatly hung and stored away so that they would not crease overnight, she could barely keep her eyes open. Wishing Lettice a whispered good night, her prayers forgotten in her fatigue, she climbed into bed and watched as the maid drew out a pallet for her own bed and laid it on the floor beside her.

With the candle snuffed, Lettice's breathing came soft and regular through the darkness. Drifting towards her own repose, Susannah's mind travelled haphazardly over all the impressions of the day, and her last thought before she fell asleep was to wonder if Daniel Gifford would be at church in the morning.

CHAPTER 4

*S*he dreamed of nothing through the night, but she woke with Daniel Gifford's smile in her thoughts, and it was hard not to wonder more about him and if she would see him today. In the morning, the family rode to church together in the usual Sunday ritual. The servants walked on behind and, to her dismay, she found herself riding alongside Edward while Eleanor rode ahead beside her mother. She had hoped she might ask her cousin about Master Gifford – it wouldn't seem strange to enquire, she decided, about a gentleman she had met in the village. She could simply claim curiosity. After all, she was new to the area and it was natural to want to know about the inhabitants. But the chance was denied her, and instead she found herself in awkward conversation with Edward.

"How is your horse?" she enquired, to break a silence that was growing uneasy.

"As you see." He gestured to his mount, a spirited grey, which was restless at the slow pace of the ride. Her own bay mare tossed her head in sympathetic impatience.

"Your mare?"

"Oh, yesterday," he recollected. "The mare that went lame. She will recover, I think. Thankfully." He turned his head towards her, appraising again, but she chose not to look away, lifting her chin instead, challenging him to dislike what he saw. "Good. That's better." He smiled when he saw her reaction. "I like a woman with a bit of spirit. Like my horses. It makes the chase so much more interesting."

"The chase, cousin?"

He made no reply but turned in his saddle and appraised her once again. Returning his stare, she took time to assess him too. She had to admit he looked very fine on a horse: his large frame emanated a sense of power and he sat easily as the gelding chafed beneath him, fidgeting and eager. The rich riding cloak with its fur trim added elegance and her mother's word, handsome, came to mind again. He laughed, enjoying her inspection, aware she assumed, of the picture he presented. They rode on in silence and her thoughts turned on his words, senses prickling and wary, until at last they reached the church.

At the lych-gate, Edward swung himself with ease from the saddle of his horse, then raised his arms to lift her down. Trapped in the side-saddle, she could do nothing but accept, turning her face away from him as his big hands closed against her ribs, his body close before her as he slid her down. On the ground her face was level with his chest and she was grateful to avoid his eyes, but he held her there for several moments longer than he needed to, and she was aware of the rapid rise and fall of his chest and the smell of him, the musty scent of horses and hounds, the faint taint of wine.

"Thank you, cousin," she said and, as if her words had reminded him of where they stood, he stepped back and released her.

Servants came and led the horses away to tether them, and as she walked along the path towards the church, she flicked a quick glance round at others who were arriving, searching for the form of Daniel Gifford, but he was nowhere to be seen. Disappointed, she dropped her head and followed her cousin along the nave and into the Hafton family pew at the front.

Last in of the family, she took her seat at the end closest to the aisle, gazing ahead at the stained glass behind the altar, the colours brilliant now with the morning sun behind them. She had been sitting a full minute before she turned her head to look around her again, and noticed with a start that across the aisle, in the opposite pew, Daniel Gifford was observing her.

Heat lurched in her belly and she dropped her gaze, fighting to control a rising sense she had never known before. Her skin flushed warm and she touched a gloved hand to her cheek as though to feel the redness there. Almost against her will she turned her head again towards him. He was dressed differently today; a fine velvet doublet above green silk breeches, clean polished riding boots that gleamed, and new spurs glittering at his heels. His beard and hair had been trimmed and neatened and though he looked a far cry from the muddied weary traveller she had met yesterday, the same sadness lurked in the intensity of his eyes. He smiled at her and nodded a greeting.

"Miss Archer."

"Master Gifford." With an effort she swung her eyes away from him towards the vicar as the service began, but she paid no heed to anything that was said, aware only of Gifford's presence across the aisle. Twice she risked a glance in his direction and both times he met her eyes with a twinkle in his own that sent the heat jolting again through her body, nerves left tingling and exposed.

When the service was over, she slid hurriedly from the pew into the aisle, hoping to escape before he could rise – she was uncertain she would retain her composure if they were to meet in front of all these people, if she had to stand right before him and meet his gaze. But as she began to move away, she heard his name being spoken.

"Sir Daniel. Welcome back."

Sir Daniel? In spite of herself, she glanced towards him and was rewarded with the briefest moment of contact. Not a smile this time, but a meeting of eyes, an acknowledgement. Then his attention was turned to the vicar who had called him, and she filed out of the church with the rest of the congregation.

In the churchyard, Eleanor took her arm. "Did you see him?" Her cousin was animated, her face alive with delight.

"Did I see who?" she replied, though she had a dreadful premonition that she knew already.

"Sir Daniel Gifford. He was sitting next to you across the aisle. Did you see him?"

"I … I … think so," she managed to stammer, stalling for time to re-order her trembling emotions. "Who is he?"

"He owns the estate to the south of ours." Eleanor pointed vaguely southwards. Susannah followed the gesture with her eyes. Now she knew what lay beyond the woods she could see from her window, and the thought of his proximity threatened to send the heat across her skin once again. She took a deep breath and forced her attention back to her cousin.

"It's called Gifford Court," Eleanor was saying. "But he's very seldom there – he keeps a small staff only to run the estate in his absence. He's been away for years. I remember meeting him when I was little more than a child." She turned to Susannah and took her cousin's hands in her own. "And now he is back. How exciting!"

Susannah managed a smile and, disengaging one hand, she drew her cousin along the path. "And where has he been all this time?" she asked. Though she had heard the answer from his own lips just the previous day, she could think of nothing else to say.

"Across the narrow sea, fighting the Spanish in the Netherlands. A soldier of fortune, so they say. But he was gone so long we feared he was dead …" Eleanor loosed her hand from Susannah's and turned back to look at the church, eyes bright and hopeful, waiting for Gifford to emerge. Susannah's eyes followed her cousin's, but she hoped he would not come.

"He went to war after his wife passed away," Eleanor went on, obviously eager to talk of him. "They said he was inconsolable, that he went to war wishing to die."

"How could they know such a thing?" Susannah asked. How could anyone know such secrets about a man's heart?

"There were letters home from his comrades, men my father knew of. They said at Zutphen he should have died a hundred times over, that he was the most fearless reckless man on the battlefield. But it seems God had other plans for him. And now he's home, apparently without a scratch."

"Poor man," Susannah murmured. "To know such grief. He must have loved her very much."

"Perhaps. But he seems cheerful enough this morning, don't you think? Chatting away to the vicar. Perhaps time has healed the wounds. Let us hope so."

"Yes. Let us hope so indeed, for his sake," Susannah agreed. But she recalled the taint of sadness in his eyes that had hinted at a private darkness deep inside. Now she understood the meaning of that look, and all her nascent hopes were crushed. He had been toying with her merely, his heart still shadowed with his grief.

Swallowing, she took her cousin's hand again and they strolled towards the gate together. Aston helped her onto her horse as Edward stood talking with his sister, and she hung back as the others moved off in file so she wouldn't have to ride beside him again. A last glance back at the church brought a final glimpse of Sir Daniel, standing in the porch, still in deep conversation with the vicar. Sadly, she turned her head away from him, touched her heels to the horse's flank, and resolved to put all thought of Daniel Gifford from her mind.

CHAPTER 5

From the corner of his eye, Daniel watched her ride away. The vicar went on asking about poor relief, and he found himself agreeing to offer his support without really having listened to a word. But no matter, the vicar was a good man and the relief of the poor his duty as a gentleman, and eventually he bid the priest good day.

By the time he stood upon the road, the Hafton party was out of sight and most of the rest of the congregation had dispersed. His own small household he had sent on ahead without him, preferring to ride alone, thoughts unencumbered by company.

He mounted his horse and jogged through the village in the opposite direction from the Haftons. A few people bid him good day, smiles to welcome him back. He returned their greetings with a nod and a smile in return, but his mind was elsewhere, turning on thoughts of Susannah Archer. When he reached the outskirts of the village, the horse slowed of her own will to a walk but he barely noticed, absorbed in his reverie, wondering how he might contrive to be alone with her again, how he might find out more about her. If he closed his eyes, just briefly, he could imagine her right there with him now, her delicate frame, her tiny hands, the pale elfin face with the violet eyes that held no fear of him – even when he knew his presence had stirred new emotions; the bright flush of her passion giving her away.

I hope so, she had said; a single unguarded comment that offered him all the promise he could wish for.

The sudden flight of a magpie from the verge sent his horse skittering across the lane, scattering his thoughts. Responding to the animal's restlessness, he gathered the mare beneath him and, touching his heels to her sides, he loosened the reins and let her go. She needed no second telling, leaping forward, the lane a blur beneath her hooves. The wind whipped through his hair and sent his cloak flying out behind him as the great horse raced along the lane.

Like flying, he thought, free like the eagle where nothing could hurt him again. He urged her faster, losing himself in the movement and the power, all thought suspended. The lane curved round to the left but he held the mare straight, heading for the hedge, white now with blossom. She took it willingly, easily, a pair of startled sparrows darting up away from them before they landed in the parkland that belonged to his estate. Then he set her head towards the house and half closed his eyes against the rush of wind: the mare would take him home.

He came to himself as they clattered to a stop in the yard before the house. The horse was blowing hard, shaking her head in satisfaction at the run. She had served him faithfully in peace and war; they understood each other well. He leaned down and rubbed her neck affectionately before he slid to the ground. Under his feet the earth felt too solid after the flight, and when a groom failed to appear straight away, he flicked the mare's reins over her head and led her to the stables himself.

By the time the groom did appear, with straw in his hair, and rubbing sleepy eyes, the mare was already unsaddled, and Daniel had begun to rub her down himself. He dismissed the groom with an angry word and set himself to finish the task instead. When the mare was brushed and ready, he fondled her ears, then left her to go inside.

The steward, Tyrell, met him as he crossed the hall. "There is a gentleman here to see you, sir."

"Who?" he barked. He was in no mood for company.

"Sir Samuel Melrose, sir," Tyrell said with a smile, guessing the news would be welcome. "He arrived just a few minutes ago. He's in the formal garden, enjoying the morning sun."

"Is he, by God?" It was welcome news indeed. "Bring us some ale, Tyrell." He strode through the house to the gardens, calling out to his friend. "Sam?! Sam?!"

The other man rose from his seat at the voice and the two men embraced, delighted to see each other again. It had been too long since they had met last, and when they broke apart they turned as one to stroll along the gravel path amongst the shrubs of the formal garden, their faces to the sun.

"It's good to see you, Sam. What brings you to Gifford?"

"I am passing through," Sam said. "On my way to visit my parents. Your parents-in-law."

Daniel ignored the slight. It had been many years since he could bring himself to face Grace's parents. "It is somewhat of a detour, is it not?"

"It's fair weather for riding – and I've missed your company."

"Well, I am most glad you're here."

Tyrell brought the ale. They found a bench to sit on with their backs to the house, facing the woods on the hill before them, and drank to each other's health. It was the first time they had seen each other since the battlefields of Holland almost half a year before, and the first conversation was hard to find.

"Who would have thought we would be here now?" Sam ventured in the end. "Enjoying an ale in the morning sun at Gifford Court, a peaceful world before us."

"I never thought I would come back, certainly. I never planned to."

"And now that you have?"

"I will continue to live my life until God does me the mercy of ending it."

"Still?"

"Still."

There was a silence. He drank off his ale and called for more. Tyrell hurried from the house with a jug.

"Leave it here," Gifford ordered. The servant put the jug down at his feet and backed away.

"You should go to London, spend some time at Court," Sam said.

"London has nothing for me."

"Court offers many distractions, Dan."

"I'm not interested." He understood the kind of distraction his friend had in mind, but he'd had his fill of trying to close the void by taking mistresses: they offered brief diversions, nothing more, and afterward his soul was just as dark, his life as blighted as before.

"Then you've changed. You were interested enough in the Netherlands."

"Distraction merely. It didn't help."

Silence settled again but it was more comfortable now, the easy friendship quickly retrieved. He was glad that Sam had come.

"Perhaps you're right. Perhaps I have changed," he said. "But I've become so used to what I've been all these years since Grace's death, I can no longer find my way to anything different."

"Then maybe it's time to forget her," his friend replied, and placed a hand on Daniel's shoulder. "Ten years is too long to carry such a burden. Grace would not have wanted you to suffer as you have."

"Perhaps." Daniel looked into his empty cup, moving it gently to and fro between his fingers. An image of Susannah Archer glanced across his mind, a good girl, too sweet to share his darkness, too innocent to be his mistress. She deserved a better fate than that. And if he married her, she might distract him for a while, perhaps, but in the end his demons would return, and she would grow to hate him. He would rather spare them both the pain of that.

"Is there someone?" Sam was watching him, the only person who could ever read him like an open book. Apart from Sam's sister, of course. Apart from Grace.

He smiled at the picture of Susannah in his head. "There is a girl …"

"Go on."

"She's just a girl," he insisted, wishing he had said nothing, reluctant to pursue a chance that would lead him nowhere. "A new girl at Hafton Hall. I met her in the church yesterday."

"You were in church on a Saturday?"

"I saw her go in," he admitted, "and I was curious."

He had glimpsed her on the road and followed her inside, intrigued to know more about her. Few strangers ever came to Hafton, and none he'd ever seen as pretty as this girl. So he had watched her as she had stood by the bible, running her eyes over the page, and she lit something inside him he thought had died with his wife. Her hair had hung in loose dark waves to her waist, swaying gently with her movement, the unsecured locks of an unmarried girl – she was still a maiden and still young: eighteen perhaps? Nineteen? It was hard to say.

When she had raised a slender hand to flick back a tendril of hair that strayed across her face, the movement better revealed her features: she had a narrow face with high cheekbones, a small straight nose, and ruddy lips that formed the most impossibly perfect bow. Instinctively he had imagined those lips against his own, the sensation of exploring their flawless softness. Everything about her was slender and delicate; beside him she would not have reached to his shoulder. But when she turned her eyes towards him, the expression within them belied the sense of fragility. She had held his gaze easily, orbs of violet blue unashamedly assessing. He had expected nervousness, or perhaps a coy lowering of her lids, the more usual effect he had on women, and the unforeseen directness had surprised him to a smile. He found himself smiling again now with the memory of it.

Sam chuckled. "You old devil."

"Ah …" He shook his head. "She's a girl. She deserves better than me, Sam. What can I give her except regret and bitterness?" The load was his own to bear: his darkness would subsume her light.

"She might make you happy."

"None of the others have."

"You didn't really like any of the others much … As you say, they were just a distraction."

Daniel smiled – his friend knew his heart too well. "Was it that obvious?"

"Only to me," Sam laughed. "Only to me." Then, observing his friend more closely, he said, "You really like this girl." It was not a question.

He nodded, the empty cup still playing between his fingers, and his eyes lowered to watch it as it turned. "She was at church this morning. I would swear she feels the same."

"Then you should go after her. If you really like her, she would make you happy."

"For a while perhaps. Then when my demons return?"

"One day you will learn to lay them to rest, and then you'll be able to live your life as God intended, instead of carrying this great burden of guilt and grief you haul around on your shoulders."

Daniel shook his head and dismissed the subject with a wave of his hand. "That's enough of me. What of you? When are you going to settle down and do your duty?"

Sam looked blank. "My duty?"

"To produce a son and heir to your family's fortune."

"Oh, that!" Both men laughed, the joke long-standing between them. In the easy quiet that followed, Daniel turned to look back towards the house with its almost yellow stone and curved gables, the tall square chimney pots, and the mullioned windows that blinked blankly in the morning sun. The house dated from his grandfather's time and had been extended in his father's, but it had never grown large and unwieldy as Hafton Hall seemed to him to be. It still felt like a house to be lived in, a home, nestled in safe and sheltered at the foot of the woods, and he had been away from it many years. Too many years.

Perhaps Sam was right, he reflected. Perhaps it was time at last to make a new beginning, Susannah Archer offering a promise of forgiveness. He smiled to himself with the thought of her. A future with Susannah might not be so bad, a life to live, instead of each day passing merely waiting for his death.

He looked up. Above the roof the clouds were drawing in once again, this time with a threat of rain. A shadow fell across the garden as they moved across the sun, and the air was cool in its wake, a dampness in its breath.

"Come inside," Daniel said. "It is almost time for dinner." And laying a hand on Sam's shoulder as they got up from the bench, he led his friend inside.

CHAPTER 6

In the days that followed, Susannah slipped in to the daily routine at Hafton Hall. The seamstress came and dresses were altered, so that she felt less out of place amidst the grandness, her gowns every bit as gorgeous as her cousin's. Slowly she began to feel settled, her old life at Abbey Leigh fading into memory, and though she still recalled her family often, the ache became less vivid as the busyness of her life at Hafton filled her thoughts and hours. She learned quickly how to please Lady Hafton, and she spent much of her time with Eleanor, playing at cards or music, practising their dancing, riding together, or simply talking. But though they were easy in each other's company, the conversation light and unstrained, she missed the closeness she'd shared with her sisters: neither of them yet trusted the other with anything that was near to their hearts. And early every morning as she rose with the dawn, she would turn away from the window, refusing to gaze out at the woods on the hill and closing her mind against the image of the man who lived beyond them.

One morning, when she had been there a little over a week, her aunt came to find her working in the garden, collecting herbs to put among the linen. The day was fine and bright, and she was happy among the flowerbeds, the air sweet with their scent, her mind wandering over nothing.

"Come," Lady Hafton ordered, startling her back to the morning before her. "I have something I want you to do."

Susannah scrambled to her feet, dipped a curtsey and smoothed out her skirts, then walked alongside her aunt back towards the house.

"I've received word that Sir Daniel has a friend staying with him at Gifford Court," Lady Hafton said.

The name lit a flush across Susannah's skin and the now familiar sensations began to plume through her insides. Furious with herself, she set her jaw against such wild emotions. Refusing to let her body react this way at every mention of Sir Daniel's name, she schooled herself to listen to her aunt.

"I think it would be diverting to invite them over for the evening tomorrow," Lady Hafton was saying. "I would like you to arrange an invitation. Most of our neighbours are elderly you know, and your cousins sorely lack younger company."

"Of course, Aunt Elizabeth." Curtseying to her aunt, she turned and walked away.

The next day, Eleanor was in a frenzy of excitement, trying on every dress she owned, every combination with every set of sleeves and kirtles, every embroidered partlet, demanding the attention and opinion of almost everyone in the household.

Susannah had already decided on her own gown; the peach taffeta that had once been Eleanor's. It had a cream beaded forepart and sleeves, and a square-cut neckline that sat low across her shoulders, showing off her alabaster skin. Her raven-black mane hung loose, held back from her forehead by a band of delicate silverwork and tiny pearls that glimmered against the sleekness of her hair like dew drops in a sunrise. It was the most beautiful garment she had ever worn and despite the heat of her nerves at meeting Sir Daniel again, she felt like a princess. She was beside herself with both nerves and delight, and though she was overjoyed to see him, she was terrified she would give herself away.

"You look beautiful," Lettice confirmed when she was finally dressed and ready.

Susannah twirled, the wide skirt bouncing round as she moved, wider with its farthingale than she was used to. She would have to manoeuvre with care to avoid knocking something over.

Grinning, accepting a kiss of goodwill from Lettice, she hurried from the chamber, through her aunt's apartments and out into the passage that led to the stairs. At the top of the staircase she stopped to steady herself, unused to moving in such a full skirt, and when she finally began to take the steps down, hand on the rail for balance, each footstep carefully placed, she found herself at the bend in the stairs at precisely the moment their two guests stepped through the door. Their eyes couldn't help but go to her. She paused for a heartbeat, gripped the banister more tightly then kept on going, her gaze lowered to the oak boards at her feet, watching her step.

She reached the bottom stair and lifted her head to greet them. "Sir Daniel. Welcome to Hafton."

His dark eyes glittered with the briefest of smiles and she saw the admiration in his eyes as he stepped forward and bowed. "Mistress Archer. It's a pleasure to see you again."

She dropped into a curtsey, her own eyes lowered now, unwilling to risk meeting his gaze again.

"Allow me to introduce my good friend, Sir Samuel Melrose."

She lifted her head and saw that Sir Samuel was observing her carefully. He was handsome too, with sandy blonde hair and a pale freckled complexion. Like his friend, he was tall and broad-shouldered and Susannah wondered if the two men had been soldiers together.

While they were speaking, Eleanor had appeared in the entrance hall, drawn by the voices of the men, and a momentary blink of annoyance crossed her features that she had not been the first to greet them. Recovering quickly, she curtseyed low. She looked beautiful, Susannah thought, her blonde hair and strong looks set off to perfection in a gown of deep blue velvet that was embroidered with gold. She watched as Sir Daniel bowed to her cousin, straining to catch if anything more than pleasantry should pass between them.

"Sir Daniel," Eleanor welcomed him. "I … that is we … are so pleased you could come."

"I thank you. I have been away a long time and it's good to renew old friendships. You were barely more than a child when I went away."

She held his gaze. "But I am a woman now. As you see." She made a gesture to herself that invited comment.

"Indeed." He nodded his agreement but did not offer the compliment that Eleanor's words had invited. Susannah let out a silent breath of relief.

"Come," Eleanor said when she understood he would say nothing more. "My parents and my brother await us in the main hall." Placing her hand on his forearm, she gave him no choice but to walk with her to the hall. Sir Samuel turned to Susannah and offered her his arm, a wry smile curling his lips. She accepted the arm with a tilt of her head and refused to allow herself to question the meaning behind the smile.

In the main hall, a trio of musicians was playing in a corner. The long table had been pushed back against the wall, and the carpet taken away: apparently her aunt anticipated dancing. As they entered, Lord and Lady Hafton rose from their places near the hearth. Greetings were exchanged and, observing carefully, she thought she detected a slight hostility between her uncle and Sir Daniel. It was nothing she could have explained, nothing but politeness on both sides, but underneath there seemed to be a sense of coldness. As she began to muse on what might have been the cause, her thoughts were interrupted by Edward's approach.

"Cousin," he greeted her.

"Edward," she replied.

Then, taking her arm, he guided her away from the others towards two stools set apart near a window.

She watched with dismay as the rest of the party gathered at the hearth, but the stool Edward had given her turned her back to the fireplace, so she could do little else but engage with him. He looked more sallow than usual tonight, all the colour gone from his complexion, and it took her a moment to realise it was the pale gold of his doublet that leeched all the glow from his skin. She turned to look out of the window, across the park. In the dying light of the late afternoon, the sky flared crimson above the trees, clouds edged with gold.

"A beautiful sunset," she said.

He inclined his head in agreement but said nothing. To fill the silence, she smoothed out her skirt with her fingers. A servant approached with a tray of pastries. She took one, more for something to do than from any sense of hunger. Another attendant offered her a goblet of wine. Behind her at the fireplace, she could hear Eleanor's rich laugh and the unfamiliar chuckle of Sir Samuel. It took all the willpower she possessed not to turn and search for Sir Daniel. To distract herself from the effort she smiled at her cousin.

"Your mare is recovered now, I hope?"

"Quite recovered now, thank you." He lifted his chin and gave her that appraising look she had come to expect. "But you don't really care about my horse, do you?"

"I am glad that your horse is well," she insisted, "it would be a shame if such a fine animal had to be destroyed." She smiled again, her primary weapon in the combat that he had urged between them, the only kind of conversation they seemed to have. "Is there something else you'd prefer to talk about?"

He gestured with his head towards the fireplace. "My sister seems quite taken with our guests."

It was impossible not to turn and look. Eleanor was still laughing at a story of Sir Samuel's, his face bright with animation, his hands moving through the air before him, tracing out the story in the air. Sir Daniel seemed to be listening, smiling a little, nodding in confirmation of a detail when his friend turned his way, but within a moment he had noticed that Susannah had turned towards him. He searched to catch her eye, and though she looked away at once, it was not before the briefest glance had been exchanged. He excused himself from his companions and moved across the hall to join her.

Much to Susannah's relief, Edward began the conversation. "My sister seems much impressed by your friend, Sir Daniel."

"It's no surprise to me if she is. Sam tells a good story. He's cheered me through a sleepless night a hundred times or more."

"You are old friends, then?" Susannah ventured, looking up.

"Indeed we are," he replied, searching to find her gaze. She let him meet it for a moment before she looked away, but she was unsure how to read the look that passed between them. "We fought together in the Netherlands," he said.

"You must know each other very well," she said, remembering the wry smile Sir Samuel had given her, wondering how well.

"Like brothers," he admitted. "I see you are settling in to your new home."

"Yes, everyone has been most kind. Edward and I were just watching the sunset."

They all lifted their gaze to the window. A faint scarlet gleam in a near-black sky was all that was left of the day.

"You missed it," Edward said, his tone devoid of feeling.

"A pity," Sir Daniel replied. "But I'm sure there will be others. Gifford Court also offers good views."

They fell silent. The musicians finished their song. Eleanor's laughter pealed in the sudden quiet, and Lady Hafton got to her feet and clapped her hands. "We should dance," she announced, signalling to her husband. "Play a galliard," she instructed the musicians. Obediently they struck up a tune. Lord and Lady Hafton took each other's hands and began their stately progress up the room. A few moments more and Eleanor and Sir Samuel had joined them. Edward bowed gallantly to Susannah, and she had no choice but to accept. She wished that Sir Daniel had asked her first and cast a regretful glance towards him. But then she was in the dance and her youthful spirit emerged, following its natural path towards delight, the movements bringing a smile and her pale cheeks flushing red. Even dancing with Edward, she found joy in the well-known steps, a lightness and a freedom. The dance ended too soon, and the dancers bowed to each other and clapped politely. The musicians began another piece that she did not recognise. Lord Hafton claimed Susannah as a partner, and as Sir Samuel bowed to Lady Hafton, Eleanor was left to dance with Sir Daniel. Susannah watched them as they passed her in the dance, aware of the pleasure in Eleanor's smile, the desire in her eyes as the partners touched hands, moving their bodies close together. However much her cousin had laughed at Sir Samuel's stories, Susannah had no doubt that it was Sir Daniel she wanted. But she saw no answering hunger in Sir Daniel's look, and the pain of her jealousy abated just a little.

The music finished once more, the partners bowed to each other, and Edward tried to reclaim Susannah as his partner for the next dance, in spite of her claims to tiredness. "But you walk out every morning," he protested. "I've seen you stride across the park without breaking a sweat. You're fit as a fiddle. You can't possibly be tired."

"Oh but I am," she insisted breathlessly. "I'm unused to dancing."

"How about some cards?'" Eleanor held a deck between her fingers. "I vote we play one-and-thirty."

"Oh very well," Edward huffed. "But only if I can be dealer."

Eleanor rolled her eyes at Susannah, who smiled, but she gave her brother the cards. Sir Daniel and Sir Samuel drew up stools to the table and Lord and Lady Hafton looked on from their places by the fire.

Sir Daniel turned to his hosts. "Lord Hafton? Lady Hafton? Would you care to join us?" he asked.

"No, thank you, Gifford," Lord Hafton replied gruffly. "I'm too old to lose money on cards anymore. Even pennies to my children."

"As you wish," he said with a smile, and took his own seat opposite Susannah. Beside him was Eleanor, and next to Susannah was Edward. Sam sat at the head and the deal began.

The game passed slowly for Susannah, aware as she was only of the man who sat across from her. Unwillingly, her eyes were drawn towards him, brief stolen glances. He seemed intent on the game, brown eyes almost black in the candlelight, the strong jaw tight with tension. At intervals, he would lift an automatic hand to his head to sweep his fingers through the wayward curls. But he barely spoke, to her or to anyone else, and she was grateful he didn't seek to talk with her. She went bust almost every hand, failing to count up the cards correctly in her distraction though her eyes never left her hands.

"Are you quite well, coz?" Edward asked eventually, when on her turn she failed either to stick or have it, even when the dealer had asked her twice.

She looked up then, startled, and for the first time met Sir Daniel's eye. He was regarding her with interest, but his expression was impossible to read. "Only … only a little tired, I think …" she managed to say and, tipping her head forward, she let a sheet of hair fall across her shoulder to shield her face.

"Then perhaps we should be leaving now," Sir Daniel said.

She looked up, torn between relief and disappointment.

"But we've not yet finished our game," Eleanor protested.

Sir Samuel laughed and gestured to the pile of pennies before her. "You are well ahead, Mistress Eleanor. I think you need have no worry."

"Very well," she smiled in reply, but Susannah sensed her cousin's disappointment. It was rare for them to have company and now she had spoiled it.

The gentlemen rose from their seats.

"It's been a very pleasurable evening," Sir Samuel said to Lady Hafton. "I thank you."

"It was our pleasure to have you," she replied.

Eleanor sidled up beside her mother, seeking to engage Sir Daniel's eye. "Well now, Sir Daniel," she said, "next time it's your turn to invite us to Gifford Court."

He tilted his head, as though considering. "Perhaps," he said at length. "But I fear you would be disappointed. It's a lot less grand than Hafton Hall."

She gave him an arch smile. "But until I see it for myself, Sir Daniel, I'm in no position to judge."

"Then you'll just have to take my word for it."

"For now," she added.

He smiled at her determination. "Indeed. For now." He bowed, cast a last glance at Susannah who caught the look and offered him a smile, then took his leave.

The cousins stood upon the doorstep to watch them go. When the horses had clattered away into the darkness, Eleanor turned to Susannah. "Isn't he wonderful?"

Susannah said nothing, preferring to keep her thoughts about him secret and close to her heart. She had no wish to anger her cousin with her own hopes for Sir Daniel.

"So dark, so handsome, so dashing."

In spite of herself Susannah laughed. "But it was Sir Samuel who amused you – you could barely stop yourself from laughing ..."

"Yes, he was funny, I know. But he has sandy hair and freckles ... sometimes amusement isn't enough." She looked across to her brother. "What did you think of them, Ed? Did you like them? Do you think I should make a play for Sir Daniel?"

"I liked Sir Samuel," he answered, after a moment's hesitation. "I think he would make amusing company. But Sir Daniel ..." He trailed off, as though the thought had left his mind half formed.

Eleanor pressed him. "What about Sir Daniel, Ed?"

"He seemed ... distracted, and a little morose, as if he would rather have been somewhere else."

"He didn't seem that way to me," Eleanor answered, put out.

"He barely said a word all night," her brother argued. "To you or to anyone else. So I wouldn't get your hopes for him up too high."

"He's probably just shy." Eleanor pouted. "And unused to female company. He has been a soldier for a very long time."

"It wasn't shyness, Nell. Do you think soldiers have no female company?"

Susannah stopped listening as the cousins fell to bickering. Edward was right, it was not shyness that had held Sir Daniel's tongue: he was too sure of himself for that, too composed. And he had talked with her easily enough in church. It was more like a deliberate distance he placed between himself and his company. A wall, the defence of a man still grieving for a wife he had loved.

She lifted her eyes to the darkness, a half-moon casting a fleeting light across the park as the clouds broke and formed again in their slow progress across the sky. Turning back into the house she cast a final look across the park where the men had departed. There was silence now, the hoof beats long faded into the night.

With a sigh she followed her cousins, who were still arguing about Sir Daniel's character. She barely heard them, immersed in her own thoughts about him, reliving each moment she had spent with him, searching to judge if his feelings had matched her own. But she had no way of telling: he was a man of the world, a widow, an adventurer. She was sure that he desired her; she had seen it in his eyes before he bowed to greet her at the start of the evening. And she had felt his eyes upon her when she danced with Edward, the look of regret that he had failed to ask her first. But for all she knew, such desire was just a passing fancy, the casual interest such a man may show a woman who takes his eye. The looks that passed between them had not seemed that way to her, but how was she to judge, inexperienced as she was?

Still pondering, she followed her cousins up the stairs, lost in her thoughts, and no nearer to an answer to her questions. She was still thinking about it when she fell at last into bed, and her sleep was filled with strange and unsettling dreams.

In the morning, a letter came from her father. She took it out into the gardens, settled herself on a low wall that surrounded a bed of rose trees, leafy green but not yet in bloom, and ripped open the seal. Unfolding the single sheet, she began reading eagerly. Her father always wrote well – long detailed letters full of humour and anecdote: the happenings of her family bright and vivid in her mind as he described them. But as she read, her pleasure in the letter turned to sorrow with the recollection that her family was two days ride away, in a different world from hers. She wondered when she would see them again, and if they missed her as she missed them.

Towards the letter's end, her eyes began to slow across the page when her father's words turned away from the world of Abbey Leigh at last and looked towards his daughter.

How are you settling in to life at Hafton? she read.

How like you your cousin Edward? Does he please you? If he does, you might think about making a life there with him. It would be a good match,

Susannah, and marriage to your cousin would keep Abbey Leigh in our family...

She stopped reading, any remaining delight in the letter swept away in three lines of writing. Disappointment threaded through her veins as she fully understood her father's logic with a sudden awful clarity. It was just as she had suspected after all – she had been brought to Hafton Hall to win approval for a marriage.

By marrying her cousin, Abbey Leigh would stay in the family as her father so dearly wished. Family is everything, her father had often told her, and as soon as she was old enough to understand what it meant to have no sons, she had vowed to respect her father's wishes in her choice of husband. But she had always nursed secret dreams that her father's choice would also be hers, and now those dreams had been shattered. In the midst of the warm spring morning, she shivered.

She lowered the letter to her lap, the sheet held loosely in her fingers, the words across it unseen, though her gaze was downcast towards them. Tears threatened behind her eyes, and she blinked them back furiously, refusing to feel self-pity. God is testing me, she thought, testing the strength of my vow to honour my parents, my vow to do a daughter's duty.

She could write back to her father and let him know her feelings: she was certain he loved her well enough not to force her into marriage against her will. But then what of her vow? And what of Abbey Leigh? There were no other cousins, and no hope for more children for her parents. Marriage to Edward, if he would have her, was the only way to honour her father's wish.

An image of Sir Daniel slid across her thoughts, desire bright in his eyes as he had looked at her in the entrance hall. Just the thought of him kindled the familiar heat across her skin, a warmth in her belly, and she had to force herself to shrug the thought away. It was no good thinking of him any more, no matter what they felt for each other. The future of Abbey Leigh was in her hands and her path was decided.

CHAPTER 7

Susannah awoke early on May Day. With the coming of the dawn the whole house was stirring, every young woman within its walls venturing out into the grey morning light to wash her face with dew.

"Do you think it works?" Lettice whispered as they knelt in the grass to bathe their faces. "Will it truly make us beautiful for the year ahead?"

"Of course it will." Susannah laughed. "As long as we have a little faith. And if it doesn't," she added, "where's the harm?"

She raised her head. The smooth green of the grass was dotted with the bright forms of women kneeling in the age-old custom. Susannah caught her cousin's eye and smiled, Eleanor's face glowing with the dew, rose pink and healthy. Eleanor smiled in return, the bathing over, then got to her feet and stood over the others as they laughed and joked amongst themselves.

It was the lightest spirit Susannah had ever seen between all the women, the festive magic of the day giving them more beauty than simple dew could do. She sat back on her heels, looking out across the park. The mist still hung low above the grass, the sun not yet risen high enough to disperse it, lending the landscape an other-worldly mystique. But the clouds were high, and the weather promised to be fair. With their faces moist and cool with dew, laughing with the hope of the day, the women went out to gather branches of hawthorn from the park, and flowers from the gardens to decorate the house.

Later in the morning, when the decorating was done and the house was bedecked with the may, a fresh spring scent lingered in the rooms. Susannah took her breakfast in the dining room with her cousins. Eleanor was cheerful and excited about the day and even the bite of Edward's cynicism did nothing to dent their mood. As soon as they had broken their fast, they set off walking to the village, arm-in-arm, the other women following in pairs, and Edward riding his mare behind with an air of bored resignation.

The lane was already bustling as people from all the outlying farms and cottages made their way towards the village green. Long before they made the bend that would bring the village into sight, they could hear the hum of the celebrations. The tinkle of the morris dancers' bells carried on the breeze above the murmur of many voices, and the sweet scent of spit-roasted meat wafted towards them in snatches as the light morning air twisted and changed direction.

By the time they reached the little green, the festivities were in full swing. A troupe of jugglers stood before a crowd who gazed in rapt attention at the swirling clubs, and beyond, near the centre of the green by the maypole, archers were practising in the butts, warming up for the competitions that would be held later in the day. Village girls flitted through the crowd, their hair bright with ribbons, and the air was alive with the buzz of the festival. Stallholders called out their wares, hawking sweetcakes and fruit and ale.

The cousins stopped to watch the jugglers for a while, gasping in awe as the troupe took up their fire clubs, arcs of flame swinging perilously through the air. Susannah could have watched them all day, captivated by their skill and the danger of the swirling fire, everything else forgotten.

❦

It was years since Daniel had been home for the May festival. He had always made sure to avoid it since the death of his wife, unable to bear the looks of pity and the memories of happier years when they had strolled the fair together. But this year was a new beginning and though the sorrow still murmured in his thoughts, it was quieter now beneath the small hope for a better future that Susannah Archer had kindled. He hoped he would see her again today, and perhaps even steal a few moments alone with her. With the thought of it he smiled and touched his heels to the horse's flank.

At the green he saw her straight away. She was watching the jugglers, and he stood some distance away from her, watching her delight in the entertainment, the way her head tilted as she followed the clubs with her eyes, the slight sway of her shoulders as she gasped or laughed in pleasure. Her black hair lifted in the breeze, floating, and though his first instinct was to cross the crowd to be with her, he held himself back, taking time to watch her unobserved.

When the jugglers paused in their act for a moment, she turned her head to take in the scene around her. Unexpectedly meeting his eyes, she gave a little start of surprise before her face lit up in an instinctive smile. Noticing the movement, Eleanor also turned, and followed her cousin's gaze.

Inwardly, Daniel cursed. He had no desire to talk to Eleanor; the coyness of her laughter grated on his nerves, and there was nothing about her he liked in spite of her open interest in him. He had little time for the brother either, sensing a wastrel under the arrogance. But by now both Haftons had seen him, and Susannah was waiting so he had no choice but to weave his way among the villagers to bid them all good day.

"Sir Daniel." Eleanor dropped into a curtsey and lifted her eyes to him in a smile, but his gaze was only for Susannah, whose head was bowed before him as she curtseyed, her own eyes steadfastly lowered.

"Mistresses Eleanor, Susannah." He bowed. "Master Edward. You are enjoying the jugglers, I see."

"Indeed," Eleanor answered. "They're fine, are they not? Though I'm sure you would have seen much better at Court."

He shook his head, a wry smile curving his lips. "I am seldom at Court, Mistress Eleanor."

"Are you not?" She seemed surprised. "Do you not find our country life a little quiet for your taste after all the excitement of the Netherlands?"

"I am glad of the peace for the moment," he replied, though he had known little peace since he first laid eyes on Susannah: the maelstrom of war seemed almost easy in comparison. He had never known such inner turmoil.

"I'm sure you will soon tire of it," Eleanor said, with feeling. "The fair is about the most exciting thing that ever happens here."

"Perhaps." But if he could spend each day feasting his eyes on Susannah, he could stay for all eternity and never tire of it. He turned politely to Edward. "Are you planning to compete in the archery?"

Edward shook his head. "I think not."

"You should. It is always a good competition."

"You'll compete, Sir Daniel?" Eleanor asked.

"I shall." He nodded. He flicked a glance to Susannah, hoping to speak to her, to win her approval, but her eyes remained cast down in their resolute position towards the ground before her feet. Why would she not look at him at least? Favour him with a smile?

"We were on our way to refresh ourselves with an ale," Eleanor said then, smiling up at him. "Would you care to join us?"

"I would be delighted." Then perhaps he might gain a glance from Susannah, he thought, and maybe a word or two.

Eleanor fell in step beside him as they sauntered across the green towards a stall not far away. He refrained from offering his arm. If she thought him rude, she was too polite to say so. Instead she turned her face towards him. "Do you plan to stay at Gifford Hall?"

"I do." He kept his eyes facing forward.

"That's good news. We shall enjoy your company. And what of your friend, Sir Samuel? Is he planning to stay also?"

"For a while." The temptation to look over his shoulder at the woman behind was almost overwhelming as he tried to focus his attention on the woman at his side. They reached the ale stall and he bought them cups of small beer. When he passed one to Susannah, she took it without raising her eyes, but their fingers touched as the vessel changed hands, and a spark seemed to charge between them. Startled, she raised her head out of instinct, and in the brief glance that passed between them, he saw in her eyes the same pain and desire that was torturing him. Dear God, he thought. No wonder she refused to look at him in company.

"Mistress Susannah," he said gently. "It is almost time for the archery. Would you care to come and watch me compete?"

She smiled, though her eyes remained averted. "I would be honoured, Sir Daniel."

Resisting the temptation to take her hand to lead her through the crowd, he led the way towards the butts, where others were already taking off their jackets, checking the tension of their bows, measuring the straightness of their arrows. Sam was amongst them.

"Wish me luck, madam," he said as they reached the enclosure.

"Good luck, Sir Daniel," she replied. "Though I'm sure you have scant need of it."

Then he took her hand, bowed his head above it, and strode off to ready himself to compete.

Susannah's fists balled tight with excitement every time Sir Daniel took his aim, willing him to shoot true. He had stripped to his shirt, the loose linen flapping against his body in the stiffening breeze, showing off the muscular shoulders and sculpted back. She could see his forearms, taut and strong beneath the dusting of dark hair as he held up the bow, the feather of the arrow against one cheek as he breathed in to take his aim. Others were cheering him also, and he laughed and bantered back. After each shot he glanced her way, seeking her approval. She smiled and clapped with the rest of the crowd, his skill surpassing all other competitors, though Sam was at least proving competition.

In the end, he won the contest with ease, and afterwards, he came hurriedly to find Susannah before she could slip away to be reclaimed by her cousins. He got to her just in time, Edward fast approaching, searching for her over the crowd. Taking her hand in his before her cousin could spy her, Sir Daniel hurriedly led her away towards the other side of the green.

"I congratulate you, Sir Daniel, on your prize." She laughed. The reticence of earlier had left her, banished by the excitement of the day and her pleasure in his attention. Her small fingers tightened on his war-callused hand. "What did you win?" she asked.

"A leg of ham," he replied. Later, he would collect it from the servant who had taken it for him, and give it to one of the families who worked his estate. They would appreciate it more than he. "Walk with me," he said, casting a quick glance back at the green. He wanted to get her alone, away from her cousins where he could have her to himself. Edward had apparently given up his search for her, distracted by the strong man competition that had taken over from the archery.

She nodded her assent and let him lead her away from the green towards the church. It was deserted now, the traditions of the May reaching back to a long-forgotten past, and a time before Christianity had taken such deep root in peoples' lives. They stepped through the lych-gate, her hand still held in his, and entered the sprawling graveyard that surrounded the church.

"You don't mind?" he asked, gesturing to the graves around them, concerned for a moment she might think it a grim place to have brought her.

"Not at all. Are we visiting someone in particular?"

"My parents," he told her.

"I'm sorry."

"There's no need to be. They died many years ago, and I've long since learned to live with their loss. They're at peace now, together. I could wish nothing more for them."

Behind the church, hidden from the lane, they stopped at a grave by a flourishing bush of rosemary, the fragrance heady in the morning air. Sir Daniel observed her, near-black eyes shrewd and observant. "How do you find living with the Haftons? Are they kind to you?"

"I have no cause to complain," she replied with a small shrug that gave the lie to her words. "Lady Hafton is my aunt, my father's sister. They are his only family, and ..." She stopped, distressed but apparently reluctant to confide any more.

He waited, and when she said no more he smiled his encouragement. "And ...?"

She looked up at him. He could see the indecision in her eyes, the desire to tell him something against the doubt if she should.

"You can trust me," he reassured her. "I have no great love for the Haftons."

She swallowed and nodded, as if he had confirmed a suspicion.

"Tell me," he said.

She swallowed again and her eyes flicked across the graveyard. He rubbed her fingers in his own and she looked up at him again. The sadness in the smile she gave him cut like a Spaniard's blade and he tensed against the pain. "My father wants me to marry my cousin," she whispered.

"Edward." The single word held a wealth of meaning, all his hurt and disappointment contained in the two barely breathed syllables.

"I have no brothers. So if I marry Edward the estate remains in the family and ..." She trailed off with a slight shake of her head, unable to say any more.

" ... and you cannot go against your father's wishes." He finished the sentence for her. "I understand."

"Yes," she whispered with the same small sad smile up at him. "I should have been born a boy."

He squeezed her hand again in his fingers. "Well, perhaps," he said. "But I for one thank God you were not."

She withdrew her hand from his, and all the joy of the day leached away from both of them. He felt desolate once more – her future as Edward's wife all but decided, her life lived a morning's walk away from him but forever out of his reach. She shrugged. "It is hopeless," she said.

"Hush," he coaxed. He would not let her go so easily – he'd waited too long to find her. "It is never hopeless."

"I wish I could believe you," she murmured, "but I do not dare to."

"Have faith, Susannah, have faith," he said. "There must be a way." He brushed her fingers with the backs of his own, and she once more grasped his hand in hers, her small cool fingers clutching at him tightly, as she moved in closer towards him. Lifting his free hand to her head, he smoothed strands of her hair back from her temple as she tilted her face up towards his.

He swallowed, passion rising in him, heat in his pelvis, surging through his limbs, the desire for life kindling within him for the first time in years, a life to be lived with Susannah. He could not lose her now. Bending his face to hers, he grazed his lips across her forehead, touched them to her cheek, then sought out her waiting lips for the briefest gentlest kiss.

"There is always hope," he murmured as she lowered her head to his chest and held him, sliding her arms about his shoulders, her slender fragile body pressed against his. He held her for a moment, his hands against her back, then gently he reached up and took her arms from around his neck, barely trusting himself to touch her, his need for her bright and hard and insistent.

"We should go back to the green," he said. But as she tilted her head back to look at him, her mouth moved so close to his that he could not help but touch his lips to hers once again, harder this time, her lips moving in response to the pressure, parting, accepting the caress of his tongue. His fingers lingered over her neck and her shoulder, sliding across the silk of her gown to cup her breast. She shuddered with the unfamiliar touch, and her mouth sought his more urgently.

Hoofbeats in the lane beyond the church and a male voice growing louder shocked them to their senses. Abruptly they stepped apart, moving away, eyes turned anywhere but on each other. Susannah ran her hands across her skirts that had crumpled up against his legs, touched fingers to her lips, still moist from his kiss.

Daniel breathed deeply, forcing down his desire: his passion for this girl he barely knew almost serving to unravel him. What on earth was he thinking, making love to a woman he could never have at the side of his parents' grave? Had he taken leave of his senses? He swung to face her. "Forgive me," he said. "I am not myself."

She nodded, unable to find a voice to answer him.

"We should go now," he said. "Before you are missed. Come."

Mastering himself, reasserting the iron control that had made him live each day since Grace's death, he touched his hand to Susannah's elbow and guided her back amongst the graves towards the gate.

In the lane they walked in silence, not quite touching, each alone with their thoughts, but he was aware of her slender form close at his side, and he prayed to God not to take away this scrap of happiness He had offered, this chance to live again. At the edge of the green they parted without words, a formal bow and curtsey before she hurried off to find her cousins amongst the thinning crowd. He watched her go, her form growing smaller as she crossed the green away from him, finding her way back to Edward.

Edward. At the thought of the name he scowled and turned away to fetch his horse. He wanted to be home.

CHAPTER 8

In the morning, Susannah awoke unrefreshed and weary from a night of fitful sleep. She rose with the dawn, the stars fading one by one and the night sky slowly lightening behind them. But despite her tiredness, she knew she would not fall asleep again.

Dressing quickly in her wool dress and walking boots, creeping out through Lady Hafton's chamber, she stole along the passage and down the stairs. The house was beginning to stir already, servants moving quietly through the rooms to light fires and draw water. A scent of new baked bread just touched the air as she passed through the entrance hall but she felt no hunger, only a need for fresh air to clear her heavy head.

Outside, the sudden hit of the cold dawn air made her shiver but she breathed deeply, looking out as the trees began to emerge in the greyness, a haze of mist floating over the parklands. It was beautiful and, drawing her cloak closer round her, she set off along the path, quickly gaining the lush soft grass of the park.

She had no real idea of where she would walk, but the park was lovely in any direction and, as always, her steps were drawn towards the woods on the crest of the hill. She had not yet ventured in amongst the trees, mindful of Eleanor's warning on her very first night at Hafton, but the knowledge that Sir Daniel's house lay just the other side of them was a temptation she had to fight against every day.

This morning the sun rose behind a curtain of cloud and the day was overcast, the mist cool as she trudged across the grass. It had rained overnight and the hem of her old woollen dress dragged with moisture from the ground. But her boots were sturdy and she strode on regardless, the movement and the fresh air her tonic. The exercise helped to stifle her agitation, her mind still turning on the thoughts of the previous day, the touch of his lips against hers, the brush of his fingers across her breast. The memory warmed her, a shudder forming inside, her breast aching to be touched again.

She walked faster as if she might leave the sensations behind, striding over the grass, the air damp against her face. But the feelings simply followed, refusing to be put away so easily. The slope steepened underfoot, sweeping up towards the line of trees, and though she had to bend forward against the incline, she kept up her pace. Her breath was coming harder now and she was enjoying the exertion. She could feel the rosy glow in her cheeks and the warmth in her muscles.

The bark of a dog behind her swung her round to face the house far below her, almost a mile away. A rider was approaching and for a hopeful heartbeat she thought it might be Sir Daniel, before she realised with a swell of disappointment that it was only Edward. Of course, she scolded herself. Of course it wouldn't be Sir Daniel coming from the Hall. She stood and waited, wondering what had brought him out so early, and what was bringing him to her.

He slowed the horse and dropped lightly to the ground beside her. He was breathing quickly, his skin flushed from the ride, reddening to health the usual sallowness of his complexion. "Good morrow, coz," he said, with a light bow.

"Edward," she returned, and bobbed into a hasty curtsey. "What brings you out this way so early?"

"I wanted to test out my mare," he answered easily, "and I saw you walking when I left the house. I thought I would join you."

Her first thought was to protest and claim this time as her own, angry at having her thoughts disturbed, but she checked herself.

There was more than a good chance she would have to marry this man and there was no point in making him an enemy. And anyway, he had not asked her permission. She nodded and turned to keep on walking. He fell in beside her, lifting the reins over the horse's head and looping them round his arm. The mare shook her head, disappointed, but followed him quietly enough as they walked on together, strolling now, all the energy of earlier lost with Edward's appearance, the fatigue of the sleepless night returning.

They reached the line of the trees and automatically she turned left to walk along them, planning to skirt the woods and head down towards the village before returning to the Hall along the lane. Edward put a hand on her arm and stopped her.

"We could go through the woods, if you like. Eleanor said you had not ventured so far as yet in case you lost your way. I know the woods well – I've been exploring them all my life."

Susannah turned her head to look at him, surprised. He seemed unusually solicitous this morning – it was unlike him to go out of his way to please her. Perhaps he had decided he must try harder to win her. After all, he couldn't be sure of the strength of her sense of duty.

"Well," she said. It was tempting. She had wanted to explore the woods since she arrived, and it was only Eleanor's warning that had kept her out of them.

Sensing her hesitation, he said, "There's a path that leads through to the eastern edge of Sir Daniel's estate. We can cut back to the village from there."

She nodded, the temptation to walk on Sir Daniel's land too great to refuse. "Then we'll go that way, if you're sure."

They retraced their steps a little, searching for the path, the horse's hooves muffled now in the long, wet grass at the forest's edge. She felt a slight bristle of apprehension, a native nervousness of forest, born of a belief in fairies and green men and witches. She looked up at her cousin as they found the path and entered the shelter of the trees. "Are there wolves?"

"Not any longer. The last wolves were hunted out in my grandfather's time. There's wild boar but we have the dogs so they shouldn't bother us."

The path was easy to follow, a well-worn track between trees of oak and elm that scattered their burden of raindrops over their heads with the breeze. Small shafts of sunlight broke through the cloud as the morning brightened, dappling the forest floor, lighting up the bluebells that grew in clumps. It was magical and, delighted, she turned to her cousin with a smile.

"It's quite beautiful. And the path is easy to follow after all."

Edward stopped walking and turned to face her with a sigh. She halted beside him, looking up.

"What's wrong?"

"Nothing is wrong, coz."

"Then why have we stopped?" A sudden sense of what was coming pulsed through her blood, but it came too late to help her. She stepped back, fear and anger flooding her veins, searching her mind for a way out.

"So that I may kiss you." He grabbed her arm with one strong hand, holding it hard between his fingers, dragging her in towards him. Her other hand he swept behind her back, pinning her firmly so she could barely move. She turned her face away from him, resolute that he would not have his way, but he took his hand from her arm, cupped her chin in his fingers, and forced her head round and up towards him.

"You're going to be mine soon, coz, so you'd better get used to it," he whispered. Then he lowered his mouth to cover hers, pressing hard, forcing her lips apart, searching her mouth with his tongue. She was aware of the smell of him, the same combination of horse and dog and wine she had noticed at the church, and the lean rangy hardness of his body against hers. He moved in closer, forcing her to step back until she felt the trunk of a tree behind her, nowhere else to go. Pressing into her, her head pinned by his mouth, he took her wrists in his hands, dragged them together above her head then locked them with one strong hand against the rough bark of the tree, leaning his weight into the hand that held her pinioned.

His free hand pressed down inside her cloak, inside the soft bodice that she wore, under the shift, searching out the nipple with his fingers, twisting it painfully between them. He took his mouth from hers for a moment. "You like that, eh?"

Desperately she shook her head, and he laughed. "Your body betrays you," he murmured. Then, clamping his mouth over hers once again, forcing his tongue inside, his hand left her breast to move down her body, searching to lift her skirts and find a way underneath.

Terrified, she began to struggle harder, kicking with her legs and, while his hand was still caught in the folds of her skirts, she managed to free one of her own hands long enough to slap him with all her strength across his face. He jerked back in surprise. On its own it would not have been enough to save her but the sudden movement startled the mare, causing her to shy, and the reins, which were still draped around his arm, snapped tight, throwing him off balance.

She didn't wait for a second chance. Ducking out from under his arm she fled, following the path further into the woods, not caring where she went, just trying to put distance between them. Every moment she expected him to be behind her, to feel his hand on her arm once again. She raced onward, running and stumbling through the trees until her chest was burning, all the breath gone from her lungs, and she could run no more.

Turning at last to look behind her, she peered through the trees, her chest heaving and painful, breath coming in long hard gasps. But there was no sign of her cousin, and she guessed he had decided to let her go this time. After all, she thought wryly, he was sure to have other chances. Cold dread seeped through her as she thought of it. She had got away from him this time, but her marriage bed still beckoned and then there would be no more escape.

Exhausted, she sank on to the leaves and rested her back against a tree, still peering back the way she had come, not yet trusting that she was safe. Gradually her breathing slowed and the pain in her chest began to ease. Above her something crashed through the leaves and she jumped, her heart starting to hammer again in the moment it took to realise it was just a pheasant taking flight.

When she finally forced herself to her feet again, she realised she was trembling. Carefully, she began to smooth out her petticoats and skirt, and rearrange her bodice. Then she ran her fingers through her hair, picking out the leaves and bits of bark that had caught in it as she ran.

Ordering her clothes served to calm her a little and when she was ready, she turned round in a circle to look about her with a sense of doubt. She had long since left the path, plunging blindly through the trees in her flight, although she guessed her instinct would have taken her away from Hafton Hall. Looking up, she wondered if she might find her way by the sun, but only small dapples of light came through, the sun too weak behind its shelter of trees to be of any help.

So she took a deep breath and began to walk, hoping to come across a path or a river, anything to stop her wandering in circles. She thought of leaving a trail for herself, a piece of string like Theseus in the labyrinth, but there was nothing she could find that would serve and so she wandered on, wondering if she had been missed yet at the house.

It seemed like she walked for hours. Hunger began to gnaw, and she remembered the scent of the bread at the house with regret. They would have breakfasted by now: they would be wondering where she was. Would they come and search for her? Would Edward admit he had seen her?

The morning passed, the trees unchanging. She stopped and looked round her once again. She must have been walking in circles. There was nothing different, nothing new from her surroundings of the last few hours. Trees simply stretched in every direction. She sighed, almost ready to give up, her strength starting to fail at last. Then, gazing round a final time in desperation, she thought that perhaps to her left the light seemed a little different, brighter somehow and more inviting, so she turned her footsteps towards it, trudging on a little further. At first she thought she'd made a mistake, the trees still thick around her, but then the ground began to drop sharply until she was half sliding down the hill, catching at passing trees with her hands to steady her balance. Then, abruptly, the trees just stopped and there, a little way down the hill, was the manor she assumed was Gifford Court. It was a pretty house, she thought, with its many different curved gables and chimneys in a light yellow stone. Smaller and neater than Hafton Hall, it reminded her more of her own house at Abbey Leigh.

Weak with weariness and hunger, she stopped and sank down on the grass, uncertain what to do next. The temptation was to go and seek help at the house, to find Sir Daniel and explain what had happened, but the repercussions of such an act did not bear thinking of. He had hardly been able to curb his passion in the openness of the churchyard with the lane just a stone's throw away. To go willingly into his house, alone, was not the action of a virtuous woman and it would be wrong to tempt him. She corrected herself: it would be wrong to tempt both of them thus – her desire had burned every bit as hot as his. She shook her head against the thought; the exhaustion and thirst were playing tricks with her mind. It had been a single kiss, whatever feelings it aroused, and she was still in possession of her virtue.

She glanced towards the house, so inviting in the late spring sun, her exhausted body craving the rest and comfort it could offer her. She dragged her eyes away and forced her mind to think what she must do. The best course, she decided, would be to skirt the house and walk back towards the village. With luck she could slip away unseen, gain the edge of the estate with no one noticing, but it was a long way to walk: without water and some sustenance, she wasn't sure that she would make it.

Undecided, she sat a while longer, resting, trying to gather the strength to try, but she had not sat long when a movement in the garden near the house caught her eye. A figure, a male figure, striding through the garden in her direction.

She had been seen.

Her heart sank within her and though she was tempted to jump up and run, she had no strength to do so. Even if she had she would not have got far. Her only hope was that the man was a servant who thought she was some kind of intruder, a traveller who had lost her way. Then she could lie to him and steal quietly away, with no one any wiser of her visit.

But the hope proved vain. Even from a distance she could tell it was Sir Daniel himself approaching. She recognised the determined stride, the set of his head as he walked. His doublet flapped open as he strode, the linen shirt loose around the collar. Slowly she raised herself to her feet and discovered she could barely stand, a heavy weariness in every limb. The anguish of her near escape must have told on her more than she had realised. She began to sway on her feet as she waited for him to reach her and when finally he got to her, it was all she could do not to collapse against him.

"Susannah?" The strong dark face was taut with concern. "What's happened?"

"Sir Daniel ..." she began, but then the swaying began again, her legs threatening to buckle beneath her.

Suddenly realising the extent of her exhaustion, he reached out a hand to steady her then moved in close, an arm around her waist, holding her firmly. She let her body rest against his, felt the warm and solid strength of him through the light doublet he wore, his arm hard and reassuring against her. With his fingers he brushed stray strands of her hair from her face and at his touch the familiar heat rose through her body. She wished she could stay in his arms like this forever.

He bent his head close to hers. "What has happened, Susannah?" he demanded. "What has brought you here like this?"

She could feel the warmth of his breath against her hair, his fingers still smoothing back the flyaway tendrils, each touch of his fingertips fanning the heat that burned inside her. Susannah lifted her head, looking up into his face. Meeting the dark intensity of his eyes, she was sure of him, her own need reflected in their depths. Softly he pressed a kiss to her forehead and she barely breathed as his mouth moved across her face to touch her eye and her cheek, before finally grazing her lips.

It was the most gentle of kisses, his mouth warm and soft against hers. She opened her mouth a little as their lips moved together and with her response his touch grew firmer, his tongue seeking out hers.

Then, as suddenly, it was over. "Forgive me," he murmured.

She felt his body go tense next to hers, a shift in his mood. Then he bent to slide his hand behind her legs and lifted her off the ground. "Come," he said, brisk now, "We must get you inside."

He carried her across the grass and through the gardens, and she held herself against him, her arms around his neck, filling herself with his essence, burning into memory every detail of his body where they touched – the curve of his shoulder, the hardness of his chest, the smoothness of the skin below the hairline on his neck. She barely noticed her surroundings, where he was taking her, so when finally he placed her down, she was surprised to find herself in what seemed to be his bed.

"You need to rest," he told her. "And I will send for a physician."

She shook her head, sitting herself up. "There is no need for a physician. I need only a little food and drink. I've eaten nothing today."

"Wait here," he said, though the command was needless: she could not have moved to save herself. Then he strode out of the room. She could hear him calling out for a servant, shouting for bread and meat and small beer to be brought. After a moment he was back, sitting on the edge of the bed, gazing down at her with concern.

"What has happened, Susannah? What has brought you here?" he asked again.

She nodded and blinked back tears, all her senses crying to tell him the truth. But she was afraid of what he might do to Edward if he knew, reckless and fearless as he was, he would give no thought to himself. And besides, she told herself, what possible good could it do for him to know? She would still have to marry Edward and she would have made of him an enemy.

"Susannah? Why will you not tell me?"

"I got lost in the woods," she said, which was true. "I walked for hours."

"Only that?" His eyes narrowed, as if he knew she was giving him only a half-truth. "If there was more you would tell me?"

"Only that." She nodded, but she slid her eyes away from his scrutiny, ashamed not to trust him with the truth and aware that she had hurt him.

"Well, you're safe now, whatever happened," he said, but his eyes still searched her face, hoping for an answer.

She said nothing, and he let it go, aware of her exhaustion.

"When you're rested," he said, "I'll take you back to Hafton. And in the meantime, I'll send a man to the Hall with a message that you're safe."

"Thank you," she breathed.

A servant arrived with the food and she ate a few mouthfuls while Sir Daniel sat in a chair at the bedside, observing her. She found she could eat very little, her weariness greater than her hunger. He took the tray away.

"Rest now," he said, straightening the covers over her as she lay down. Her last thought before she slipped into welcome sleep was the sweet sense of being in his bed, with the scent of him around her.

CHAPTER 9

*I*t was late afternoon when she woke and she was ravenous, but her strength had returned and after she had straightened her clothes and washed her face with a bowl of water that had been set for the purpose, she hurried from the chamber to look for Sir Daniel.

She found him in the formal garden behind the house, discussing shrubs with the gardener who was delighted to have his master back and someone to make the decisions. She watched him for a moment before he saw her, observing him in his life without her, but he sensed her presence straight away and turned at once to greet her. With a final brief word to the gardener, he strode to the door to meet her.

"Did you sleep well?"

"Like a child," she replied. "And now I could eat a horse."

He laughed, the stern face softening. "Come inside. It is almost time for supper. I'll have my man set another place."

She followed him back inside the house and for the first time took the time to look around her. She was in the dining chamber, a spacious airy room, oak panelling lining the lower part of the walls, and an enormous stone fireplace that took up the entire far wall. An ancient pair of crossed swords hung above it. A good fire was burning well and the room was warm and comfortable against an afternoon that was turning cool. A table that could have hosted a banquet occupied the middle of the floor with stools drawn up either side of it.

He opened his arms in a gesture that encompassed the room. "This is where I live. This is Gifford Court."

"It is lovely," she said, gazing round. "Truly."

"You're very kind. It isn't half so grand as Hafton Hall."

"Perhaps not. But there's more makes a fine house than grandness, do you not think?"

He studied her for a moment. Then he said, "Yes. I do think that."

"You think what?" Sir Samuel's voice swung them round. "Ah, Mistress Susannah, you are awake at last."

"Indeed I am, Sir Samuel. And looking forward to supper."

"No lasting damage from your ordeal in the woods, I hope?"

A moment's hesitation in her answer brought a questioning glance from Sir Daniel, but she covered it quickly. "No, none at all."

"But perhaps you should take care not to walk in the woods alone again," Sir Daniel said.

"Yes," she agreed, but she kept her gaze averted. His eyes were still searching hers, and she could not have met them again and told the same lie. "It was foolish of me. I shan't do it again."

"Then I'm glad." He gestured to the table. "Please, sit."

They took their places at the table. Servants came with platters, but it was far less formal than dining at Hafton Hall, the food not so lavish but no less delicious for that. She took small mouthfuls of wine which her host kindly watered for her, and Sir Samuel did most of the talking, keeping her laughing through the meal with his stories of life in camp and on the march. None of the stories, however, touched on Sir Daniel's experiences except very briefly, and she understood the closeness of the friendship where such discretion could be trusted. Sir Daniel said very little, content to let his friend do the talking, but his eyes rested often on Susannah, a question behind them she wasn't sure she could answer.

After the meal, when the supper had been cleared, they moved to sit near the hearth. She settled into the deep cushions scattered before the grate, arranging her skirt in a pool around her. Sir Daniel stretched out in a hard-backed chair to one side, Sir Samuel on the other.

"I spend most of my time in this room," Sir Daniel explained. "Mostly I am here alone and one room suffices for my needs."

"I like it very much," Susannah said, looking around it again. "It truly feels like a home."

A silence fell, heavy and awkward.

"Did I say something wrong?" she asked. She was sorry the mood had changed; she thought she had never felt so content.

Sir Daniel took a deep breath and bit at his lip as if considering. Sir Samuel busied himself rubbing at a mark on his boot with a thumb.

"Sir Daniel?"

"This was my wife's favourite room," he said. "She used to use the exact same words to describe it."

Heat burned across her neck and cheeks and she lowered her head. She was devastated that she called him back to his grief, however unwittingly, and cast a shadow over the day. She could feel his eyes still observing her across the hearth.

"I'm so sorry," she whispered. "I did not know."

"Of course you didn't. How could you?"

There was another silence. Sir Samuel looked up from his boot. "I think I'll go and check on my horse. He was favouring the near foreleg earlier ..."

Sir Daniel said nothing as his friend left the room.

"He is a good friend to you, I think," Susannah said when he had gone.

"I would trust him with my life." He hesitated. "Grace ... my wife ... was his sister."

She nodded. There seemed to be nothing she could say, but the relationship made sense – the two men brought closer in their grief.

"I am assuming that you have heard what happened to Grace?"

"I heard only that she died."

"She was killed in a riding accident. She was going too fast and the jump was too high. She fell as they landed and broke her neck."

"I'm so sorry."

In the silence that followed he observed her, and she thought that perhaps he was going to say more. Twice he opened his mouth as if to speak then closed it again, changing his mind. Then, in another change of mood, he leaned forward to reach for the jug of wine, pouring more into his goblet, holding it out in offer to her. She shook her head.

"So," he said, brusquely, standing up, looking away from her. His tension was almost palpable. "Now you know. But it happened many years ago."

She lifted her face to look at him. "Some wounds take a long time to heal," she said.

He made no answer, lifting the goblet to his lips and draining it off. When it was empty he wiped his lips with his hand and turned to her. "I should take you home."

She dropped her eyes. It was comfortable here by the fire, and though she knew he had yet to tell her everything, there was the beginnings of a confidence, a trust that was building between them. She imagined he must have sat like this before the fire with his wife before she died, sharing thoughts and secrets. It was a life she could wish for herself, if she had any choice, if she were not constrained to marry Edward.

Edward. The thought of him made her shudder.

"You are cold, Susannah?"

"Perhaps a little," she lied.

"I hope you're not coming down with a fever."

"I am fine," she assured him, forcing a smile. "Truly."

"You should stay here at Gifford Court tonight, just in case. The evening is cold, and there is a dampness to the air. It would be well not to take chances."

"As you wish," she replied, but she kept her head down so the delight in her smile would be hidden. "Thank you," she said, and she wondered if he could hear the smile in her voice.

~

Later, after games of cards and backgammon that he allowed her to win, he took a candle and led her upstairs once more.

"You can have my chamber. It has the most comfortable bed and the room is warm. I had them light a fire for you."

"But where will you sleep?" she asked. "I cannot turn you out of your bed."

"Gifford Court is a big house, madam. There are beds a-plenty."

"Of course … I didn't mean …"

"Good night, Mistress Archer."

"Good night, Sir Daniel." She shut the door behind her.

She should have locked it also, he thought grimly, on guard against him: it was a mistake for her to imagine she was safe in his house. His need for her had burned throughout the day, every sense aroused and raw, her presence both exquisite and a torture, stirring new desire in him for life, forbidden for him to take. Whatever had he been thinking, inviting her to stay? Putting her in his bed, no other women in the house. A lamb with a wolf, he thought, innocence deceived.

He forced himself back downstairs to the dining chamber where Sam had already made himself a bed amongst the cushions beside the fire, breathing deep and regular. There was a chamber made up for him as there was every night, but Sam preferred the warmth of the hearth, and so many years as a soldier had turned him against a taste for soft beds.

Daniel put the candlestick on the table and sat down, his mind still turning on the woman in his bed, the woman who threatened to unravel his sanity. He cast his mind back across the evening. That her passion burned as bright as his he had no doubt. If she had spurned his feelings he would have walked away from her without a second thought – he had no interest in forcing himself on a woman who was unwilling. But her soul cried out to his, her need as keen as his own. She had welcomed his touch, his kiss, and she had come to him in her distress this morning, though he knew she had not yet told him all. He suspected Edward Hafton to have had a hand in her woe: they were a cold bunch, the Haftons, calculating, greedy. His father had traded strong words with Lord Hafton on many occasions, though his own long absence seemed to have cooled the hostility that once lay between the families. And soon Susannah would be one of them, a Hafton, against her wishes, against her desire. How could he save her? he wondered. How could he make her his?

Pouring himself more wine, he settled back in the chair and stared into the flames above the sleeping form of his friend.

~

Susannah lay in the bed with her eyes wide open, staring up into the folds of the rich canopy that hung above the bed, just visible in the light of the dying embers in the hearth. Her long rest during the day and the pleasure of the evening had robbed her of all desire for sleep. Now, trying to force her body to be still was asking the impossible. She tossed and turned, searching to find a position that was comfortable but in vain. In the end she gave up the effort. Sitting up, she drew back the curtains that surrounded the bed, picked up the candle and took it to the fire to light it from the embers. Then she set out to explore the room.

She had taken little notice when she had woken there earlier in the daylight. Then, she had been anxious to go downstairs and find Sir Daniel, but now the fact that it was his room and he had cared enough to give it up for her lit in her a curiosity that had to be appeased.

She padded around the bed on bare and silent feet, the oak boards warm and smooth against her soles until she felt the soft weave of a turkey rug underfoot. Wriggling her toes in its luxury, she smiled at herself, enjoying the childish pleasure. A sudden noise beyond the door, a creak of a floorboard, stilled her heart and she held her breath, waiting, until she heard it again. Footsteps in the passage outside – a servant, perhaps, doing the last rounds before bed, or Sir Daniel, as sleepless as herself.

Soundlessly she crept to the door, the candle before her throwing misshapen shadows that flickered at the corner of her eye. She had just reached out for the latch when it turned of its own accord and the door swung softly open. Gasping in shock and quickly snuffing her candle, she stepped back across the room towards the fire as a hand appeared bearing a candle of its own, followed by a muscular arm and the unmistakeable body of Sir Daniel, his face in darkness, unrevealed by the small light he held out before him.

"Susannah?" he whispered. "Is that you?"

"Yes, it is me," she whispered back, instinctively clutching at the neck of the shift that hung loosely off one shoulder, holding it close about her. She had never appeared so exposed before a man, not even her father.

"I saw a light moving under the door as I passed," he explained. "I wanted to be sure there was nothing wrong."

"There's nothing wrong. I just couldn't sleep. Too much sleep this afternoon no doubt."

He nodded and placed the candle on a side table that stood by the fireplace. Then he crouched before the hearth to throw more logs on the flames, poking the glowing embers back into life. Flames began to lick at the new wood, crackling, heat lifting into the room. When he was satisfied, he stood up and moved back away from the sudden warmth into the darker recesses of the room.

"Come by the fire," he said to her. "The night is cool."

She stepped forward to stand by the hearth, holding out her hands to it for a moment. She had not been cold, but the flames were bright and attractive, and it was pleasant to stand before them. She was aware of Sir Daniel's nearness and the hunger in his eyes, but keeping her eyes on the fire, she tried not to think of the sheerness of the linen shift and her nakedness beneath it. She swallowed, and her skin burned with a heat that had not come from the heat of the fire. Every sense within her was alive, raw and sensitive, as though his hands were on her flesh already. A tension crackled through the space between them like the promise in the air before a thunderstorm.

So this is how a woman falls, she thought. In pleasure and desire.

"I must marry Edward Hafton," she whispered, as if such words might shield her from their need for each other.

He moved forward from the darkness of the room into the firelight and her eyes never left his face, straining to read him, to understand the thoughts that lay behind his eyes. He was still watching her, but she could make no sense of what she saw, the tension in his jaw, a hardness in his gaze.

"You're not contracted to him yet," he said.

"Nonetheless, I must marry him," she replied. Her conscience still strove towards her duty, even when she was shaking with her passion. Need and longing surged through her body with every breath she took. If he took her in his arms now, she would respond in kind without question – he could undo her in a moment and ruin them both.

"And you would go to him pure." His voice was harsh above the crackle of the fire. It was not a question.

She inclined her head, her resolution failing with his proximity, the power of his presence so close. "It would seem ... honest."

He flashed her a brief half-smile. "Is that what you desire? To marry Edward Hafton?" he said.

Her lips tightened at the unkindness of the question, and she braced her body against the blow. "You know the answer to that."

"Tell me."

She turned away from him towards the fire and folded her arms across her chest, anger threading through the passion.

"I want to hear you say it." He reached a hand for her arm and, grasping it, swung her round to face him, but she kept her head averted, eyes down, uncomprehending of this sudden streak of cruelty. "Tell me."

Susannah said nothing and he let her arm go, turning away from her to lean his palms against the mantel above the hearth, staring into the fire, tapping at the grate with a booted toe. She could see the conflict in every inch of him as he fought to deny his desire for her and honour her promise to Hafton. He turned his head towards her, and she watched him, still trying to read the thoughts behind his eyes. Stepping closer, she touched her fingers to the muscle of his forearm beneath the rolled-up sleeve. The feel of his skin against her fingertips sent waves of need roiling through her, desire bright and sharp: she had never felt such longing.

"Forgive me, Sir Daniel," she managed to say.

He closed his eyes a moment and shook his head.

"Then ...?" She looked up at him, aware of her weakness against his strength and her nakedness beneath the linen shift but still she trusted him – he was no Edward Hafton to force her against her will. Gently, he placed a palm against her cheek, then in a sudden movement bent his head to hers to find her lips, pressing his mouth against hers.

She pulled back. "We cannot," she gasped. "We must not."

He paused for just a moment, weighing her words, before his hand shifted from her cheek to cradle the back of her head, holding her still as he lowered his mouth to hers again, harder this time, more insistent. For a heartbeat she resisted, the last thread of duty holding on, but her desire won the battle and she began to respond, her lips moving, tentatively at first, then gaining confidence, her tongue meeting his.

She raised her arms to hold him against her, tracing the lines of the muscles of his shoulders, hard and unyielding, and as he drew her close to him she could feel the hard warmth of his chest against her breasts. She wanted him with an abandon she had never known was possible, the pleasure of him overwhelming her senses: the taste of him, the hardness of his body, the urgency of his fingers on her skin.

Then, breathless, they drew apart. Cupping her face in his hands, he searched her expression, looking for traces of fear or doubt or regret, but she knew all he saw in her eyes was the mirror of his own desire and the pleasure she was taking.

He lowered his mouth to hers again, more gentle now, taking his time, lightly biting at her lip with his teeth, then sliding his mouth across her chin to find the soft skin of her throat. His hand held the back of her head as she tipped it back, exposing her neck to the caresses of his lips, his tongue, his teeth, while his thumb gently stroked along the delicate line of her jaw.

She was totally in his power, aware of his strength and his experience, but she felt no fear of him. Her trust in him was complete, offering her body as a sacrifice, her virtue as a prize, sure he understood the value of the gift.

"Why you?" he breathed. "Of all the women I have known, why have I fallen for one who is promised to another?"

She was silent, her whole being focussed on the host of new sensations as his hand traced along the line of her shoulder, his fingers warm, sending shivers across her skin. She saw him smile at the pleasure he was giving her, and as her head tilted back, his hand found her breast, fingers running lightly over it, teasing through the linen. She shuddered, the sensation unfamiliar, waves of liquid heat rolling through her until her limbs seemed weightless, her body supported by his arm behind her back, all sensation centred on the movement of his fingers. Suddenly he stopped, waiting as she steadied herself before he moved around to stand behind her. She turned her head to see, to follow him around, but he put his face against hers and nudged her head back to face the fire.

She shivered and leaned into him behind her as he lifted the curtain of hair from the nape of her neck, slid his tongue against the soft skin, tasting the sweet salt of her warmth. One hand crept across her shoulder, sliding furtively inside the shift, cupping the breast, kneading skin against skin, while the other moved along the line of her hip, finding the curve of her buttock, his fingers hard and strong as they held the young flesh between them, massaging, kneading.

She moaned, all thought lost in his caresses. His mouth was still warm against her neck and her shoulder as his hand slid round from her buttock across her hip, finding the soft flesh of her inner thighs, stroking, working its way towards what lay between them. She could barely breathe, aware only of her skin under his touch and the sensations that spiralled through her body.

Quickly, lightly, he rubbed his palm across her groin, sliding his fingers between her thighs across the sheer fine linen, until she felt her legs almost give way beneath her. Then, with expert ease, his fingers ravelled up the fabric of the shift, finding their way beneath it to touch the soft warmth between her legs. She gasped, her body tensing as his fingertips started to explore her secret place, strumming gently against the moist folds of flesh, shudders rippling through her from his touch.

Heat began to form in a ball in her belly, threatening to explode and shatter her into fragments. The feeling was exquisite, all-consuming, and she pushed back against him, his body hard behind her, all that was keeping her upright.

But she was barely aware of him, all her existence coiled in the sensation between her legs as his fingers slid inside her, throwing fuel on the fire that burned her whole body, raging through her, uncontrolled. Her legs buckled, and she felt his arm tighten round her, holding her up, his fingers still probing, the pleasure almost too much to bear.

Tears of ecstasy caught at the corners of her eyes, but she let them come, surrendering to the awareness of her physical body, a state of bliss she had never known was possible. All thought was suspended, and just when she thought she must drown in the flames, over-whelmed by their force, he slowly withdrew his hand, trailing it deliciously back across her belly, across her breasts, skimming the bare skin of her shoulders. She held her breath, waiting for what came next, anticipation keen inside her. His hands ran over her shoulders until they were cupped in his palms.

Then he turned her round to face him. Slowly, deliberately, with his lips curved in a smile of pleasure, he undid the bow that held her shift across her shoulders, loosening it an inch at a time, savouring the moment she would become naked before him.

The shift dropped in a pool at her feet, and it was hard for her to resist the urge to cover herself, her natural modesty even before this man that she loved, who would soon take complete possession of her body. He stepped back to see her better, dark eyes travelling over the lines of her form. She imagined how her body looked to him: the small upturned breasts, the nipples hard with desire, the narrow waist and slim hips, the strong slender legs, the dark triangle between them.

"You're beautiful," he said.

His voice broke the spell. Naked and exposed before him, Susannah found a sudden clearer understanding.

What they were doing was wrong.

Against God, against the law, against her family, against her future husband.

Her hands flew to cover herself as she squatted to scrabble for the shift at her feet. She got up slowly, uncertainly, her breath still ragged, the heat still in her belly. But she held the flimsy fabric before her, hiding her body behind it as she lifted her head to face him.

"This is wrong," she whispered, and the simple word almost broke her heart, her spirit crying out in protest, her body screaming with desire for him. "We cannot do this. It is wrong."

He said nothing, barely breathing in his anger and his disappointment.

"I am still a maid," she breathed. "And I am to be married. But not to you."

For a moment she was unsure what he would do. He stood silent, fists clenched at his sides, his breathing rough and uneven. His face was shadowed but even in the half-darkness of the single candle she could see the rage in the cruel set of his lips and the hurt in the way he slid his eyes away from her. A log slipped in the fireplace, fire catching with a snap, sparks flying up and lighting the tension between them.

With a sudden movement he stepped forward towards her and took her chin in his fingers, gripping hard and tilting her head so that their faces were close. His eyes were black and in the thwarted desire there she saw a light of fury burning too. She held her breath, suffused with a sudden fear of him, that he would not heed her words, that his hands would touch her flesh again, for if they did she knew she would be lost to him: she had no more strength to refuse, her blood crying out to submit to him and to follow the passion that held her body in thrall. If he touched her again, she would fall.

He held her head for what seemed an age, searching for the answer in her face to some question she did not know. Then he let her go, roughly, so that she almost stumbled backwards.

"Then we shall stop," he said. "If that's your wish."

"It's not what I wish, Sir Daniel. But it is what must be. You know it must."

He nodded curtly and turned to go. "Forgive me, Susannah," he whispered. Then he was gone, the door latch falling into place behind him. The candle guttered madly with the sudden draught, throwing gruesome shadows on the wall.

She stared after him for a moment, the pleasure of his presence already just a memory. Why had she needed to speak? she asked herself. She could have been in his arms now, in the bed, skin against skin, giving and receiving a bliss she had never known existed until this night. She wanted to wail and cry and beat at the floor in frustration, but instead she snuffed out the candle, threw herself into the bed that still held the smell of him, and over many hours of the night, cried herself to sleep.

CHAPTER 10

In the morning, she went downstairs reluctantly, aware from the looking glass of the picture she presented – her eyes were red from crying with dark circles underneath them, and her complexion was white from weariness. But she entered the dining chamber with her head held high, refusing to let him see her as beaten and sad as she felt. Both men were already at the table but only Sir Samuel looked up when she entered. She saw the momentary shock in his eyes, but he was too well mannered to pass comment. Recovering his composure in an instant, he greeted her with a smile and a nod.

"Good morrow, madam."

"Good morrow, Sir Samuel."

"Sir Daniel." She spoke politely, but the coldness in her tone was unmistakeable.

"Good morrow, madam," he replied, but if he lifted his eyes from the table, she did not see it and the atmosphere hung heavily between them.

"Come," Sir Samuel offered, "join us," and he gestured to a place at the table.

She sat and he poured her a mug of small beer. She sipped it, took a morsel of bread from the tray and lifted it to her mouth, forcing it past her lips, but she could barely bring herself to swallow.

I must eat, she told herself. I must not let him see how miserable I am.

Taking another mouthful of bread, she washed it down with a swig of the beer. She had never felt so wretched in her life.

"Madam?" Sir Daniel lifted his gaze towards her, and she turned her eyes to meet his, holding his gaze until it was he that looked away. She could not read what she saw there, his expression impassive and cold. "I have some business to attend to this morning," he said, "but if you are recovered enough to ride, I will have a man escort you back to Hafton this morning."

"Very well."

There was a pause, a moment of hesitation. Then he went on, "But only if you feel able to ride. If you need to rest here longer, you would be more than welcome." He turned his eyes again towards her and in them Susannah now saw the mirror of her own misery. He was offering an olive branch of sorts, a chance to start again, and though she was tempted to take it, she knew that staying could only cause more heartache. It was better to go and be apart so they could not hurt each other anymore.

She softened her tone, aware of his pain. "You're very kind, Sir Daniel, but I am quite well enough to travel. Thank you."

"Perhaps I could escort you, Mistress Susannah," Sir Samuel offered. "It's a beautiful morning for a ride."

Sir Daniel shot him a glance that came close to hatred. He said, "As you wish, Sam."

Then he turned again to Susannah, who looked on with a dispassionate expression, her emotions reined in tightly. "Are you a strong rider, madam?"

She thought of the pretty dappled mare she had left behind at Abbey Leigh, remembering the races across the Downs with her sister, the ditches they had taken in their stride, the logs they had leaped at a gallop.

"I am not without some skill, sir," she replied.

"Good. Then you may ride the chestnut gelding. His name is Regent. He will suit you well, I think."

A look passed between the two men that she could not read but then he was calling for a servant, giving instructions for the readying of horses, and her sorrow to be leaving wiped all other thoughts from her mind.

Daniel watched them go. She had been right, God damn her, he thought. And he had almost ruined her, almost taken his pleasure in spite of her protests, even knowing as he did so he would come to regret it, her virtue on his conscience for the rest of his days. But it had not just been desire that had moved him, though God knew how much he desired her. It was love that had stirred him and the knowledge that last night might have been their one and only chance to love each other as they wished.

He recalled how she looked as he had left her, her hands still clutching the shift in front of her, her raven hair loose and messed around her face, a strand across her cheek. Her face had been ashen, eyes staring and afraid, and her fear of him had cut to his heart.

The ride began in silence. Regent, skittish and high spirited, fretted against the bit that held him back, angling sideways at a jog before she managed to soothe him to a walk. She knew that Sir Samuel wished to talk to her, offering his company as some solace in her distress but that he lacked the right words to begin. She was grateful for his good will, and his gentle friendly nature drew her out of her despair.

"I thank you for offering to accompany me," she said, to ease the way. "It's pleasant to have company on the ride, though I think Sir Daniel would have preferred one of his men to escort me."

Sir Samuel's lips curved into a smile. "He is jealous of the time I will spend with you, is all."

"And afraid, perhaps, of what we may talk about."

"He trusts my discretion."

"I do not doubt it," she answered quickly, "and I would never ask you to betray that trust. He is a fortunate man indeed to have such a friend."

"Thank you." Sir Samuel tilted his head in acceptance of the compliment.

Then, deciding that after all she had nothing much to lose by directness, she said, "He must have loved your sister very much."

"He was devoted to her. We both were."

"He told me she was killed in a riding accident."

Sir Samuel flicked a glance to her that she could not read. "Yes, that is so," he agreed, but his tone suggested he had no wish to say more on the matter. She decided to let it drop.

"I am sorry for it. It must have been a great blow for both of you."

"Dan ... Sir Daniel took it hardest."

They walked on in silence, the horses' hooves thudding rhythmically on the mud of the lane, the strident song of a blackbird calling the alarm from the hawthorn at their approach. Behind the hedge, the acres of Sir Daniel's estate stretched across the gentle hills and, on the other side of the lane, meadows gave way to steep climbing slopes and the woods she had stumbled through only yesterday though it seemed now to have happened in a different lifetime. Beyond the woods lay the edge of the Hafton lands. Edward's lands. She tried not to think of it.

A magpie flitted up from a ditch at the side of the lane and Regent took fright. Rearing, it was a moment before his forelegs hit the ground again, and he began to plunge and snort, threatening to bolt. Susannah held her seat, fighting to keep him steady, and gradually she settled him into a gentle sideways jog. When she was sure of him again, she patted his neck and looked across to Sir Samuel, laughing.

"Sir Daniel was right; he is spirited."

But Sir Samuel had gone pale, his face lined with fear. "He should have given you a different mount," he breathed through lips that were tight with tension. "What in God's name was he thinking ...?"

She stared, the reality biting. What indeed was he thinking, when his first wife had died from just such a horse? "I was in no danger," she said softly, but it was more to reassure herself than Sir Samuel. "He is not beyond my skill to handle."

Sir Samuel made no reply. She could see the fury in his eyes, his jaw clamped tight with rage, a muscle twitching in his cheek as Regent still skittered sideways in the lane, tossing his head against the reins that held him in check.

Sir Samuel took a deep breath, brought his anger under control, then he turned his head towards her. "Are you all right, madam?"

"I am fine, thank you, Sir Samuel. But I'm touched by your concern."

His lips tightened into a grim smile. "If anything were to happen to you while you're under my care, he would never forgive me."

"If anything had happened to me then, it would not have been your fault."

"You ride well, madam. Luckily."

It was Susannah's turn to smile. "Perhaps we should canter a little way and hurry the journey along before anything else untoward can happen."

"If you wish."

Their horses needed no urging. The chestnut cantered willingly along the lane, his stride smooth beneath her, and though he fought for his head to go faster, she held him easily in check. One touch to his flank and he would have flown. The pleasure of such controlled power reminded her of happier days with her sisters, racing over the hills at Abbey Leigh. He was a beautiful horse and despite Sir Samuel's misgivings she was glad Sir Daniel had chosen him for her to ride.

At the gates to Hafton Hall, they slowed to a walk and as they passed between the great iron gates, all the elation of the ride drained from her in a wave. She felt as though she were entering a prison.

Sir Samuel noticed the change in her. "You look less than happy to be home."

She turned to him. "It has never felt like home, Sir Samuel, and I doubt it ever will, even when I become its mistress."

An image of the evening she had spent in the dining chamber at

Gifford Court fluttered at the edge of her thoughts: she had felt at home there from the moment she stepped through the door. She sighed. Whatever Sir Daniel's intentions towards her, whatever her feelings for him, she had made her choice last night – Gifford Court would never be her home.

"I think Gifford would suit you better, madam," Sir Samuel said softly. "In spite of what you may think."

His words sent a flush of heat across her skin and she swung her head to face him as he rode alongside. "What do you mean?"

He hesitated, the reticence that was born of his discretion doing battle with his wish to help. He said, "I mean only that … Daniel's affections are not given lightly. But once his affection is won, he will be loyal to the end. You … you hold his heart, Susannah, and I would not wish to see you break it."

She was silent, heart hammering, uncertainty sweeping through her, all her resolution crumbling in the face of his words. Break his heart? She had not thought it possible. She knew she roused desire in him, yes, but love? She had not dared to dream of so much. It is never hopeless, he had told her, and she smiled with the memory, a small spark of hope lighting inside her. Then she recalled the events of last night, his eyes flashing anger by the bed when she denied him, and his coldness towards her in the morning. It did not seem like love to her.

"You are kind, Sir Samuel, and you mean well. But you are mistaken," she said carefully. "It is not in my power to break Sir Daniel's heart."

Sir Samuel's expression hardened and closed. "Forgive me, I should not have spoken. I only thought to …"

"To what, Sir Samuel?"

"To be sure you understood. Dan is not always an easy man to read."

"Then I thank you," she replied more gently, aware he had offered his thoughts in good faith. She took her eyes from his face and looked toward the great house looming before them. "But I fear it is here my future lies, not at Gifford Court."

"It is Daniel's fear also," Sir Samuel murmured so softly she barely heard it above the clop of the horses' hooves on the stones. Then he touched his heels to his horse and broke into a trot for the last few yards of the ride. Regent tossed his head, eager to follow, but she held him in check and continued the steady walk, needing more time to order her emotions and prepare herself to meet her cousins.

Eleanor flew out of the door to greet her. "Are you all right? I told you not to go into the woods alone. You must have been terrified. Thank God you are unhurt. Are you well?"

Susannah slid from the chestnut and gave a last smile of understanding towards Sir Samuel before she allowed herself to be bundled inside by her cousin.

"There is no need to fuss," she said, but her cousin would have none of it.

"You're very pale. You must come into the dining chamber and eat." She called to a servant, ordered food and ale to be brought, put an arm around Susannah's shoulders to guide her towards the great hall where a good fire crackled in the hearth. In spite of herself, Susannah was glad of the warmth, and she took the stool she was offered before it.

Sir Samuel followed, ignored by Eleanor but greeted at last by Lady Hafton who apologised for her daughter's manners and settled him across the hearth from Susannah. The two travellers exchanged a glance and she was glad that he was with her. He at least understood a little of her heart and her thoughts. She wondered what he would relate to Sir Daniel on his return, if he would berate him for his choice of horse. She hoped not – she had grown quite attached to the chestnut.

"We were so worried," Eleanor was saying, sitting on the rug at her cousin's feet, gripping her hands. "Edward said he had seen you out walking early, but we thought nothing of it until the time to break our fast had passed and still you had not returned. Then we began to worry. Mother sent servants out all over the estate to search for you. We thought perhaps you had turned on an ankle or fallen somewhere. But it never crossed our minds you might have wandered into the woods. Whatever possessed you, sweet cousin, to go into the forest like that?"

Sir Samuel turned his eyes from the fire to wait for her answer.

She hesitated, unsure under his searching look. "I … I … cannot say," she stammered finally. "The foolish whim of a moment, I suppose."

He slid his eyes back to the fire, apparently unconvinced. She hated to lie but what choice did she have?

"You foolish girl!" Lady Hafton approached with cups of ale. "You had us all worried half to death."

"I'm so sorry, Aunt Elizabeth. I don't know what came over me. I was lost in my thoughts, not thinking …"

"Well, no harm done, thanks be to God."

Susannah took her ale and sipped at it slowly, eyes lowered. Then she said, "Where is Edward?"

"He has gone to see friends at Easterleigh Manor. He left yesterday afternoon."

Relief tumbled through her that she would not have to meet him yet. She had a few days more to prepare herself, a few days more of precious freedom from his presence. Sir Samuel caught her eye and she looked away, unwilling to give her thoughts away.

Lady Hafton turned to their guest. "You will have dinner with us, Sir Samuel, before you return? It is almost noon, and you must be hungry after your ride."

"I am indeed." He nodded, and they made their way from the great hall to the dining chamber where servants stood ready with platters of dressed meats and game pie. They took their places in silence and in silence they began to eat.

Eleanor fussed over her for the rest of the day despite Susannah's protests and, after Sir Samuel had left, the cousins sat together in

Lady's Hafton's sitting room, where the light was best for sewing. Susannah's needle flickered through the fine fabric of a shirt she was working on, a detail of blackwork embroidery for the collar. It was a gift for her father, and the thought that soon she would be sewing shirts for her husband, for Edward, raised a swell of sorrow inside that brought tears to her eyes and made her prick her finger.

"Cousin Susannah," Eleanor cooed. "You should be resting. There is no need for you to be sewing."

"I would rather be busy," she replied. "I have no wish to be idle." She blotted the bubble of blood on her finger with a rag, then checked the shirt carefully to make sure she had made no stain.

"So tell me about Gifford Court," Eleanor said. "What is it like?"

Susannah swallowed, and when she spoke she took care to disguise the emotion in her voice. "It is smaller than Hafton Hall, similar to Abbey Leigh, but it's well appointed. It nestles near the foot of the hills and the trees reach down towards it."

"So the rooms are dark?"

"Not at all. The trees are on the north side. The house itself faces south across gardens and parkland."

"What of inside?"

She tried to think how best to describe it but her images of the house were so bound up in her feelings towards its owner it was hard to find any words of description.

"It is lovely," she said, finally.

Eleanor narrowed her eyes, observing her cousin, and Susannah stared harder at her sewing to avoid the scrutiny. When Eleanor said nothing more, Susannah glanced up, curious. Her cousin was still watching her. To break the tension, she smiled. "Why do you stare at me?"

Eleanor said, "You've told me nothing of Sir Daniel. Or Sir Samuel."

"There is nothing to tell, cousin. They looked after me, that is all. In the afternoon I slept, at supper we ate soup and ... some capon, in a lemon sauce, I believe. After that we played cards and backgammon and then we retired. It was altogether uneventful."

Her cousin nodded, as if satisfied, and gave up her scrutiny, lowering her eyes to her sewing. Susannah regarded her thoughtfully for a moment longer, wondering at her suspicions. Then she saw something that brought a genuine smile to her lips.

"Eleanor," she said, "there is straw in your hair." She reached forward to tease the offending piece from her cousin's locks but Eleanor jerked back her head as though Susannah had slapped her, driving her own fingers through the ends of the fine blonde mane instead, finding the piece of straw and dragging it free. She rubbed it between her fingers for a moment and when she looked up, her face was dark, her jaw set firm with fury.

"I went to the stables this morning to check on my mare," she snapped.

"Of course," Susannah replied, though she wondered at her cousin's reaction.

There was a moment's silence, Eleanor's needle flicking hastily through the linen until she stopped and looked up. "You know my brother was worried about you," she said. "He even delayed his journey until we had received word of you and knew that you were safe."

"I regret I worried anyone," Susannah replied, keeping her tone even.

"My brother is very fond of you."

"He has made his intentions plain to me, Eleanor. There is no need for you to play matchmaker."

"I know." Her cousin smiled. "But he is worried he has made a bad beginning."

Susannah repressed a temptation to laugh. It was either that or cry, she thought.

"Do you care for him at all?" Eleanor asked softly. "He would make a good husband for you."

"Perhaps," Susannah answered, reluctant to confide her marriage plans to her cousin. In spite of Eleanor's protestations of friendship, Susannah suspected her first loyalty would always be to her brother. She knew by instinct it would be wise to keep her feelings hidden.

"You will consider him?"

"I will consider him."

Eleanor smiled and resumed her sewing, plying her needle with skilled and even care. "I am glad. I should welcome you as a sister."

Susannah returned the smile and another silence fell between them as they worked.

CHAPTER 11

*I*n the early morning, a rider arrived from Abbey Leigh.

Susannah stared at him in surprise when she was called – she knew him straight away as one of the grooms – he had helped her to her horse a hundred times. He stood in the main hall, muddy and weary, and he looked as though he had ridden through the night. It must have been on urgent business indeed to take such a risk. A single rider on the road after dark risked robbery at the very least, and possibly much worse.

"Mallors?" She approached him across the hall. A sense of dread tempered her pleasure at seeing the familiar face. "Dear God, Mallors, what has happened?"

He gripped his hat in his hands before him, twisting the brim in his fingers. His face betrayed bad news. "Forgive me, Mistress Susannah, but I bring the gravest news."

Her heartbeat quickened, and she ran her tongue across her lips, mouth dry with dread.

"Your good father has been taken poorly. He is not expected to live out the week and he's been asking to see you. Your mother sent me to fetch you straight away."

She swallowed and turned away, hands on hips, battling to control her breath, to stop herself crying out. Then, drawing herself up, breathing deeply, she swung back towards him. "Thank you,

Mallors," she said. "Go to the kitchen and take some breakfast and rest. They will take care of you there. I must prepare to go immediately."

"I was to bring you back myself," Mallors said.

"You're exhausted. You may follow on later when you and your horse have rested. Now go to the kitchen."

He nodded and backed away with a bow, and she turned to her cousin who had been looking on.

"Can you arrange a horse and a man to take me, Eleanor, please? I must go at once."

"Of course." Eleanor hurried across to the door, her skirts swinging out behind her in a swish of emerald silk.

Susannah followed her out and ran up the stairs to make ready her things for the journey.

Within an hour she was ready, mounted on her favourite bay mare and with a groom she did not recognise beside her on a sturdy grey. A small bundle containing one change of dress was strapped tight behind him. They left the house at a canter, the horses keen and willing, and though she missed the eager gait of the chestnut, the mare was smooth and strong beneath her. A gusty wind whipped at her skirts and a lowering sky promised rain. "I do not plan to stop," she told the groom.

They rode at a steady canter most of the morning, slowing now and then to a walk to rest the horses. Halfway through the morning the rain began, a steady drizzle at first, cool and damp against her face, but then gradually falling harder, the day darkening in its wake. The wool of her skirts soon soaked through and dragged cold and heavy against her legs. Her arms ached, and her back began to hurt from the unbroken hours sitting side-saddle. As a girl she had ridden astride whenever she could, secretly, away from the eyes of her parents, her skirts pulled up above her knees. It had been heaven to sit straight on, the horse's power between her knees, easier to harness and command. It had been a far more comfortable way to ride.

Now, turning in the saddle this way and that to try and ease the soreness in her spine, she wished she still had such freedom. It was going to be a long ride.

~

They arrived after dark, wet through and shivering. She had never been so relieved to see the hearth at Abbey Leigh in her life. Her sisters were delighted to have her home, and after she had hugged them all in turn, they fussed about her with a clean rough sheet to rub her dry, and warm wool clothes for her to wear. She was impatient with their attention, anxious to see her father, the chill in her own bones of no consequence.

"How is he?" she demanded, shaking them off, sodden clothes steaming before the fire. She took the spiced wine her mother gave her and nursed the warm goblet in her hands. She was still shaking with the cold. "Can I see him?"

"Let us get you warm and dry first. We have no need of two deaths in the family."

"But … "

"No buts." Her mother's sternness was strangely comforting, a reminder of how her life used to be. Before the Haftons. Before Sir Daniel. "Drink your wine, then go upstairs and get changed. Olivia will help you. When you are once more presentable, I'll take you to your father."

Upstairs in the bedchamber she had shared with Olivia, she let her sister peel the wet layers away, warmth returning slowly, the shivering subsiding. But the quickened heartbeat remained; anxiety about her father, her urgent need to see him. Olivia seemed to take forever with the gown even though they barely spoke, focusing instead on their task. At last she was ready, and when she stepped out into the passage her mother was waiting. "How is he?" she asked.

Her mother shook her head. "He is dying, my sweet. It's his chest, his breathing. It gets worse by the day."

She swallowed down her grief. On the long ride from Hafton she had prayed there had been some mistake, hoping against hope she would arrive at Abbey Leigh and find him recovered and well, the old smile on his lips at her coming. Her mother's words cut down such imaginings.

"How long have you known?" she managed to whisper, following her mother's brisk stride along the passage towards his chamber.

Her mother stopped abruptly, turned to her daughter then hesitated. "His breathing has been hard for many months."

Susannah stared. "Many months?" she demanded. "Then why did you not tell me? How could you have sent me away if you knew?"

"It was your father's decision, Susannah. He wanted to see you settled before he ..."

Susannah shook her head: she did not want to hear the word. "I must see him."

"Of course." Her mother laid a hand on her arm, soothing. She smiled. "He will be pleased to see you. You were always his favourite, Susannah. His first and most precious child."

They reached the chamber: her mother turned the handle gently, the door creaking lightly open. That hinge had creaked ever since Susannah could remember and no amount of oil had ever been able to fix it.

In the doorway, her mother stopped and turned again. "Prepare yourself, you will find him much changed."

She nodded, gathering her strength, swallowing down her fears as her mother risked a small smile of reassurance then led her daughter inside. The chamber was warm and dimly lit by candles in brackets on the walls, and a fire that glowed bravely in the hearth. She stopped, taking in the scene before her. Her father was propped up in the bed, and even from the doorway she could hear the harsh rasp of each breath he was fighting for.

"My dear father." She ran to the bed and sat beside him, taking his hands in her own. Her mother had been right – he was just a husk of the man she had bid farewell to a few short weeks before, his skin grey and stretched across his frame, his hands pale and claw-like as his fingers searched to grasp her hand.

"Susannah," he breathed. "I am much pleased to see you. I feared you would not come in time."

"Hush, sir. I am here and all is well. Pray do not try to talk."

"All is not well. But I will soon be at peace and I hope I have done my duty by my family. By my eldest daughter at least?"

"Of course you have, sir. Of course."

"Then your cousin is not displeasing to you?"

"No, sir." She slid her eyes away for the lie but his own eyes were barely open, struggling to focus, and she guessed he could no longer read her as he used to do.

"Then marry him and I may die in peace ..." His pale lips stretched into the semblance of a smile. " ... knowing you are settled and Abbey Leigh is safe. It would bring a smile to your grandfather's face to know it."

"Yes, sir."

"As long as you are happy, child."

She nodded, tears creeping from her eyes as her father fought again for breath, his whole body trembling with the effort.

"Stay with me a while," he whispered, squeezing her hand. "I have sorely missed your company."

She returned the pressure with her fingers. His eyes gently closed and after a while his breath seemed to come more easily. There was no more rasping and the rattle in his lungs had ceased.

A movement behind her made her turn. It was her mother, creeping closer to take her place in the chair that was set on the other side of the bed. She took her husband's hand in hers and lifted her eyes to her daughter. "Then it is over," she whispered. "God be praised. He suffers no more."

Susannah stared in disbelief. "No. It cannot be. I have only just arrived."

"He was only waiting to take his leave of you. Now he is at peace at last. He has suffered greatly; I would that God had not spared him for so long." She stood and, bending over her husband's body, laid her lips gently, one last time, on his forehead.

"Go and call your sisters, Susannah. We will make a vigil."

Susannah was up in a moment, fleeing from the room, her world crumbling around her as she stumbled down the stairs and into the main hall. Three pairs of eyes swung towards her with an understanding in them that dragged at her heart. There was no need to say the words. One by one they rose from their places by the hearth, placing down their sewing with care, needles neatly tucked, before following one another across the room and filing up the stairs to bid their father a final farewell.

~

The day of the funeral it lashed with rain, the graveside slick and treacherous with mud. Susannah was glad of the storm, her tears washing away unnoticed in the rain. It was a strange household in those few weeks after her father's death. Abbey Leigh had lost its captain and struggled for a while in the aftermath. Susannah stayed for as long as she dared: she saw the fragile woman in her mother, the mask of bossy sternness slipping in her grief. So she remained to offer courage and support, and lend the fortitude her mother could not find.

It was not the time to talk of her marriage. Her father's dying words had sealed her fate, and now, as they mourned, there was nothing more to talk about. But in time, when the mourning was over, she knew the process would begin – letters from Lord Hafton to her mother, the drawn out brokering of a deal that would bind her for her life to Edward Hafton, and deliver Abbey Leigh into his hands. Dread lurched through her, cold with misery every time she thought of it, the memory of his body up against her in the woods, his hands inside her dress.

And over all her thoughts hung the image of Sir Daniel, desire rising with each memory of his touch, pain following hard behind with the recollection of how it ended. He was a shadow that confused and disturbed her, a distraction from her sense of duty, infusing her with guilt. She had come so close to falling, to giving him her body, but he had undone her, nonetheless. She had given him her soul, her thoughts, her love: possession of her body seemed almost trifling in comparison. Grief for her father mingled with the tears she wept for Sir Daniel and when, finally, it was time to make the journey back to Hafton, her soul was heavy with her sorrow.

~

The day dawned fair, a warm June breeze to speed her way, the bay mare smooth and calm beneath her as they set their steps away from Abbey Leigh. The farewell was tearful: she would never more return there as a maid, and though the words remained unspoken, her mother's eyes were eloquent enough. At the gates she did not look back, the image of Abbey Leigh clear in her mind, but set her gaze instead firmly forward to face a future she could no longer escape.

Now, with her home some hours behind her, her tears long dry, she was glad of Mallors' company, a familiar friendly face, a face she trusted and a reminder of her life at Abbey Leigh. They spoke little but his kindly presence served to soothe a little the growing unease inside her, the sense she was returning to her doom.

The first day's ride passed peacefully, the weather holding fair. The sky was still light when they drew in at an inn for the night, dusk not yet approaching and the long June evening light still before them. But she was weary from her thoughts and her grief, and the comfort of an inn was a pleasant prospect.

Mallors took the horses to the stables while the inn-keeper's wife showed Susannah to a chamber that was simply furnished with a bed and a little table next to the window. It was small and low ceilinged, the heavy beams passing close to her head, but it was clean and the window gave on to the village so that she would be spared the noise of horses coming and going from the stables at the back overnight.

She took her supper in her room, looking out at the village as she ate. The warm summer evening had brought people out of their homes – a small group of women stood gossiping in the street, young children playing around their skirts. An old man passed by and one of the women called out to him something she could not quite make out, but he laughed, and the other women laughed too, and their cheerfulness helped to soothe her troubled thoughts.

She finished her supper of fowl and cheese and bread, and

drained the cup of small beer, but with nothing else to do, she remained at the window looking idly down into the village, watching the world go by with vague unfocused attention. A rapid clatter of hooves scattered the village women smartly from their places in the road to let the rider through, drawing their children to them out of the horse's way. The sudden activity sparked her interest and drew her gaze to the road before the inn. In spite of herself, she leaned closer to the glass, bored and curious.

For a moment she stared, convinced she must be mistaken. But she had made no mistake. The horse that stood now in the road outside the inn was none other than Regent, the chestnut head tossing proudly, mane flying in the breeze. Her pulses quickened, and her breath came short as she watched in disbelief that Sir Daniel could be at her door. He dismounted and, touching a hand to his horse's bridle, he glanced up at the façade of the inn, casting his eyes across the windows. Susannah drew back abruptly, heart hammering.

Why? She railed inwardly. Why, of all the inns in Somerset had he chosen to come to this one?

Then, because she could not help herself, she peered out through the glass again, but both horse and rider had gone, the road empty of all save the village women, who had gathered in their huddle once more. Shaken, she wondered if he had been there at all, or if she had dreamed of him, the phantom of an overwrought mind.

Daniel led Regent to the stables himself. He had travelled too much and too widely ever to trust his horse completely to strangers and he would see the gelding settled before he took his own rest. The ostler eyed him with dislike, offended, but Daniel paid no heed, and only when the horse was unsaddled and fed and watered, did he turn away to stride back across the yard, hungry and thinking of his supper. Out of habit, he ran his eyes across the other horses in their stalls as he passed, until one of them unexpectedly caught his eye. He stopped abruptly, supper forgotten, looking again to be sure. It was the Hafton's bay mare, Duchess. He knew her well – he had raised her himself before he went away to war. It was the same bay mare he knew that Susannah often rode, and a flare of hope lit in him that she might be here in the inn, on her way back to Hafton at last.

He walked back to the ostler, who was rubbing down a fine grey gelding.

"Master Ostler?" The man looked up from his work, laid a practised calming hand on the horse's shoulder.

"Yes, sir?"

"The bay mare, in the corner stall." He gestured towards it with his head. "Did you happen to note who was riding her?"

"A young lady, sir," the ostler replied. "She was travelling with a single servant and hardly any luggage."

"I thank you." He flicked the man a coin and turned away, wandering thoughtfully back out to the yard, his hunger forgotten. Susannah was here, he was sure of it: he must search out the innkeeper and find out her room.

In her chamber, Susannah paced the small square of floor between the window and the bed, hands twisting restlessly before her. Just that one small glimpse of him had set her pulses racing, heat coursing through her blood. She could feel the warmth of the flush across her skin, knew how red her cheeks would be.

She had dismissed straight away the first fear that he had seen her. The window that looked onto the road was small, and the little lead-lighted panes would have reflected back the daylight to anyone looking up. So, she reasoned, there was little chance he would know she was there, and precious little hope of seeing him unless he should chance to have a room close to hers. Then, she thought, there was a possibility, however small, that they might meet in the passage. She shook her head to clear it of the thought. She didn't want to meet him. Especially not here in an inn, where she was completely alone with nowhere to run to if he tried again to seduce her.

She had turned the events of that night in his chamber over and over again in her mind, reliving each moment, and the pain of it was greater than the pleasure, for she could believe only in the truth of his desire. His coldness when she refused him and the rough way he had left her gave the lie to Sir Samuel's words that his friend truly loved her. If that were so, then why had he been so cold in the morning? Why had he not escorted her to Hafton Hall himself? There was only one conclusion to be drawn though she had battled these past few weeks to find a different answer to the riddle. He had been cold because he hated her: she had spurned his advances and refused to fall. She guessed he was used to more successful seductions and she imagined he was not a man who liked to fail.

A knock at the door distracted her from her thoughts, a servant, she assumed, come to clear away the supper, so she opened the door without a second thought. But her breath caught in her throat when she saw Sir Daniel standing there in the gloom of the corridor, cloak thrown back across one shoulder, a dark and pained intensity in his eyes.

"Madam." He bowed.

She dropped into a curtsey, breathless, unable to speak.

"I saw the bay mare in the stables," he offered by way of explanation. "I guessed you must be here."

"Yes," she replied, rising, barely able to find her voice. She had not thought of the horse. "As you see."

A servant passed along the narrow corridor, tray in hand, and Sir Daniel moved closer into the doorway. Instinctively she stepped back, though his sudden closeness filled her senses, all of them raw and alive to his presence, crying for his touch. But he seemed hesitant, and when the servant had passed, he stepped back away from her as though he understood she needed more space to breathe.

"I hoped," he began, "you might agree to take a turn around the village with me. It is a beautiful evening …"

There was an uncertainty in his voice she had not heard from him before, a fear that she might refuse him. Swallowing down the suspicion that it was simply an act to deceive her, she lifted her face to his. He was watching her as though he would read every thought in her head, desperate for her answer.

"Yes," she heard herself saying in a shaky voice, though her head was commanding her to say no. "I would like that very much."

She took the key from the lock on the inside of the door and stepped into the corridor beside him, aware of the danger, that she was as a lamb consorting with a wolf. But her need for him was too great and there was a part of her that still sought to believe that he loved her – it was a risk she was willing to take.

He moved back while she locked the door behind her and then he was leading her down the stairs, through the warren of passages that led out to the main entrance on to the road. Outside, the evening sun was bright after the gloom of the inn and they stood before it for a moment, blinking, eyes adjusting to the sudden light. Then he said, "This way, I think," and she fell into step beside him.

They walked a way in silence, a hard tension between them that she could find no words to relieve, until they found themselves at the churchyard gate.

She smiled. "Must we always meet in church?" she said.

He laughed, the darkness lifting from his eyes. "It seems that way, does it not? Perhaps we shall walk a little further?"

"Let's," she agreed, and they wandered on, beyond the edges of the village until they came to a grassy bank that gave on to a bubbling stream.

"Here?" he asked, and when she nodded, he swung off his cloak with a practised sweep and placed it on the grass for her to sit on. She sat carefully, arranging her skirts around her, glad she was wearing deep green, a colour she knew became her.

Sir Daniel sat beside her, one knee raised, and a forearm resting there. He looked out across the water to the opposite bank where a flock of ducks were holding court beneath a willow tree. She followed his gaze, then slid her eyes to meet his as he turned his head back towards her.

"I'm truly glad to have met you today," he said. "I am so sorry about your father. I've thought of you often since I heard the news. I know he meant a great deal to you."

"Thank you," she replied, touched by the kindness in his words. "I arrived just in time." She remembered standing at the graves of his parents in Hafton and knew he understood her grief.

"He was waiting for you?"

"I believe so." Waiting to ask if she would marry Edward Hafton, waiting for her assent to die in peace. She should not be here, she thought, the wolf beside her, tempting her from her duty. She should be back in her room at the inn, safe and alone. On her way back to Hafton Hall and marriage. She steeled herself against her feelings, her eyes following the ripple and rush of the stream.

"Your family must have been glad to have you there," he said.

"Yes," she agreed, slipping him a brief glance before returning her gaze to the stream. "But it was strange and awful. I've never seen my mother ..." she searched for the word, "... vulnerable, before. She has always been so strong. But yes, it was good that I was there – I was able to take care of things until she came back to herself. She has an able steward though, so I think between them all will go on well until ..." She stopped, unable to bring herself to talk to him of her marriage. She dropped her eyes to her hand which brushed at imaginary creases in her skirt.

Sir Daniel finished the sentence for her. "... until you are married."

"Yes," she whispered, looking away across the stream once again. The ducks had waddled down to the water now and were swimming peacefully to and fro on the stream. "Until I am married."

"Susannah?" He turned again to face her, hesitated, searching for his words.

His hesitation made her turn towards him. She was used to his confidence and self-assurance and this new uncertainty in him touched her. "Yes?"

He dropped his eyes as though ashamed, his fingers picking absently at blades of grass on the bank between them. He took a deep breath before he spoke. "I ... did not behave well towards you last time we met ... and I think perhaps I earned your distrust with my behaviour. I cannot blame you for that."

She was silent.

"You say nothing. Then I am right ... you thought I would seduce

you, and that having failed, I wanted nothing more to do with you
…"

Tears pricked at her eyes and she turned to look upstream. A cottager on the far bank was collecting her laundry from the bushes, shaking out the linen before she folded it, and a young girl was helping her, learning early the skills of a housewife. She blinked the tears away but still she could not bring herself to face him.

"Look at me, Susannah," he said softly. "Please."

She kept her eyes averted as he shifted closer, reaching across to touch her face and turn her chin toward him. She did not resist, looking up into his face, into those deep dark eyes that seemed to hold so many secrets. Did she dare to trust him? His lips were close, and she remembered the touch of them on hers, the taste of his mouth. Desire trembled through her body – if he kissed her now, she would be lost.

"Listen to me. And believe me." His voice was barely a whisper. "I wanted you that night, more than anything I have ever wanted. More than I ever wanted Grace. More even than I wanted to die after her death."

She gasped. His fingers moved from their hold on her chin to smooth the wayward hair back from her temple.

"But I didn't just want you for that single night. I wanted you for all nights. For all my life. I still do. I would make you my wife, if you would have me."

She dropped her head, unable to bear the desire in his eyes. His fingers continued to caress her forehead, her cheeks, and she rubbed her head against his touch. Tears threatened again behind her eyes. "I cannot," she said.

"Because of Edward?" His voice was rougher; she could feel the anger rising in the firmer touch of his hand.

She lifted her face. "It was my father's dying wish."

"But did you tell him the truth?"

"It was always his dearest wish to keep Abbey Leigh in the family. I should have been born a boy, but I am a woman, and all I can do to honour his wish is to marry my cousin."

"Even though you love me."

She shook her head, tears starting to fall unchecked. He ran a thumb gently over her cheekbones, wiping the tears away. "Don't cry, Susannah, please. It hurts me to see you cry."

She dropped her head against his chest, and he held her gently, fingers running through her hair, his cheek resting on the crown of her head, as though he were filling himself with the scent of her.

"I would be a better husband to you than Edward. A better custodian for Abbey Leigh. I would cherish it as I cherish Gifford Court. And it would prosper under my care."

She shook her head under his hand.

"Look at me Susannah," he said again, and with both hands he raised her reluctant head so that their faces were close. "Do you really think that Edward will care for Abbey Leigh? That he will look after it as your father has done? What interest has he ever shown even in Hafton? He will not care for it, nor its people, and it will founder…"

"There is a steward. And my mother. And there is me."

"And not one of you will have the power to go against your master."

She drew in a deep breath. Then, pushing away his hands with her own, she scrambled to her feet. Looking down on him, her hands on her hips, she said, "It was my father's dying wish. What would you have me do?"

He said, "He would not have wanted you to be unhappy, Susannah. You lied to him to make his passing easier, that is all. He loved you and he would want you to be happy. You know this."

He pushed himself to his feet to stand beside her and placed a hand on her arm to stop her walking away. At his touch she swung towards him so that they stood close, close enough that with one movement of his head he could have kissed her, both of them breathing hard, the moment charged with their emotion. With his hand still on her arm, he drew her gently closer towards him so that her breasts touched the leather of his doublet and she could feel the hardness of his thighs through the fabric of her skirts. She offered no resistance when he took her face in his hand and bent to kiss her, letting his lips touch hers for a moment, her breathing quick and short. But when he tried to move closer in, she pushed him away with her hands against his chest and turned from him, walking along the bank, her head lowered, her face in her hands.

Her thoughts were in turmoil, her resignation to her fate thrown into doubt by his words. All that he said made sense – her father would have wanted her happiness; he never knew the truth of things. There was a moment of silence, her own breathing hard above the gentle rush of the stream. Then she turned to him. "I need some time to think, Sir Daniel. I had not thought these past weeks that marriage to you was even possible. I had thought your intentions were … otherwise."

"Then you will consider my suit?"

She nodded, the pleasure of his company stilling the maelstrom in her mind. With him beside her, pleading for hand, it seemed that only one future could exist. It was impossible to imagine they might ever be apart. "I will consider your suit." She smiled then and took the arm he offered as they began to stroll back towards the village alongside the stream.

"Are you on your way back to Hafton, Sir Daniel?" She looked up at him, hopeful. It would be wonderful to have his company for the rest of the journey.

"Alas, no," he replied. "I am on my way to Bristol. I have business there I must attend to."

"Business, Sir Daniel?"

"Aye, Susannah, business." He smiled at the tone of her question. "I have been away from England a long time and there are matters relating to the estate that I must take care of."

"Of course," she said. "I only wondered …"

"You know well the matters that relate to the running of an estate. If … *when*…" he corrected himself, " … *when* you become mistress at Gifford Court, you will know much more. I would welcome your help indeed."

"I should like that," she replied. "Very much."

They said their farewells at the door to her room. "I shall think on all you have said today," Susannah said. "I have much to consider – it is not only our own wishes at stake. I must think of my family also."

"Then my happiness is in your hands," Sir Daniel replied.

They stood close in the dim light of the corridor. She could hear the soft rise and fall of his breath, and her own pounding heartbeat. He glanced along the passage to check they were alone and when he was quite sure, he tucked a finger under her chin and lifted her face to his. His mouth met hers, his lips soft and warm, gentle, for the briefest of kisses. Then it was over, and he had stepped back from her with a small bow.

"I shall call on you as soon as I return from Bristol," he said.

"I shall look for your coming," she replied.

She stood and watched him walk away until his head had dropped out of sight on the staircase, but he did not look back. Then she fumbled with the key in the lock and let herself into her room.

CHAPTER 12

The first person she met when she arrived back at Hafton was Edward, who was returning to the house from the stables. He stopped when he saw her and stood for a moment regarding her, his breath coming quickly, as if her presence made him nervous. She dropped a small curtsey but she was less afraid of him than before, girded by the knowledge of Sir Daniel's love for her.

He bowed in response. "I am sorry for your loss," he said. "And glad to see you looking so well."

"Thank you, cousin."

"I will not detain you any longer: you have had a long journey." He bowed again. "Good day to you, cousin."

"Good day," she replied with another small curtsey, watching him cross the yard and round the corner of the house.

She stood for a moment, perplexed by his courtesy. Then, shaking her head to dismiss it from her mind, she followed him inside the house where Eleanor came flying down the stairs to greet her with a delighted smile.

The days passed slowly at Hafton Hall. She wrote to her mother to ask for her advice. In the cold light of Sir Daniel's absence, Susannah was no longer so sure of him, and was afraid that her feelings – of love for Sir Daniel, of dislike for Edward – might cloud her judgement about the right path to take. For it was not only her happiness at stake, but the future of her family and all who lived at Abbey Leigh.

She had been back little more than a week when Lord Hafton sent for her to come to his office. She was surprised by the summons – her uncle rarely paid her any attention, and a sense of foreboding weighted her limbs as she rose from amongst the herbs in the garden she had begun to think of as hers, where she and Eleanor were making plans for planting.

Eleanor lifted her eyebrows with a whispered message of good luck as Susannah followed the messenger out of the garden, into the house and along the passage towards her uncle's office. At the door, the messenger bowed and backed away, and she lifted her hand to knock on the heavy panels of oak.

"Enter!" Lord Hafton's voice carried through the thick wooden door, and reluctantly she turned the handle and went inside.

It was a beautiful room she had never entered before. Tall mullioned windows admitted the bright morning light, glass-covered bookcases lined the walls, and a large oak desk stood bathed in a shaft of sunlight. Beyond it, Lord Hafton sat back in a high-backed chair, his fingers clasped together before his chest. She curtseyed.

"Susannah," he greeted her. "Come, sit down." He gestured to a stool that stood on her side of the desk and she went towards it, still looking around and admiring the room.

"It is a fine room, is it not?" He smiled. "Now you know why I spend so much time in here."

"Indeed, Uncle. And so many books."

"Would that I had time to read them …" He paused, growing serious, and observed her across the strewn papers on his desk. "But I didn't call you here to admire my office."

"I thought not," she replied.

"I have received a letter from your mother," he said.

"Oh?" Her stomach tightened with a sense of dread. She clasped her hands together tightly in her lap and took a deep breath to steady herself.

"She has asked me to stand as witness to the character of Sir Daniel Gifford. He has been courting you, apparently, and she wishes to know more of his reputation before she can give permission for the courtship to proceed."

Susannah lowered her head. She should have realised her mother would do such a thing. Of course she would seek Lord Hafton's advice. Why would she not? She should have thought.

"I was not aware that Sir Daniel has been paying you court, Susannah. He certainly has sought no permission from me to do so. I rather thought that your interest lay with my son."

She swallowed and said nothing.

"You have nothing to say?"

She looked up, wondering how best to defend herself. "I wrote to her, sir, asking only for advice. Sir Daniel expressed his interest. I was unsure what I should do."

"You should have asked me," her uncle replied testily. "I stand for you *in loco parentis* while you are here. It is my counsel you should have sought."

She bowed her head.

"And I would have counselled you to forget about Sir Daniel Gifford – he is a rogue and a murderer."

Her head snapped up at his words and she stared, speechless.

Gratified by her reaction, he gave her a grim humourless smile. "He killed his first wife, you know."

"I heard she was killed in a riding accident, sir." She heard the tremor in her voice, the heat of disbelief coursing through her blood.

"Oh, she fell from a horse, right enough," her uncle agreed with a dismissive wave of his hand. "There is no one would argue with that. But she should not have been on such a horse, nor leaping such a fence at so great a pace. She was never up to the challenge. Anyone with eyes could see her skill was wanting, but still he made her do it.

She broke her neck." He paused to gauge her reaction, but she set her expression against the turmoil inside, his words hateful to her, painful to listen to.

"It was the talk of the county," he continued, "and a scandal he was never brought to justice. He should have hanged. And I am not the only one who thinks so."

"I did not know," she murmured. Confusion and fear rolled through her in waves – she knew now the darkness she had glimpsed inside him, the cause of his years of grief.

"So," Lord Hafton went on. She had to force herself to listen. "I will be writing to your mother to tell her that I consider Gifford a most unsuitable match, and that all contact with him has been broken. I will also assure her that your courtship with my son is continuing unhindered and that I expect in the fullness of time to be announcing your betrothal."

"No," she murmured then, finding her voice, thoughts falling into place. "I must speak with Sir Daniel."

"There is no need," her uncle snapped. "I know him, as I knew his father before. Both of them rogues. He will deny everything. I forbid you to see him again."

She drew herself up. "Forgive me, sir, but it is not in your power to forbid me. I am of age and though I would have the blessing of my family, neither law nor church require it."

Lord Hafton sat back, appraising her, the same expression she had seen many times on the face of his son. She met the stare, blood drumming in her veins, heat across her skin, but she maintained her composure, determined he would not see her fears. He leaned forward across the desk towards her. "You are in my house," he breathed, his tone dangerous, "And you will do as I say, or you will face the consequences. Do I make myself plain?"

"Yes, Lord Hafton," she said.

"And I say that you will not see Sir Daniel Gifford again."

She rose from the stool without giving him an answer. Then she curtseyed low before she turned away and walked out of the room. It was an effort not to run.

Outside the door, she stood in the passage, breathing deeply, trying to calm her racing nerves. Her first impulse was that she must speak to Sir Daniel and hear the truth from his own lips. She wanted to take the mare and ride to Gifford Court straight away, to confront him, but she knew he was not yet back from Bristol – he had promised he would come to her as soon as he returned. So she must swallow down her impatience and force herself to wait. She moved away from the door, walking blindly through the passages of the house, her footsteps leading her out and away from the hateful words of her uncle.

In the gardens the air was clear and fresh, and she breathed more easily as she turned her footsteps toward the stables. Entering the yard, she thought she saw a flash of blue velvet skirts, Eleanor's gown, slipping into one of the hay barns, but her mind was too full of her own cares to pay much attention.

She found Duchess and, leaning against the stable door, she fondled the bay mare's ears, the soft voice of reassurance she used to the horse helped to calm her own troubled thoughts. It was cool in the stables out of the heat of the sun, and the mare butted her head up against her gently, enjoying the attention.

Her uncle's words played again and again in her mind, and it was not hard to believe the truth of them. She had seen the darkness in Sir Daniel's eyes herself, and deep down she had known there was more to be told about the death of his wife: thinking back, she was sure he came close to telling her the night she stayed at Gifford Court. Her heart went out to him, and she felt no hatred, only sorrow that he had suffered so much for so long for his guilt. Sir Samuel had said he had adored his wife – no wonder he had wanted to die on the battlefield, crying out to God for his punishment.

But God had chosen to spare him, to give him a chance to atone, and in His wisdom, He had brought him to her. Then she remembered Sir Samuel turning ashen when the chestnut gelding reared and shied, and her heartbeat quickened with the memory of it. She no longer knew what she should do, whom she could trust. She wanted to believe in Sir Daniel – he held her heart in his hands, the promise of a life together all that she could wish in this world. She must hear it from Sir Daniel himself. Only then would she know. Only then could she decide.

Wishing she could go for a walk but too afraid of being caught again by Edward, she remained in the stables long past the hour for dinner, no appetite, just the dull ache of longing to see Sir Daniel to tell him what had passed and hear the truth of things. There was a dread too, of meeting her cousin. She was sure her uncle would have related their conversation and she was not sure if she could bear the smug expression of Edward's sense of triumph.

Eventually, a stable lad approached. "Are you quite well, Mistress?" he enquired. "Only you've not moved this last hour or more."

"I am quite well, thank you," she replied. But it seemed she could delay no longer. Bidding the mare farewell with a final pat on her neck, she squared her shoulders and walked across the yard back into the house.

Edward found her after supper, when she was taking a turn in the formal garden in the hope the fresh air might dispel a growing headache.

"Cousin." She greeted him coldly, hoping her tone might send him away, though she doubted he would be so easily put off. She had no fear of him within the boundaries of the garden, judging she was safe enough, but she was in no mood for his games, the battle of wills that threaded through their every conversation.

He bowed. "Permit me to walk with you a while. It is indeed a beautiful evening."

She cast her eyes at the summer sky, still bright and clear, no sign in its colour yet of the coming night. A narrow sliver of moon hovered above the trees away to the east. She would be glad when this summer sultriness was over, her hair hot against her neck as it had been all day. She lifted a hand to flick it free, allowing air to caress the nape.

"My father spoke to me today," he began.

"What about?" She let her eyes slide sideways briefly, but he was watching his shoes as they stepped slowly over the smooth path of grass.

"About you," he replied, turning a quick glance towards her.

"I'm sure you could have found a more interesting topic." She laughed, though she knew she had scant cause for mirth.

"Do not be coy, cousin," he said, stopping the stroll and turning to face her. "It doesn't become you."

She said nothing.

"He told me he warned you about Sir Daniel." He waited, still facing her, so she nodded to confirm his words. "Were you surprised?" he asked.

"A little," she said carefully, wary lest her answer arouse his temper. She wondered why he was interested, how much he knew.

"So now you can forget about him," Edward hissed. "Your family sent you here as a bride for me, and I intend to honour that intention. You will see nothing more of Sir Daniel Gifford. You are mine. And it would serve you well to remember it."

"But why, Edward? Why do you want me when you have so little regard for me? Why would you want me as your wife?"

He lifted his chin in that familiar look of appraisal. Then he smiled, a cold smile that held a trace of cruelty. "Why?" he repeated her question, gave a hard bark of laughter. "Why? Because I like you, cousin Susannah, and I want to make you mine. Why should that surprise you? Do you think I am immune to your charms when apparently Sir Daniel is not?" He grabbed her arm, his fingers digging in to the flesh above her elbow.

"Let go of me!" She tried to drag herself away, but his hold was strong. She recalled the last time he had held her so and the same fear thrilled through her blood as he stepped in closer. Caught in his grasp, she fought to move away from him when he used his other hand to cup her chin and drag her face up to his. The familiar smell of him filled her and she struggled to avert her head as his mouth pressed against hers. One kiss, and he let her go with a laugh.

"Soon, cousin, you will have no choice but to submit. Your father chose me for you, remember? Would you go against his final wish? Soon I will be your master. You will call me husband and I will bed you as and when I wish."

He kissed his fingers and blew them to her, and she recoiled as though she had been struck. Then he turned and walked away from her, still laughing, his arrogance plain in the set of his shoulders and the jauntiness of his step. She watched him until he was out of sight behind the bushes. Then she turned and fled inside.

"Susannah, what is wrong?' Eleanor asked, looking up from her game of patience in the main hall. "You look as if you've seen a ghost."

Susannah slid on to a stool at the table with a wary glance towards her aunt and uncle at their places by the unlit fire. Lord Hafton was talking loudly about one of his hounds, and his wife was nodding, her mind apparently elsewhere. Eleanor picked up the cards and tidied them into a nice neat deck, then lifted her eyes to her cousin. "Pray tell me what is wrong, Susannah. You have been very strange all day."

She shook her head. She was tempted to confide, the burden hard to bear alone, but much as she loved her cousin, she knew Eleanor's loyalty would always be to Edward. Whatever version of the story he chose to tell would be the one that Eleanor would take as true. "It is the heat, merely. It saps my energy. I wish it would rain."

"And when it rains," her cousin smiled, "you will wish again for the sun."

Susannah returned the smile. "Perhaps."

Eleanor shuffled the cards. "A game of one and thirty? Or shall we wait for Ed?"

"We'll play," she replied, forcing her voice to be even. "He can join in later if he wishes."

To her great relief Edward stayed away all evening. Even so, the hours still seemed to stretch out unending despite the distraction of the cards, and when her aunt finally decided to retire, Susannah was only too eager to help. But even when the household was finally abed and she could curl up in the privacy of the dark, the oblivion of sleep failed to come until the early hours when she fell at last into a drifting sleep of dreams and nightmares.

The weather broke overnight, and Susannah woke before the dawn to explosions of thunder like a barrage of cannon fire overhead. The tumult wrenched her from her dreams and she sat up on her bed, the room lit like daybreak by shards of lightning that split the night sky. Cool air circled against the bare skin of her shoulders, welcome after the heat of the last few days. She rolled out of bed and lifted the curtain, a sisterly smile to Lettice as the maid came to stand beside her, and together they watched the lightning shattering the sky and lighting up the grounds that shimmered ghostly and silver in the unnatural light.

A sudden desire to be outside in the storm stole over her, a yearning to feel cold rain on skin that had only felt heat for so many days now. Curbing the impulse, she forced open the window instead and held out her hand, letting the water catch in her palm till she was cooled by its freshness. She could have stood there all night but finally she snapped the window shut, wiped her hand on her shift and lay herself down again to go to sleep.

The next morning the rain had eased. A light mantle of drizzle covered the park and the air had a new coolness against her skin when she climbed unwillingly out of bed before her aunt awoke. Lettice got up sleepily beside her and together, with deft and practised fingers, they helped each other dress. Then her aunt called, and they went to help Lady Hafton with the more complicated, drawn out process of attending her ladyship.

Downstairs, the household was readying itself for the Sunday trip to church. Susannah ate little for breakfast, wearied by the sleeplessness of the night and outside, afterwards, the fresh air was welcome. The bay mare tossed her head in greeting as Susannah rubbed the velvet nose. Francis Aston caught her eye and smiled before coming across to help her mount.

They set off at the usual ambling pace, Aston walking at the bridle of Lady Hafton's mount, leading her sedately. Susannah hung back, allowing her cousins to fall in abreast so that she could ride at a distance behind them. Edward ignored her and Eleanor merely smiled before turning to her brother with a laugh. Susannah could make no guess at their conversation.

At the church she saw the chestnut gelding tethered straight away. Heat shot through her limbs, her lassitude forgotten, pulses thrilling to the knowledge of his presence. In spite of all she knew of him, the pleasure of seeing him again was undimmed, the chance to hear the truth from his own lips. She slid hurriedly off the mare and gave the reins to one of the stable lads, her eyes searching across the churchyard for a glimpse of him.

She found him easily enough. He was standing on the path with Sir Samuel, the two men in conversation with her cousins, their backs turned towards her. Eleanor was laughing, flirtatious, and jealousy threatened to steal up from her gut as she watched. Hurriedly straightening her skirts, flicking her hair behind her shoulders, she steeled herself and bent her footsteps towards the gate. He saw her as soon as she set foot inside the churchyard. Hastily excusing himself from her cousins and oblivious to their reactions, he came to her at once. Seeing him approach lit a heat of misgiving inside her – surely her uncle was wrong about him. Surely.

He stopped before her at a courteous distance. Aware of their audience, she dropped into a curtsey which he returned with a bow. They did not meet each other's eyes.

"I am most glad to see you again," he murmured.

She said nothing.

"Come." He offered her his arm. "We will talk after church."

In front of everyone she had no choice but to take his arm. But she kept her eyes averted as they walked together along the path and into the church.

Once the service began she heard not a word the vicar said, repeating the liturgy with automatic lips, her thoughts intent instead on the man who sat across the aisle, just within touching distance if both reached out their hands. When at last it was over, she stepped out and away from the pew to let the Haftons leave before her, and though she saw Lord Hafton hesitate with a glance of fury and a curt bow to his neighbour, Sir Samuel engaged his attention with his usual light-hearted charm and led him away along the aisle. Hafton threw one last look of rage across his shoulder as Sir Samuel's hand guided him towards the door and gradually the little church emptied of all save Sir Daniel and Susannah.

"Madam." He bowed.

She dropped into a curtsey, breathless, unable to speak. Sir Daniel stepped forward towards her, moving closer, and instinctively she took a step back though his sudden closeness filled her senses, all of them raw and alive to his presence, crying for his touch.

"Susannah." Sir Daniel reached out his hands for hers and she took them, relief at his presence warming through her. "I've missed you. Come," he said, gesturing to the pew, "Sit with me and tell me your news."

She sat beside him, taking a moment to smooth her skirts and prepare the words she needed to say. "After last we met, I wrote to my mother, to seek her advice," she began, glancing towards him, a small nervous smile on her lips.

His face grew serious, and he took her hand in his own, hoping to offer some reassurance. She let it rest, though she had hoped to keep a little distance between them. "Go on," he murmured.

"She wrote back not to me but to my uncle." She turned again to him. "I'm so sorry, I did not think. I should have known she would ask for his counsel. I should have thought …"

"What of the letter?" Her pulse had quickened, sensing the trepidation in his words. His hand was strong and warm as he rubbed his fingers over hers.

She dropped her eyes, and he waited for her to speak again. "She asked him for a report of your character."

"He told you this?"

She nodded. "He said he would never approve the match. He said I would marry Edward. And he forbade me to see you again."

"That is not his place to do."

"Yes. I said as much."

"Did you?" He smiled. "Good girl."

There was a pause. She ran her tongue across her lips, searching again for the words she needed, harder now to find a way to say it. Sliding her gaze away from him, she hesitated, aware of his eyes on her face, searching. She was afraid to ask, afraid to hear his answer. "He also told me something else …" she began, then stopped, her courage failing. Perhaps it would be better not to know, she thought. Perhaps some things were better left unsaid.

"What did he tell you, Susannah?"

She shook her head, too close to tears to speak.

"You must tell me." He turned his body on the wooden pew to face her, lowered his head towards hers, peering up into her face, and when she turned her head away from his gaze, he lifted a hand to her chin and turned it back. Caught, she let his eyes meet hers for a moment before she lowered them away,

"Tell me," he insisted. "Whatever it is, you must tell me." His voice was soft, but she knew from his tone that he would not let it go.

Keeping her eyes lowered so that she would not have to see the pain her words would cause him, she whispered, "He told me that you killed your wife. That you made her ride a horse she lacked the skill to handle, forced her to jump a fence that was too high …"

He slid away from her along the pew as if she had burned him, and she heard the sharp intake of breath as he fought to control his emotions. He rested his elbows on his knees, stared down at the space between his boots. Moments passed.

"Sir Daniel?" she whispered.

He turned his head towards her without lifting it up and what she could see of his face was contorted with pain. "Did you believe him?" he breathed.

"Yes," she said. "I did."

"Then why are you here?" He sat up abruptly, voice harsh. "You wish to mock me?"

"No!" She turned her eyes towards him, steely, daring him to think such a thing. "No!" She held his gaze then, pinning him, choosing her next words carefully. "I am here," she said, "because I wanted to hear the truth from your own lips. I think you have paid enough: you have spent ten years in darkness. I am here because I believe God spared you in the Netherlands to bring you back to me. To atone." Now that he was before her, their hands entwined, she could no longer doubt him, trusting the judgement of her heart.

"Is that all?" he whispered. "Is there no other reason?"

"And I am here ... because ... I love you."

He swallowed, straightening himself up. "I am glad," he murmured. "Very glad."

He turned towards her then, reached a hand to smooth back the hair from her forehead. She lifted her head to his touch, like a cat that rubs itself against the hand that strokes it. "You don't hate me, now that you know?"

She shook her head against his hand, and he smiled. When he spoke again, she could hear the effort it cost him to utter the words, his eyes shadowed with the darkness she had seen in him the first time they met. "It is true that I made my wife ride a horse she was not strong enough to hold. I cannot deny it."

"Why?" she asked. "Why did you do it?"

"I thought ..." He hesitated, as if the remembrance was still painful to touch. "I thought she could do it. I thought she was strong enough. I believed it was only the confidence she lacked ... but I was wrong. And she paid with her life for my mistake."

She took his fingers in hers, his rough dark hands against her pale narrow fingers, the skin cool to his touch. "It was an accident," she whispered. "You acted in good faith."

"I was a fool."

"And you have paid."

"Not as she paid. What right do I have to happiness, when she is in the ground these last ten years?"

"God in His mercy has given you a second chance."

He gripped her fingers tightly. "Then marry me," he whispered. "Marry me."

"But what of Edward? My family ..."

He did not hesitate, pressing on, she supposed, while he sensed she might be willing, before hard cold reason commanded love to stand aside, and her resolve to follow her heart gave way to her sense of duty.

"Handfast with me now, Susannah," he urged. "Say the words that will bind us together. We can win your family round. I promise you we will have your mother's blessing before our marriage. Only say the words that will bind us together until then. Once we're betrothed no one can part us – we will be bound in law and spirit."

"Here? Now?" She barely knew what to think, her body trembling with fear and excitement and desire for this man at her side, who wanted her as he had never wanted anyone. To marry him was everything she could have dreamed, but she could not go against her family so boldly, in spite of all she wanted. She must have her mother's blessing.

"Sam can stand as our witness and no one else need know until we receive your family's consent," he was saying. "But you will be safe, promised to me, and no one can take you from me."

She remembered Edward, swearing to make her his wife, his lips hard and rough on hers, the smell of him up close against her. She thought of Lord Hafton who would move heaven and earth to see it done. Contracted to Sir Daniel, she could no longer be forced into marriage with Edward – the choice would have been made. It was tempting.

"I couldn't bear to lose you, Susannah," he said. She could hear the desperation in his plea, the pain that lay behind it. Sir Samuel's words came back to her mind – *you hold his heart in your hands.* She prayed she might be gentle with it, cause him no more suffering.

"You have come to be my light …" he whispered, "… without you there is only darkness. Say you will have me as your husband. Only say the words and it is done."

She swallowed, overwhelmed by the fullness in her heart, the love for him that flooded through her blood, her whole being wrapped in his, rapt, enchanted, until nothing else could ever matter again. How could she refuse him, she thought, how could she leave him in such pain when his love was all she wanted? She must, she thought. She must.

"I cannot go against my family," she whispered, pain sliding through her. "I cannot. We must wait. I will write to my mother again, and explain all …"

His fingers tightened on hers at her words and she flinched at the strength of his grip. Abruptly, he let her hand go. "Forgive me," he said. "I did not mean to hurt you."

"I know," she replied. But she could not stop the tears from coming then and when she lifted her face to his, her cheeks were wet. He wiped them away with his thumb but more replaced them until he touched his lips to her cheekbones instead.

She shivered with the intimacy. Gently, slowly, he moved his lips across her face, kissing her eyes, her nose, her cheeks, his breath warm against her skin, his mouth soft, caressing. She forgot to breathe, aware only of the touch of his lips. Finally he sought out her mouth, his lips brushing hers for a kiss so brief, so gentle she thought she might have dreamed it. She gasped, breathing again, lifted her gaze to look at him. Intent pools of darkness answered her gaze, hunger in his eyes.

She was barely breathing, desire for him in every fibre of her body screaming out to change her mind. His mouth found hers again, the same light touch as before, teasing, leaving her desperate for more.

"Marry me," he murmured.

The kiss grew firmer, his mouth pressing harder now, sensual and passionate. She parted her lips and moved them against him, then shivered as his tongue entwined with hers, probing and caressing, warm and strong inside her mouth.

His fingers trailed along her throat, sending quivers of desire across her skin, through her blood. His hand slid across her breastbone, touched the top of her gown, but her breasts were hidden from his touch, safe behind the stiffened bodice. Instead he took his mouth from hers and placed his lips against her throat. She tipped back her head, felt the warmth of his tongue on the delicate skin, the brush of his lips. Fire burned inside her, a longing for more; desire to give herself to him, receive him in every part of her being and meld her body with his. She shivered again, overwhelmed by sensation, all thought lost in his touch.

He rested his hand on her thigh, caressing the muscle through the silks of her skirts. His other hand was behind her back, holding her close, his arm hard and strong, supporting her. Heat scorched through her, almost too hot to bear. She felt as though she were a part of him, one and the same, no longer two separate beings but two halves of a whole.

"We are in church," she managed to gasp. "We cannot."

His lips grazed her collarbone, his hand shifted against her thigh, brushing between her legs. "Handfast with me now, and I will stop," he murmured, lips moving against the soft skin of her neck.

"I cannot," she breathed.

"Yet you say you love me."

"Yes," she whispered. "I love you."

His hand moved again on her thigh, gently drawing up the fabric of her skirts, his fingers brushing skin on skin as with expert ease he found his way beneath the petticoats. Strong fingers gripped her thigh, his hand rough against the delicate skin as very gently he began to brush the soft flesh of her inner thigh, slowly working closer to the goal. She moaned, anticipation building, the need inside her desperate for fulfilment.

"Say you'll marry me," he urged.

"Stop. Please stop," she whispered, but the words held no meaning anymore. Her body moved treacherously against him in pleasure as his fingers inched tantalisingly higher. Waves of rapture rolled across her, like being taken by the tide. How could she refuse? His fingers paused beneath her skirts, resting on her inner thigh, so close to their final destination.

"Swear with me," he murmured again. "Say you'll be my wife."

His strong arm still held her behind her back, his mouth lay close to hers, the warmth of his breath against her cheek, as she waited, breathless. She gave no answer to his plea, made silent by desire, but in her mind she had given him her surrender, unable to resist anymore – she was his to take.

He gave her a moment, waiting, but when no answer came, his fingers reached to touch the folds of her moist warm flesh, exploring gently, sliding into her. She gasped in the moment between shock and pleasure. Then his fingers started to move inside her, rhythmic, expert, until finally she gave herself up to him utterly, drowning with the tide, wave upon wave of the most exquisite bliss crashing through her body. She had never known such ecstasy existed. All thought, all sense of the world was subsumed in the movement of his hand. All that existed were the sensations he created, her love, her spirit, her soul bound to him in her acceptance of his touch. He possessed her completely, her heart in his hands.

Slowly, the sensations began to subside, the tide of pleasure ebbing at last. Great shudders wracked her body, and tears filled her eyes as Sir Daniel softly withdrew his hand from beneath her skirts and held her gently against him. Sated, she curled against him, his body hard and safe and strong: she never wanted to leave his side again.

"Handfast with me now, Susannah," he urged once more as he held her, still trembling in the aftermath. "Say you will be my wife."

"I will swear," she whispered. All her strength to resist was in pieces, shattered by the pleasure he had given her, already his in all but the words. "I will swear."

He smiled then, and the darkness left his eyes. Tenderly, he caressed her temple, running the back of his fingers over her face, his lips against her hair. "Thank you," he murmured, lips moving against her hair.

A door slammed somewhere beyond the chancel. The vicar,

Susannah supposed, closing the vestry before he left, but the sudden noise roused her from her languor. Remembering where she was, she straightened and shifted away from him, lifting her face to his with a smile. She could hardly believe what was happening, and she refused to allow herself to doubt.

"I'm a lucky man," he said, returning the smile.

But she thought that she was the luckier.

"Come," he said then. "Straighten your skirts and we'll fetch Sam from outside."

Weakly, she stood up, her legs still unsteady beneath her, her limbs still light from the pleasure. Folding down the rucked-up skirts with care, she ran her fingers through her hair to smooth it.

"You're beautiful," he said when she was finished.

She smiled, then eagerly he took her hand and led her from the pew along the aisle to find Sam, who was outside in the churchyard, wandering through the graves looking bored. He lifted his eyes in surprise as Sir Daniel led Susannah by the hand across the grass towards him.

"Is something amiss?" he asked. Then, as Susannah drew close, he bowed. "Good morrow, Mistress Archer."

"Sir Samuel."

"Sam," Sir Daniel said, turning all his attention to his friend, though Susannah's fingers still lightly lay in his. "I …" He turned to look at Susannah with a small eager smile, squeezed her hand. "That is we … we would ask a favour of you."

"For you, Dan, anything."

"Would you stand witness to our betrothment?"

"Here? Now?" Sam looked from one to the other, surprise quickly turning to a grin. "No celebration? No announcement?"

"Yes, now, if you please." Sir Daniel's reply was testy.

His friend bowed. "It would be my honour." He glanced across the churchyard towards the road and village beyond. Small knots of people moved in the road. He said, "Shall we perhaps go inside the church?"

Reminded that they were out in the open where they could easily be seen by anyone, Sir Daniel tightened his hold on her hand again and led her back inside the church.

"Where?" Sam asked, once the door was closed.

"It matters not," his friend replied impatiently. "Here will do." So they stood near the door by the carved stone font, Susannah's hand clasped firmly in Sir Daniel's as they repeated the vow that would bind them.

"I, Daniel Gifford, do promise myself to thee, Susannah Archer, that I will be thine husband, which I will confirm by public manner, in pledge whereof I give thee mine hand."

The heat of his hand on hers as she repeated the same words after him seemed almost to scald, and beneath the heat she could sense the tremor in his blood, the urgency to make her his so he could never lose her to another. She murmured the words as if in a dream – it seemed impossible that her fate could be decided so easily. She would marry Sir Daniel after all, and spend her life at the hearth at Gifford Hall. A life of love, as she had hoped.

"God be with you both," Sam said when it was done.

Sir Daniel gave his friend a brief smile and dug a coin from a pocket for the poor box. It clattered as it fell against the wood, loud in the quiet hush, and the rattle brought Susannah back to reality. Thoughts of her father, thoughts of Abbey Leigh slid across her mind. What on earth had she done? She swallowed and straightened her shoulders towards the future. There was no going back now. Sir Daniel took her hand once more, and in spite of everything, his presence made her smile as he led her back into the body of the church. Sam turned tactfully away. In the aisle Sir Daniel turned to face her, her hands held in his.

"What now?" she whispered, looking up into his face. The dark eyes blazed with a passion she had not seen before, a determination that almost frightened her.

"We will say nothing yet. You can tell the Haftons you spoke to me today to reject my suit. It is better they believe I am no longer a threat – as long as they believe I'm a rival, they will try to hurry your marriage to Edward. This way buys us more time."

She nodded. His words made sense, but the enormity of what she had done was beginning to press in on her. She had gone against her family, defied her father's dying wish, and now she must be secret and a liar. She prayed she would be up to the task.

"I will write to your mother," he said. "And you must write again also. You must tell her your feelings for Edward, about his character – surely she would not want you to wed such a man as he."

Susannah shook her head. Her father might have understood if there had been time to tell him. Her father would have wanted her happiness over everything. But her mother would be a harder nut to crack: she would hold to her husband's last words, his ardent wish for Abbey Leigh to stay within the family. For all his faults, Edward Hafton was family, he was blood, and her mother's loyalty was absolute.

"She will not be easy to persuade," she said.

"We must try. Don't forget, Susannah, she has already written to ask about my character – were she set implacably against me I think she would not have done so." He must have seen the worry in her eyes because he smiled and touched a finger to her cheek. "Don't fret. All will be well. I promise you. We are bound together now and nothing and no one can set us apart."

Then he lowered his head to kiss her and with the touch of his lips on hers, all thoughts of Edward and her mother slid from her mind and all she could think of was the man who held her, whose happiness was now bound to her own.

She was called to Lord Hafton's office as soon as she set foot through the door of the Hafton Hall. The servant who was waiting to summon her led her swiftly upstairs and along the passage although she could have found her way alone and, before she knocked, she breathed deeply, trying to gather her courage as Sir Daniel had bidden her.

"Enter!"

She went in. Her uncle was standing before the desk, Edward

lounging by the fireplace. She felt his eyes inspect her with ill-disguised desire as she dropped a hasty curtsey at the door.

"Come here, girl," her uncle said, pointing to a spot in the middle of the room. She stepped towards it, blood pounding, her throat dry. Have courage, she told herself again, taking strength from the hope of a future that no longer lay within these walls. She stopped at the place he had indicated and lifted her head. She would not be bowed by this man, she determined. He had no power over her any more. She held his gaze, waiting. Pale watery eyes stared back at her from the florid face, jowls tight with anger.

"How dare you?!" he hissed. "In front of everyone."

"You misunderstand, sir," she said, surprised by the evenness of her tone. Her voice sounded strong and clear in the quiet room.

"I think not. I think it was plain for the entire congregation to see …"

"I spoke to Sir Daniel, yes," she interrupted. "But only in order to tell him I would no longer accept his suit. Surely you can have no objections to that, sir?"

His eyes narrowed, but she was steadfast under the hostile scrutiny. At the edge of her vision she was just aware of Edward, his gaze still appraising, wanting – his attention was far more disturbing than all the anger her uncle could threaten. She kept her eyes facing forward, shutting him out. She would not give him the pleasure of seeing her discomfort.

"Indeed?" her uncle said at length. "And how did Sir Daniel take the news?"

"Like a gentleman, sir," she responded. "As I expected."

Lord Hafton broke into a rattling laugh and, turning his gaze away at last, he moved back to take his place in the chair behind the desk. He did not invite Susannah to sit, and she remained standing, hands clasped neatly before her, no trace of the emotions inside.

"Like a gentleman, eh?" He chuckled again. "D'you hear that, Edward? Your cousin is impressed by Gifford's manners." He fixed his gaze on her again, and the humour left his eyes. "It takes more than manners to make a gentleman. But still," he turned to his son, "if you wish to woo your cousin, Edward, perhaps you should brush up your manners. It seems she sets great store by them."

"Will that be all, sir?" she said, cutting across their laughter.

"For now," Lord Hafton replied. "I will write once more to your mother, and when she replies we will talk of this again."

"Then I bid you good day." Dropping into the briefest of curtseys, she turned and walked swiftly out of the room and as the door closed behind her, she heard the great guffaws of laughter at her back.

Hateful, hateful men, she thought, gathering her skirts and heading out into the garden for air where she was brought up short in her thoughts by Eleanor, heading for the bench by the ornamental pond, a prayer book in her hand.

"Come sit with me," Eleanor said.

"It is cool to sit. Shall we not walk?" She was too restless with emotion now to be still. Movement helped to absorb the nervous energy and made conversation possible.

"As you wish." Eleanor stood up and linked her arm through her cousin's as they began to stroll along the neat gravel paths that led between the shrubs. "Did my father deal harshly with you? He was furious."

"You are aware of the reason?" It was harder to lie to Eleanor and she kept her eyes on the path before her feet.

"Edward told me. He is afraid you will be ruined by Sir Daniel."

Susannah nodded. She could feel Eleanor's gaze against the side of her face, searching, and the curious scrutiny of her friend was far harder to bear than her uncle's outright hostility.

"He is dear to you, I think," Eleanor said softly.

"He was," she replied carefully. "But now it is over and I will see him no more." She flashed her cousin a brief smile, and hoped she would take her word, but the doubting crease in Eleanor's brow told her otherwise.

"You would rather marry Sir Daniel than my brother?"

Eleanor's gentle tone threatened her resolve: she could feel the tears beginning to rise, responding to her cousin's kindness. She swallowed them down, bracing herself. "I do not wish to discuss it."

Eleanor stopped walking and, drawing her hand from its place under Susannah's arm, she turned to face her cousin. Susannah gazed away at the mist that still hung over the parkland, the damp air cool on her skin, but she could feel her cousin's eyes, searching her face for the truth.

"You may tell me truly," Eleanor said. "We are friends. Are you in love with him?"

"Not in love," Susannah said, her stomach turning at the words. "A brief attraction merely. And now it is over."

Eleanor smiled and laid her hands on her cousin's shoulders. "Over perhaps, but not forgotten. I can see the sadness in your eyes."

Susannah took a deep breath, steeled herself to meet her cousin's look. "Your brother will make me a fine husband, I am sure. Sir Daniel was but a passing fancy."

Eleanor regarded her for a moment, thoughtful. Then she said, "I think you are simply being brave, coz, but no more. We will talk of other things."

Relieved for the moment but aware the danger was not yet passed, Susannah let herself be led among sweet-smelling roses, and half-listened as Eleanor talked instead of a new gown she was hoping for and the plans for a trip to Bristol for the satin and beads to make it. But as her cousin talked, Susannah composed in her head the letter she would write to her mother as soon as she was free.

CHAPTER 14

*L*ady Hafton, when she travelled, did not travel light. Accompanied by a cart of belongings and numerous servants, messengers rode on ahead to procure rooms along the way. But the weather was perfect for a journey. The wind and rain of June had given way to cool bright sunshine in July, and the roads had begun to harden again so the cart rarely got caught in the mud. The three women rode together, taking it in turns alongside one another on the narrow road, and though a part of her was grateful to be riding away from Edward and the hated Hafton Hall, she regretted her mother's answer had not come before she left. It would be many days now before she could receive an answer and the uncertainty wore at her nerves, desperate as she was for her mother's blessing. There had been no chance to see Daniel again since the morning in church, and at times she could barely believe it had happened. Surely she could not truly be betrothed to him? So sweetly, so secretly. The thought of it brought a smile to her mouth, and she looked out over the hedgerows and across the fields beyond where the barley harvest was just beginning.

They arrived in Bristol late in the afternoon, and Susannah was delighted when she found the inn where they would lodge lay close to the floating harbour, where the air was fresh from the sea, and the breeze was heavy with the noise from the ships, the shouts of men and the creak of ropes, sails snapping tightly. They retired early to their rooms though the night was still light, twilight lingering above the water, and the two cousins sat at the window seat of the room they were sharing, the casement pushed open into the breeze. Pointing out the tall masts they could see, they imagined where the ships had come from, and what cargoes they had carried, excited to be so close to such exotic wares.

Then, as the air began to grow cooler with the coming of the night, Eleanor leaned out and drew the windows closed. Susannah felt a pang of disappointment – the game had been a good distraction from her thoughts. In the semi-darkness Eleanor turned to face her cousin. The handsome face was serious as she took Susannah's hands in her own, and she offered a quick nervous smile before she began.

"I have something I would ask you to do for me," she said at last, speaking quickly, words tumbling out in haste.

"Of course, what is it?" Susannah could not imagine what Eleanor might be about to ask but she had never seen her cousin so anxious, so fearful.

Eleanor swallowed, squeezed Susannah's hands a little tighter. "I must ask that you fetch me a midwife." Her words were barely more than a whisper.

"A midwife?" Susannah was astonished.

"Ssshh!" Eleanor hissed, though there was no one who could hear them. "Yes," she whispered. "A midwife. I am with child, God forgive me, and I've heard tell that midwives know the herbs I can take to be rid of it."

Susannah stared, still too shocked to speak. "But …?"

"We must do it here," Eleanor urged. "And do it quickly. Here we can be secret. Just you and I. Once we are home there is no hope for secrecy. I will be discovered, and my father will … my father will … well …" She turned her head away, gazing out again through the crooked windowpanes. "I'm sure you can imagine what my father will do."

Susannah lifted a hand to her mouth in horror. Her own crimes paled in comparison to this. "Dear God, Eleanor. How long?"

"I believe a few weeks only. I hope not too late. Now go. Find me a midwife. It must be soon."

Susannah rose from the window seat, took her cloak from its peg on the wall and went to the door. "I will return as soon as I can," she murmured.

"Don't come back until you've found her," Eleanor warned, then she turned away to stare out of the window once more, her hands clasped above her belly in the unconscious posture of a woman with child.

Susannah nodded and stepped out into the passage. She was nervous going out in strange streets in the gathering dusk, especially so close to the port. In the street outside the inn, she stopped, looking around her. She had no clue where she needed to go, and she knew that just beyond the road where she stood, the streets by the river would be alive with seamen and alehouses, and women of the night who would just be beginning to ply their trade with the falling of the dusk. How would she ever find a midwife? And how could she keep herself safe while she searched? The task was all but hopeless.

Two gentlemen in silks and velvets walked past her, leaving the inn, heading towards the port for a night's entertainment. For a moment, out of desperation, she considered following, but then another thought came to her and she turned back inside the inn to search out the innkeeper's wife.

Eventually, after many false turns, she found the woman in the kitchen where several servants were sharing a rowdy conversation above their ale. The heat from the stoves was almost overwhelming, and all eyes turned to her as she approached. The innkeeper's wife looked up from her conversation with the cook and stepped towards the visitor.

"Goodwife, may I have a word?" Susannah said, shifting her eyes towards the men. "In private?"

The innkeeper's wife, whose face was not unkind, nodded and drew Susannah out into the passage where it was quiet and cool and they would not be overheard.

"Forgive my intrusion, Goodwife, but I must beg help of you," she began. "My companion has been taken ill: it is her woman's disorder only, but I must find a local midwife who knows the herbs to help."

The innkeeper's wife narrowed her eyes, suspicious, but without directly accusing her guest of lying, she had no way to voice her doubts. She considered for a moment. Then, apparently deciding the problems of the guests were their own affair, she said, "It isn't fit for a lady like yourself to be out on the streets at this hour. I'll send a boy to fetch someone. Go back to your chamber and I will send her to you anon."

Susannah reached into the pocket of her cloak and withdrew a few coins. "For the boy," she said, giving the coins to the innkeeper's wife. "To speed his way."

The innkeeper's wife smiled and closed her fingers over the coins. "I'll see that he gets them."

"I thank you," Susannah said and, turning back along the passage, she hurried up the stairs to tell Eleanor what had passed.

The midwife was with them in less than an hour and was not best pleased when she discovered the true reason for her summons. She was of the middling sort and respectable, a merchant's wife, Susannah guessed, and beneath the plain linen cap her brow bore the creases of many years of worry.

"I am an honest midwife," she breathed. "I have a licence from the bishop to assist at childbed. Not for this."

"I would save you the trouble of my childbed," Eleanor begged. "Only please, you must be able to do something to help me."

Susannah had never seen her cousin so afraid, so desperate, and she could only have respect for the steely courage it must have taken to hide her fears for so long.

"I could lose my licence for this," the midwife hissed.

"No one will ever know," Eleanor whispered. "You have my word."

The midwife nodded and, taking a seat on the edge of the bed, began to unpack her bundle. Eleanor flashed a nervous glance to her cousin and then both of them watched the midwife's hands as she made up a draught from one of many bottles.

"I must go to the kitchen," the midwife said, standing. "This needs to boil a while."

The girls waited for what seemed an age, silent, Eleanor still before the window, Susannah pacing the small square of floor until the midwife returned with an evil-smelling potion in a mug. "Dragon-water," she told them, "known for your purposes since ancient times."

"And it will work?" Eleanor asked, taking the mug, disgust crinkling the handsome features as the vapours touched her face.

"Nothing is ever certain," the midwife replied. "But aye, it has been known to work."

Closing her eyes, screwing up her nose, Eleanor drank off the draught in one breath.

"It's vile," she breathed when she had finished. She held out the empty mug to the midwife, who took it without a word. "It had better work."

"How long will it take?" Susannah thought to ask then.

"You can expect no sleep tonight. By morning it should be done."

"We thank you," Susannah said, showing the midwife to the door, finding more coins in her cloak.

The midwife took the coins, examined them critically, then left without another word.

They waited through the night, speaking little. Eleanor huddled at the window, staring out into the darkness, and Susannah had not the heart to question her, though there was much she would have liked to ask. Finally, in the early hours, they fell exhausted into sleep across the bed, but the draught had not taken and when they woke in the morning, Eleanor was still with child.

Distraught, she lay curled in a ball on the bed, wailing. "Dear God in Heaven! What now? What do I do now?"

"Perhaps we can find a wise-woman who might know a different herb," Susannah suggested, caught up in her cousin's fear and desperation. "Perhaps the innkeeper's wife knows of another."

"Don't be a fool!" her cousin hissed. "We've failed."

A silence fell across the room. A team of horses clattered by on the cobbled street outside. Susannah went to the window and drew back the curtain to let in the early light. Eleanor watched her for a moment, then sat up abruptly, finding again the iron self-control that had got her this far. The transformation was remarkable. "And how will we find a wise-woman, pray tell?" she demanded. "How shall we ask the innkeeper's wife again? Sorry, it didn't work. Do you know anyone else who can help me kill my child?"

Susannah turned away with a deep breath, and stared out of the window. The street was already busy though it was barely dawn, travellers leaving the inn with the day's first light, workers heading to the quay to begin the day's labour. Her cousin was right; they had missed their chance in Bristol. She turned back in towards the room, her hands resting behind her on the windowsill.

"Perhaps in Hafton?" she said.

"So the whole village will know? I think not. That was my only chance and it has passed. And now I must put on a brave face and go to buy fabric for gowns that in a few weeks will no longer fit me." She paused. Then, "Perhaps I should tell my lady mother now and then at least I might get a dress I can wear." She stood up and began pacing the chamber, her skirts sweeping out behind her every time she swung her body round.

There was a silence, Eleanor's footsteps and the swish of satin the only sound, nothing Susannah could say that would help. A knock at the door broke the tension, a servant with some bread and cheese and ale, but neither one of them was hungry and the tray sat untouched on the small table where the servant had left it.

At last Eleanor stopped her pacing with a sigh. Then she sat in the window seat, forcing open the latch of the window and letting in the morning air. It was salt and cool and refreshing. Susannah took her place beside her.

"Eleanor," she said, softly. "How did it happen? Who?"

"It is of no matter," her cousin murmured, her eyes still trained on the scene outside. "No matter at all. We will not speak of it again."

Another knock sounded at the door and the voice of Eleanor's mother roused them from their weary torpor. Susannah rose and opened the door and her aunt stepped into the chamber, still in her night gown, a rich brocade wrap held around her body. Her quick eyes took in in a moment that all was not well, the uneaten breakfast, the girls' dark eyes and undressed hair.

"What has happened here?" she demanded. "Where are your maids?"

"Nothing," Eleanor snapped back.

"We are tired, is all, Aunt Elizabeth," Susannah said lightly. "We talked until late in the night, and bid our maids let us sleep this morning."

"You are old enough, both of you, to know better." She turned to Susannah. "Make yourselves ready. Quickly. We have fabric to buy and seamstresses to go to and the morning grows late."

Eleanor lifted a complicit eyebrow at her cousin, and Susannah smiled. Then Lady Hafton returned to her own chamber with a rattle of the door, and the two cousins put on their faces for the day.

In spite of everything, the girls were excited by the busyness and bustle of the city. They walked along the quay behind their aunt, with the maids following on behind. The ships rocked gently at their moorings, creaking lightly, the tide slapping at the wharf. Rowing boats plied between them, shouts being traded. The quay was alive with activity and foreign faces, dark skins, other tongues mingling with English from all across the realm, languages Susannah had never heard, couldn't even guess at.

Men stopped working to watch them pass and though Susannah lowered her gaze and hurried on, Eleanor lifted her eyes and smiled, enjoying her audience. They passed casks of oil and olives from Spain, barrels of wine, cases of oranges and lemons, and one ship yet to be unloaded that was redolent with oriental spices. Pallets of woolskins lined the quay, waiting to be loaded for export, and everywhere they turned there was something else to see.

Three sailors on the wharf interrupted their conversation to ogle them, and shouted something out but their words were lost in the hubbub, and the cousins hurried on to keep up with Lady Hafton as she strode between the people and the goods, heading towards the old city on the other side of the river.

There, across the bridge, they found the stalls in the Corn Street market, and in the mercer's shops a finer choice of fabric than they had ever seen, silks of every kind – damasks, lampas, velvets, brocades, shot silks; fine linens, delicate gauzy hollands and lawns. And Lady Hafton surprised them both by haggling the price as gamely as any merchant's wife. But by mid-morning the excitement had died, the weariness of the sleepless night beginning to tell and the cares of their secrets wearing them down.

Lady Hafton showed no patience with either of them, hustling them through more stalls and shops before finding the one draper's shop she was seeking, where she would find the seamstress she had been recommended. The girls were measured one after the other and Eleanor explained to the seamstress what she wanted made from the green silk velvet her mother had just paid for.

Then the seamstress turned to Susannah. "And what are we going to do for thee, madam?"

Aunt Elizabeth held Susannah's shoulders from behind, squaring her up straight before the long gilt-framed looking glass on the wall. "Mistress Archer," her aunt began, "will soon be in need of a new dress for her wedding. So something rather special, I think. We have bought some peacock blue silk which will complement her skin."

But Susannah was no longer listening, aware only of the sound of her heartbeat and the washing of her blood from her skin. She clenched her fists, forcing herself to stay upright, to keep breathing. The thought she might soon be Edward's wife filled her with dread. In spite of all she had shared with Sir Daniel, she still had nothing but his word, and her mother had yet to give her consent. She wheeled round to face her aunt who broke off her sentence, startled. "I cannot accept such a dress, Aunt Elizabeth. I cannot."

Lady Hafton stared. "What foolishness is this? I insist."

"I cannot take it."

"And what will you wear to marry my son? One of Eleanor's cast offs?"

"They have done very well till now," she replied.

"Madam," Eleanor interjected. Lady Hafton stepped back and turned her head towards her daughter. "I don't think Susannah's objection is so much to the dress …" Eleanor began.

Susannah's mouth went dry, her palms prickled hot.

"I think it is more the fact of the marriage itself she objects to."

Lady Hafton swung round to address the seamstress who was waiting patiently with the measure in her hand. "Leave us," she commanded, and the seamstress dipped a hasty curtsey and fled the room.

Lady Hafton faced Susannah, a muscle twitching in her cheek, her lips set in a thin and furious line. "What is this nonsense?"

"It isn't nonsense, Madam," Eleanor assured her. "Susannah does not want to marry Edward. Do you, Susannah?"

The sense of betrayal after what they had shared the previous night almost took Susannah's breath away. She stood rigid, her fists clenched, breath coming hard and fast with her anger. It seemed that Eleanor was more like her brother than she'd guessed: all that pretence at friendship and all the time the same streak of spite running underneath. At that moment she hated both of them.

Drawing herself up, her shoulders square, she dug deep for her resolve. "Your son has not yet asked me, Aunt Elizabeth," she said, "And my mother's consent has not yet been sought."

"Your mother will give consent. She wouldn't dare not to."

Susannah ran a tongue across her lips, taking the moment to calm her ragged breathing. "I think it would be wise to move forward one step at a time, do you not?"

"Don't play games with me, girl," Lady Hafton breathed. She was as hard as her husband underneath, Susannah thought, as different from her brother, Susannah's father, as apples from snow. "You know full well what is planned. Edward has never made any secret of his intent – the marriage is as good as made."

A slew of possible answers slid across her mind but any one of them would have carried the argument further and rent a greater rift. It would be wiser to hold her tongue and say nothing more. With some difficulty she schooled herself to silence, biting her lip against the words that gathered there, before she lowered her eyes and dropped her head in apparent submission. "Yes, Aunt Elizabeth. I am aware of it."

Her aunt watched her for a few moments more as if she were judging whether or not to pursue the argument further. Susannah waited, tensed and ready to answer, but apparently Lady Hafton had decided it had gone far enough. Turning away from her niece, she called out for the seamstress to attend on them again, the deep voice ringing out imperiously. Hurried footsteps sounded beyond the door. Then, swinging back quickly to Susannah, she murmured, "You will have the dress, whether or no. Do I make myself plain?"

"Yes, Aunt Elizabeth," she replied obediently, and then she stood ready and waiting to be measured when the seamstress hurried to resume her work.

In the evening, when they had finally returned to their bed after interminable hours of cards and backgammon in Lady Hafton's bed-sitting chamber, the two cousins sat on the seat in the window. Susannah pushed the casement open, drawing in the cool salt air, the room stuffy with having been closed up all day.

Eleanor sat observing her, hands folded across her belly.

"You would be better not to fold your hands like that," Susannah said, more for something to say in the awkwardness than any real remaining concern for her cousin's plight. "It's how women sit when they're with child. You'll give yourself away."

"What do you care?" Eleanor spat, and turned her face to the window.

Susannah observed her cousin in profile, the strong heavy jaw, the long nose, the high forehead and the blonde hair tumbling prettily about her shoulders.

"Eleanor?" she said. "May I ask you something?"

Her cousin turned, that same appraising look in her eyes that Susannah had seen so many times in Edward, the same sneering bitterness.

"Why did you say that to your mother today? What possible reason could you have had?"

"I thought someone should say what is glaringly obvious to anyone with eyes. You have made no secret of your dislike of Edward. And your interest in Sir Daniel is no great secret either. If my mother is too blind to see what is front of her face, then someone needed to tell her."

"It isn't that she hasn't seen it, cousin. It is more that she just doesn't care. My wishes are of no more account to her than they are to your father or brother. Or to you, it would seem."

Eleanor sneered, the handsome face turning ugly. "If you have a single shred of sense you will marry Edward: he is the son of a viscount, after all. Then not only will Abbey Leigh remain in your father's family, but your children will bear titles."

Susannah turned away, shocked by her cousin's coldness; the same cool detachment as the rest of the family. She had thought Eleanor was different, she had thought that they were friends of sorts, but it seemed she was mistaken, and the realisation saddened her.

"I'm going to bed," she said, finally, though it was not yet dark, the long summer dusk still spread across the sky.

Sleep couldn't claim her quick enough, and when finally she drifted off, her dreams were filled with images of falling.

CHAPTER 15

The rest of the time in Bristol was hateful. The cousins barely spoke, and Lady Hafton seemed to find it an effort even to look at her niece. Time weighed heavily on Susannah's hands, and she could hardly wait to get back to Hafton, where she hoped that letters awaited her; letters that would release her from the Haftons and send her running and delighted into the arms that waited across the woods at Gifford Court.

Happily, Lady Hafton cut the visit short by a day, deciding late on Thursday afternoon they would return the following day. The long light of their last evening in Bristol was spent in preparation, the activity much easier to endure than another night of tense and awkward card games in her aunt's apartments.

They left not long after daybreak next morning, and at last they were on the road once again, trudging with tortuous slowness to keep pace with her aunt's slow amble on the ancient cob. The journey was mostly silent; the only sound the steady, repetitive thud of hooves on hard earth, and birdsong in the trees that lined the road. The women barely talked – under the stern bad humour of Lady Hafton there seemed to be nothing to say, and even when she rode beside Lettice, little conversation passed between them.

Finally, on a golden day that sent the afternoon light shimmering across the grass, they turned in at the gates of Hafton Hall and, despite the warmth, Susannah shivered. Her longing to return and find the precious letter faded as the house loomed up before her, its gables and chimneys vivid against the summer blue sky, its many leaded windows winking back the brightness of the sun. She remembered her thoughts when she saw it for the first time, how impressed she had been by its grandeur; older, bigger, statelier than the house at Abbey Leigh. Now she had come to hate every brick of it and all it represented – she felt as though she were entering a prison.

~

There was no letter. There was post for her aunt, and a single missive for Eleanor, but there was nothing at all for her. All the possibilities ran across her thoughts: she wondered if her uncle had taken it in her absence, if it had been lost on the road. It seemed impossible that her mother had not yet written back – Mistress Archer was a practical woman and had never in her life been afraid to make a decision. Whatever her mother had decided, Susannah was sure, the decision would have been made by now.

"No letter from home?" Eleanor raised a fine sly eyebrow as she sat by the fire, strumming the lute, watching her cousin unpack her things. "That must be rather disappointing for you."

"Strange, rather than disappointing," Susannah replied, shaking out a petticoat before kneeling at the chest to fold it away. "It is very unlike my mother to take so long to write."

"Perhaps she is afraid to deliver news that will upset you. Had you thought of that?"

She stood up from the chest, and crossed the room to the window, knelt again at the travelling trunk and withdrew a neat pile of folded shifts that still held the sweet lavender fragrance of the laundry soap. She lifted them to her face, inhaling the scent with pleasure. Then, still kneeling, the linen lowered to her lap, she turned to face her cousin.

"My mother is not afraid of anything," she said.

Eleanor smiled. "We are all of us afraid of something. Even the bravest among us has his fears. Tell me, cousin, what is there that frightens you in the dark stretches of the night when sleep eludes you? What horrors fill your nightmares?"

Susannah said nothing, wondering what answer she might give that her cousin would accept. She smoothed her fingers across the linen and pulled at a thread that had come loose in the embroidery.

"My brother, perhaps?" Eleanor suggested with a touch of spite. "If I were in your position, he would certainly frighten me."

"I am not afraid of your brother," she snapped, which was untrue. The thought of being caught again by Edward was terrifying. More than once since that morning in the woods she had woken from her dreams in the early hours, sweating and afraid. And though the risk of it remained, her nightmares haunted by his presence, she drew her courage from the knowledge that Sir Daniel loved her, and her future lay along a different path. She got to her feet and crossed the room once more to put away the shifts in their place in a different chest.

"Or perhaps …" Eleanor went on, picking out a few notes of an unfamiliar tune before lifting her eyes from the instrument to examine her cousin. "… it is the thought of losing Sir Daniel that frightens you."

Susannah smoothed out the creases in the shifts. With her eyes still lowered, she murmured, "I cannot be afraid of something that has already happened."

"No," her cousin agreed, returning to her picking. "I suppose not."

Susannah turned from her place at the trunk, still on her knees, one hand resting on the linen. "And what are your fears, cousin?"

"Nothing," Eleanor said smoothly, in direct contradiction of her earlier assertion. "I fear nothing at all."

A hostile impulse surged through Susannah. "You lie," she said.

Eleanor stopped her playing and looked up in surprise at the venom in her cousin's voice. "How so?" she demanded.

"I was with you in Bristol, remember?" she replied, knowing even as she said them that the words were both unkind and unwise. But they tumbled from her lips nonetheless and she drew a kind of reckless satisfaction from watching their effect. "I saw your fear in the bed when you realised at last that the herbs had failed, that soon you would become an unwed mother. I saw fear in you then, make no mistake."

White-faced with fury, Eleanor threw the lute aside and scrambled out of the cushions to her feet, running at her cousin, fists raised, eyes flashing with rage.

"How dare you?!" she screamed, raining wild blows around Susannah's head and shoulders. Susannah put up her arms to defend herself, cowering under the attack. She had not thought to provoke such a violent reaction, and though she was well used to defending herself in sisterly scraps, she knew better than to retaliate now. "How dare you?!"

Eleanor was still screaming, still slapping and punching, grabbing fistfuls of her enemy's hair when Lady Hafton came running into the room with Lettice, who was pale with fear and horror, a few steps behind her.

"Stop it this instant!" Aunt Elizabeth yanked at her daughter's arm and hauled her away from her cousin. "That is no way to behave! Whatever the provocation. Do you hear me?" She shook Eleanor's arm the way a parent shakes the arm of a screaming infant and, overpowered, Eleanor fell immediately into silent sullen submission.

"What happened?" Lady Hafton demanded, looking from one to the other. "What is the meaning of this?"

Susannah lowered her eyes beneath the question and said nothing, cautiously using her fingers to draw her hair back from her face strand by strand.

"We argued," Eleanor said.

"That much is obvious," her mother snapped. "But about what?"

"It is of no matter. A trifle merely."

"A trifle?!" Lady Hafton's tone was incredulous. "You came to blows over a trifle?"

"Apparently so."

Eleanor's breathing was heavy in the silence as Lady Hafton's gaze flicked between them, searching for the truth. Finding nothing, both girls' eyes resting resolutely on the rugs at their feet, she said at last, "Well, if it was merely over a trifle, then you must kiss and make up and be friends again."

Susannah swallowed and took a deep breath, lifted her face towards her cousin. Hatred was still smouldering in Eleanor's eyes, the vivid green clouded with hostility. Warily, reluctant, still eyeing each other like cats before a fight, they took obedient steps towards each other, pausing within touching distance, searching for the willpower to embrace. Susannah found the strength first and held her cousin close.

"I will not forget this," Eleanor whispered, her lips close to Susannah's ear. "So don't imagine this is over."

"That is better," Lady Hafton said, when they had let each other go and moved apart to a more comfortable distance. "Now, Eleanor, come with me. Lettice, you may remain here and help Susannah unpack."

"Yes, m'lady." Lettice dropped into a curtsey as Lady Hafton and her daughter swept out of the chamber. Eleanor slammed the door behind her, and in the wake of the crash they heard Lady Hafton berating her daughter beyond it, the scolding voice fading gradually as they moved away down the passage.

When they could hear them no more, Lettice turned to Susannah, a worried frown between her brows. "Are you all right, Mistress? She looked to be landing you some nasty blows."

"I am unhurt," Susannah assured her airily, though she knew she would have bruises on her shoulders come the morrow. "Come, let us put these gowns away." She wanted to be busy, to put the whole hateful episode behind her.

Lettice smiled uncertainly, unconvinced, but when Susannah began to sift through the gowns in the travelling trunk there was little the maid could do but follow her lead. Movement calmed her, the careful ordered placing of the clothes in their proper places, and gradually her racing heart began to slow. But as her quivering senses began to settle, a headache commenced to threaten, pounding in the hollows behind her temples. She shook her head against it, paying it no mind, and with an effort of will turned her thoughts again to the matter of the letter.

It was baffling her mother had sent no reply. She could think of no possible reason for such a long delay and she began to worry for her mother's health. Reason assured her that one of her sisters would write if her mother were ill, but what other cause could stay her mother's hand for so long? A sense of dread enveloped her – to lose her father was bad enough, to lose her mother too so soon would grieve her sorely. She could hardly bear to think of it, and tears began to prickle at her eyes. She blinked and set her lips in a determined line – she was not going to let herself cry. Pushing away such morbid thoughts, her mind turned again inevitably to Sir Daniel. Consent or no, it had been too long since she had seen him.

"Mistress Susannah?" Lettice said softly when they had almost finished the unpacking. Her voice drew Susannah's thoughts back to the present, to the reality of life at Hafton Hall.

"Yes, Lettice? What is it?"

"I don't mean to speak out of turn or anything …"

Susannah nodded her consent, grateful for the interruption to her thoughts. Reassured, Lettice went on. "But are you quite well?"

"I am well," she replied. "Only a little distracted."

Lettice gave her a small smile that showed she was unconvinced. Then, because she could think of no other course to take, Susannah said, "May I trust you, Lettice? With a matter that can only be between ourselves?

Lettice frowned. "Of course you can trust me. If my loyalty is not to you, then where else would it be?"

Susannah took a deep breath. "I need you to take a note to Sir Daniel, but it must be secret. No one at Hafton must know."

"Of course." The maid hesitated. Then she said, "I can go all right to Gifford Court without suspicion. I was born on the estate. My family are tenant farmers there, and my brother's a lad in Sir Daniel's stable. He said as how you rode the chestnut gelding – he thought highly of you for that. I walk to and fro all the time, through the woods and everything."

Susannah laughed with relief. "So how is it you came to work here, at Hafton Hall?" she asked.

"I was just a child when Lady Grace died, that was Sir Daniel's first wife, but soon after that he went away and only kept on a very small staff, so when it came time for me to go out to service, I was lucky to find a post here. It's not like working for the Giffords of course, but at least it's close to home."

"Tell me about Lady Grace." She tried to sound casual, but her heart was hammering with the question, her breath coming quick and uneven.

"I didn't know her myself, only what others have said, but I have heard Sir Daniel adored her, and that her death tore him apart."

"The Giffords are good masters?" she asked.

The maid nodded. "Always. The family take great pride in it. No one has ever gone hungry that belongs to the Giffords, however poor the harvest."

Susannah smiled, turning Lettice's opinion over in her mind. The way a man treated his servants surely told a great deal about his character. "And Sir Daniel?" she asked. "What kind of man would you say he is?"

Lettice hesitated, reluctant to pass judgement on her betters.

"Tell me," Susannah coaxed with an encouraging smile. "I would value your thoughts very much."

"He is well respected in the village, and well-loved amongst his servants, not like Master Edward ..." She trailed off, fidgeting nervously, coming to the end of what she thought her mistress should hear, apparently wishing she hadn't begun. But Susannah was not so easily put off.

"But Master Edward?" she prompted.

"It's not my place to say."

"Come on, Lettice, you have said this much, and if you tell me no more I can only think the very worst of him."

"Well ..." Lettice dropped her voice. "... 'tis said that Master Edward has a bad reputation in London ... with the ladies ... 'tis said he keeps a mistress." She looked up with fearful eyes in case she had said too much.

"How do you know this?" Susannah asked gently.

"Master Edward's man, Patrick, goes with him everywhere.

Knows all the master's business. He's no tittle-tattle but servants will talk, especially when the ale is flowing ..."

"Of course. Thank you for telling me."

The maid smiled, pleased with the praise, while Susannah slipped into her chamber and wrote a hasty note for Lettice to take to Gifford Court.

CHAPTER 16

On the morrow she was early to the church, tethering the mare to the rail, stepping carefully through the lych-gate. It had rained in the night and the grass in the graveyard glistened now with its burden of raindrops. Overhead a bright sun warmed the morning through the gaps in a swift shifting curtain of cloud that blew across the sky. A gust caught at her hair, whipping it across her face. She paused to tease it gently back into place with her fingers.

Inside the church there was no one as yet and she went to the rail to kneel and pray, asking God's forgiveness for her sins, for choosing love above her duty to her father, for the lies she had told in its pursuit. And she prayed for her mother's understanding, that she would give them her consent.

The sudden scrape of the door on the flagstones brought her to the end of her prayers. She rose from her knees and turned to walk back along the aisle. Sir Daniel was waiting for her, arms outstretched, a smile on his face, and she had to stop herself from running to him, letting him enfold her in his embrace, safe, warm, loved.

"Sir Daniel!" she murmured in delight, stepping forward towards him. It was a pleasure to be in his company.

"*Sir* Daniel? What is this *Sir* Daniel? I can see no need for you to call me *Sir* Daniel anymore. We are betrothed, and you will soon be my wife, my dove – you may call me just Daniel. Or even Dan, if it pleases you more."

She laughed, considering the choice he had offered, rolling the names on her tongue. After a moment's hesitation she made her decision. "I think that Dan doesn't quite become you," she said, "but Just Daniel I like. I believe I shall call you Just Daniel, from now on."

He touched a finger to her cheek, laughing, his delight in their meeting as great as her own. "And what should I call you, Miss Archer? Susannah? Susy?"

"My family sometimes calls me Su," she said. "Except for my mother, who always calls me Susannah."

He laughed again. "Then I shall call you Su. My Su. It is truly wonderful to see you again, Su. I have missed you. Come, let us sit."

He led her into the nearest pew and took her hands in his as they sat beside each other on the cool smooth wood. It was marvellous just to be in his presence, all her fears and worries melting in the pleasure of his company. Lettice's judgement of his character rested in her thoughts, and now that she was with him her fears for her mother seemed foolish – she was sure there was a good reason for her mother's silence. A letter would come soon, she was sure, and all would be well. There was a silence, their arms brushing as they sat side by side. She looked down at her hand in his, running his fingertips across her palm and her fingers, caressing the place that she hoped would soon bear his ring.

Then, finally, Daniel lifted his head and they both turned to look at each other. He said, "Your note said you have news …"

"Yes," she nodded. "I have had no word from my mother, and I am beginning to worry. Has she written to you? I thought perhaps she might have replied to you instead." She knew by his face before he answered that he had received no word either.

"Nothing has come."

"It is most strange. My mother is not a woman to delay a decision, or to hesitate. We should have heard from her by now."

"'Tis strange indeed," he agreed. "Perhaps her letter has gone astray on the road. Perhaps you should write again."

"I shall do so," she nodded. "I shall do so today."

"Then we must be patient a little while longer, though it kills me to be so." There was another silence. Then he said, "I also have news."

She looked up sharply at the tone of his voice, his reluctance. He met her gaze and held it, a gravity deep behind his eyes. Her heart leaped, an inkling of bad news.

"I have been summoned back to Court. I must leave for London right away."

"London?" Disappointment seared through her, the thought of him so far away amid all the temptations that London could offer.

"There is talk of a Spanish invasion. The Earl of Leicester has summoned me himself."

She stared at him in horror. "You will not have to go to war again, surely?"

"I pray it never comes to that, and if it does, I swear I will come back to you. We will be married, Susannah, you have my word." He lifted a finger to her chin, tipped her face up to look at him.

"I would I was your wife already," she whispered.

"Aye," he agreed, and she smiled at the bare desire in his eyes. A movement in the chantry, the vicar on his way towards the vestry, roused them to recall their surroundings and they shifted apart a little. The memory of the last time brought a flush to her cheeks and when she met his eyes again, they were smiling with the same fond recollection.

"How are things at Hafton Hall?" he asked. "How is Edward towards you?"

Her cousin's name snatched her back from the sweetness of her memory. She said, "I have barely seen him since my return. He is unwell, I am told, and keeping to his chamber. I wish him no ill, but I am much relieved not to see him."

"Of course," he agreed, though he was unaware of the true reason for her fear of him, the secret of that morning in the forest still untold. She wondered now if she would ever tell him, unwilling to rouse the anger it would light, afraid of what he might do.

"Have no fear of him, Su," he said, and she started, afraid he might have read her thoughts. "We will be together soon."

"If only my mother will give her consent." She sighed. Now that

Daniel was going away, out of reach, her distrust of the Haftons revolved into fear that they would hatch some act of treachery to keep him from her always, to deliver herself and Abbey Leigh into their grasping hands. The door to the vestry shut with a slam and both of them jumped, startled, before they laughed at themselves.

"We should go," he said. "Before we are discovered."

She nodded, reluctant to leave him, unsure when next they might meet. "Write to me from London," she said. "Write to me at Lettice's family and they will see it safely delivered. I think a letter from you would not reach my hands at Hafton."

"I will write," he swore, stroking the hair back from her forehead, his fingers cool against her skin. "And I will be back for you as soon as ever I can."

"I know," she whispered.

He kissed her then, a brief gentle meeting of their lips that left her breathless, longing for more, before he helped her to her feet and walked her to the door, dragging it open, scraping again on the flag-stones. On the threshold, he paused for an instant, wondering, she supposed, if it were wise to walk outside together. But it was only for a moment and, smiling down at her, he took her arm as he led her to the horses and helped her up on to the mare.

"When we are wed," he said, looking up at her. "You shall have the chestnut gelding. He has missed you."

She laughed. "I would like that very much. Tell him I have missed him also," she said as Daniel stepped back out of the way.

Then, touching her heel to the horse's flank, she urged the mare forward, away from him and on into the main street of the village. Just before she rounded the bend in the lane that would hide the village from view, she looked back over her shoulder and saw him as he swung himself into the saddle, sitting on the sidling horse with ease. A moment later the lane veered left, and he was hidden from her view.

CHAPTER 17

When she returned to the Hall, she was met by Edward in the stable yard as she slid down from the mare.

"Good morrow, coz," he greeted her, inclining his head with unusual courtesy as a groom came to take away the horse.

"Cousin." She returned the greeting, all her senses alert and wary. She almost preferred him smirking and arrogant: at least that was what she expected. A courteous Edward could surely only bode ill.

"I trust you enjoyed your ride?"

"Very much," she answered. "It is a beautiful morning." She patted the mare, and the groom led the animal back to the stables. Watching her walk away, she thought how much she would like to ride the chestnut again.

"Ah, the weather." Edward squinted up at the sky, as if he had never considered it before. "It interests you does it not?"

"As much as anyone." She shrugged. "I hope you are feeling better?"

"Right as rain." He smiled. But he did not move, his tall frame standing a little distance before her so that she could not easily get past him into the house.

"Was there something in particular you wished to say to me, cousin?" she demanded, losing patience. She was safe here in the stable yard with the grooms about and she still had the residue of confidence about her that had come from meeting Daniel in the church.

"We see little of you these days," he said. "No more walks in the park, shutting yourself up in my mother's chambers. I would have thought the summer months would have drawn you out more. The early mornings have been quite glorious of late – I am surprised you do not take advantage. I know how you like to walk."

"I used to like to walk," she replied, forcing herself to politeness against the anger that poured through her body, tense and restless. She kept her eyes on the cobbles of stable yard between them. "Now I prefer to observe the view from my window."

"Since you found yourself lost in the woods, I presume? I little guessed a girl such as yourself would be so quickly discouraged. I would have imagined you to be straight back into the saddle."

"A girl such as myself, cousin?" This time, she lifted her head to face him so that he might see the hostility and the challenge in her face.

He smiled, enjoying her only half-suppressed fury. When he smiled, truly smiled, she thought, there was a trace of the man he might have been, humour lending the strong handsome face a lightness that replaced the habitual sneer. She pitied the woman who would become his wife.

"Yes," he said. "A girl with your spirit. I must confess myself surprised at how easily you have allowed yourself to be beaten."

"Oh," she replied, with a smile of her own. "But you see, cousin, I am not beaten yet." And so saying, she made to walk away.

He laughed, lips curling into the familiar mocking sneer. "You deceive yourself. Whatever your hopes you will soon be my wife. Your father's first loyalty was to Abbey Leigh and to the family line. Father to son, custodians of the land since the days of Henry Tudor. I am family. Blood. I am the son he never had, his father's grandson and a fitting heir. You know this. Your happiness is as nothing compared to blood. And inheritance. It is all that men live for. Yet you would choose to betray your family by marrying elsewhere? Your father must be turning in his grave."

"You are hateful," she hissed, fingers itching to slap the smugness from his face, to jolt him from such detestable self-confidence.

"You will marry me, coz," Edward said. "By special licence. My father goes to Wells on business next week and I will accompany him. While we are there, I plan to pay a visit to the office of the bishop and obtain our licence. When I return, I will marry you. By the end of the month, cousin, you will be my wife."

She thought of Daniel on the road to London now, out of reach, and the anger in her blood drained to dread. For a moment she toyed with the notion of calling to the groom to bring back the mare, riding after him, but a woman on her own on the London Road risked a much worse fate than she could ever face with Edward. "You cannot force me to marry you against my will."

"Oh, I think you'll come round. Trust me. In the end you will be only too relieved to be my wife."

"I will never marry you," she spat.

Then pushing past him, furious, she strode into the house and ran to hide herself in the small inner chamber that served as her room so that she could cry out her rage and her fear undisturbed.

She kept to her bed for the rest of the day where she knew that Edward would not bother her. His words had put real fear in her heart. A forced and illegal marriage was not impossible – well-bribed chaplains had been known to look the other way in the past. And once a marriage was made it was hard to unmake, whatever the impediments.

Daniel was on his way to war against the Spanish, and Sir Samuel fighting with him. They could be gone for weeks or even months. By the time they could return and declare the match invalid, Edward would have used her as his wife many times. By then she could be with child and Abbey Leigh would be in the Haftons' hands. She twisted on her bed in helpless frustration.

An unwelcome thought sliced across her mind. Was this her punishment by God? After all, she had set aside her father's dying wish and forsaken her God-given duty as a daughter. She had lied to her family, let her desire lead her into sin. Edward had called it a betrayal and so it was in a way, though she believed she had good reason – her father had never known the truth about her cousin's character. She remembered Daniel's words at the riverbank – *your father would not have wanted you to be unhappy. You lied to him to make his passing easier, that is all. He loved you and he would want you to be happy.* Then, by Daniel's side, it had been easy to believe.

But what of her vow? Of her promise to do her daughter's duty? She was but a woman, she reminded herself, her will subservient to her father's. And whatever her thoughts, her private feelings, it was not her place to make such decisions. The inheritance of the estate was her father's affair; it was not for her to change the terms with the wishes of her heart. She twisted again, winding herself tighter in the sheets, and wished for the thousandth time she had been born a boy.

The arguments circled in her mind through the afternoon and on into the evening. Lettice stole in to see her twice, bringing bread and cheese and ale, and some almond gingerbread she had begged from the cook as a treat that might cheer her mistress's spirits.

"Don't let Master Edward bully you, Mistress Susannah. You stand your ground. And if you need anything, any messages taken, just be sure and let me know."

"God bless you, Lettice," she replied. "You are a good kind girl, but Sir Daniel is too far away for messages, and I must fight my own battle now. Go now, before you are missed."

The girl crept away, and she drank a little of the ale, forced down a few mouthfuls of the bread and fell to dozing, her dreams filled with images of Edward, pressing close, suffocating her, taking every-thing, even the breath from her body.

In the morning when Lettice drew back the curtains early to rouse her from her sleep, she woke as one who had been drugged. Her head was pounding, her eyes sore and it was as much as she could do to lift her head up off the pillow.

"Bless you, Mistress, but you're sick. I must tell your Aunt, if I may have permission. You need to be looked after in a proper way, more than I can do."

She nodded, too weary to care. Her whole body ached, soreness in every limb. An image of Daniel skimmed her thoughts: she tried to focus on it, tried to remember the conundrum that had so upset her yesterday, but the details evaded capture, her mind too hazy to recollect. Only a vague sense of unease remained, the absence of someone dear and the threat of something dark she could no longer recall.

Chasing the memory exhausted her, the memories too indistinct to pin down, faces too faint to determine. Weariness circled her mind, and in the end she gave up the struggle, letting her thoughts wander as they liked. But always behind them lay the awareness of a problem to be solved, its darkness casting shadows over all her other thoughts. Sometimes she thought the riddle was solved in dreams of Daniel riding the chestnut in the sun, of quiet evenings by the hearth at Gifford Court, and she would recall he had asked her to marry him, her life bound to his. Then the darkness would intrude again, Edward pressing hard against her with no escape from the pressure of his weight.

The hours blurred together, time passing unnoticed as she drifted unaware from sleep into wakefulness and once more into sleep. From time to time brief flashes of lucidity cleared away the fog: for a moment she became aware of Lettice at her side, a cool hand on her brow, the bitter taste of a draught on her lips. Then the mist would descend once more, and her thoughts would go rambling in search of an answer to an unknown puzzle.

On the morning of the third day she rallied from the fever, waking with the dawn, grey light seeping in through a chink in the curtains. Lettice was lying on the floor at her side, a blanket drawn over her fully clothed body, her face pale and drawn. She stirred with her mistress's movement and when she opened her eyes to see Susannah watching her, the weary face lit up with delight. Throwing aside the blanket that had covered her, she scrambled up to embrace her mistress, and Susannah felt the girl's tears against her shoulder.

"I was that worried about you, I thought you were going to die."

"I'm still here." Susannah smiled, and the movement brought a tenderness to the muscles of her face. She lifted a hand to her cheek, checking for something to explain such soreness. "I feel like I've been beaten black and blue. Everything aches. Why does everything ache so?"

"You've had a fever fit to kill you," Lettice said, smoothing down her skirts, tucking stray dark curls back into her cap before she turned away to draw the curtains back, letting in the dull steel light of the dawning day.

Susannah blinked in the sudden light, her eyes unaccustomed to the brightness.

"You'll need a few days to get right again, I should say," Lettice said, coming back to kneel beside her.

"I'll be good as new in no time," Susannah said, shifting carefully in the bed, testing how it felt to move. The sheet was damp underneath her, her shift moist with sweat.

"Fetch me water and soap," she said, her voice cracking. She cleared her throat gently. "Some of the Castile soap we bought in Bristol. I must wash the remnants of this sickness off me before I dress."

Lettice curtseyed and left, eager to please. Gingerly, Susannah pushed herself up to sitting. The unaccustomed movement sent her head spinning like a top and she paused, allowing the dizziness to settle before she got to her feet and stepped across to the window, gazing out across the park to the woods, seeing in her mind's eye the house at Gifford Court beyond them. Then she remembered that he was no longer there but a long way away from her, his mind occupied with the business of war and keeping England safe from the Spanish. He would have no time to think of her now, she told herself. His thoughts would be turning on matters she knew nothing of, playing his part in the defence of the realm. But it was easy to imagine him in such a world and a sudden sense of pride welled up inside her.

Lettice's return with the water brought her reverie to an end. She withdrew from the window and left her thoughts of Daniel with reluctance as Lettice began to sponge her down with warm water and the sweet-smelling soap.

"How long was I ill?" she asked.

"Two days."

"Only two days? It seemed much longer." Indistinct images flitted through her thoughts, memories of the moments of clarity. "You cared for me well, Lettice. I remember you barely left my side. And you gave me draughts to drink. One especially I remember as evil-tasting."

Lettice laughed. "My mother keeps a herb garden. She is wise in all kinds of herb lore and she insists I always keep some of her potions about me."

"Thank your mother for me. When I am quite recovered I shall visit her and thank her myself."

"She would like that." The maid smiled as she loosened the neck of the shift to expose more of her mistress's body, sponging down the skin with the warm soapy water. It felt like heaven. Susannah stood quiet and still as Lettice washed her all over, cleaning the sickness away, freshening. When she was clean and dry, she dressed in fresh linen and a gown of blue brocade with a blood-red forepart and sleeves. Gradually, she began to feel something more like herself. "And what news have I missed while I've been ill?"

"It's been very quiet, Mistress Susannah. The master and Master Edward have been off hawking these last few days, and Mistress Eleanor has also been ailing and keeping to her chamber. Lady Hafton's barely left her alone."

"Ailing how?" she asked quickly, though she could guess well enough.

"She has been vomiting."

"Do they know why?"

"We've all got our suspicions, Mistress, but we know better than to give them voice."

So Eleanor's condition was no longer a secret. She wondered how long till it became common knowledge. "I'm guessing Lord Hafton is not yet aware of it?"

"No, not yet," Lettice replied. "But I think there's not much more hiding it from her mother."

A woman's shriek from another part of the house startled them both. A quick glance passed between them and they both made hurriedly for the door. One of Susannah's sleeves was not yet properly fastened and it flapped against her shoulder as she ran. The sudden movement sent a wave of giddiness over her and at the door she had to stop, supporting herself on the doorframe, leaning her head against the wood while the fit of unsteadiness passed.

Lettice turned back in the passage. "God in Heaven! You're not fit enough to be running about the house. You should be resting. Go back and sit yourself down and I'll see what has happened. Then I'll come back with news."

"No." Susannah shook her head. "It is passed already. It was just the sudden movement made my head spin a little, is all. I am quite well now."

She pushed herself away from the doorframe, took a breath to see if her words were true, then finding that she could move well enough without feeling faint, she followed the maid along the passage. They could hear raised voices, the deep threatening boom of Lady Hafton and the shriller, tearful pleas of her daughter growing louder as they approached.

A servant appeared from the stairs. "Is everything all right, Mistress Archer?"

"I'm not quite sure, Stevenson," Susannah replied. "But I will call you if you're needed."

"Yes, madam." He bowed and backed reluctantly away, his curiosity besting his discretion.

"Go to," she commanded again, waiting until he was gone before she lifted a hand to the door of Eleanor's chamber and knocked.

The shouting stopped immediately and silence followed. Then her aunt's footsteps strode across the wooden floor and the door was snatched open. Lady Hafton filled the doorway, breathing deeply, her face grey with fury. Instinctively, Susannah stepped back and dropped into a curtsey.

"Oh it is you, is it? You are recovered. What is it that you want?"
Aunt Elizabeth barked.

"We heard a shriek, Aunt Elizabeth," she said, rising, raising her
head to look at her aunt.

"Susannah?!" Eleanor's wail was heart-rending. "Susannah!
Cousin. Help me. Please!"

Susannah waited, her aunt still facing her in the doorway,
blocking out the view of the scene within.

"Madam!" Eleanor cried. "Please let her in. Please!"

"Very well." Lady Hafton stood back just enough for Susannah to
squeeze through the gap, and as she crossed to where Eleanor lay
curled like a child, holding herself on the bed, she heard her aunt
send Lettice to fetch Lord Hafton. Eleanor heard it too and threw
herself from the bed, across the room and on to her knees, grasping
her mother's skirts, wailing and crying, hysterical.

"No! No! I beg of you, please don't tell my father, not yet, not yet.
Please, madam, Please!"

Lady Hafton dragged at her daughter's arms, tried to prise her
fingers free.

"Get up, girl!" she hissed. "Get off your knees now. It will avail
you nothing. Get up and compose yourself to face your father. He
will not be impressed by hysterics. Now get up."

Eleanor let her mother's skirt go but she did not rise, slumping
instead, shoulders rounded, head down, hands hanging loosely, as if
someone had simply snuffed out all the vitality that a moment ago
had given her life. Susannah went to her, crouched down beside her,
and put a comforting arm around her shoulders. God knew she had
no love for her cousin, but it would need a heart of stone to feel
nothing for her woe. Gently, stroking Eleanor's hair, rubbing her
shoulders, cooing as she had done a hundred times or more to give
comfort to her sisters, she managed to coax her cousin up to her feet,
guiding her gently to sit down on the edge of the bed.

Lady Hafton watched, bitterness and gall written deep in every
line of her face. When Eleanor was finally seated, still slumped, eyes
staring hopelessly at the rug at her feet, her mother stepped forward
to stand over her.

"You hateful child, to do this to us," she breathed. "Hateful."

Eleanor lifted her face to her mother, life returning to her eyes, which glinted with a hatred of their own.

"The apple falls not far from the tree," she murmured. Then she smiled, a bitter twist of her mouth that held no humour. "We are all of us the same. Edward and I, you and my father. We children have simply become what you made us."

Susannah watched, appalled and fascinated by the scene taking place before her, waiting for her uncle's arrival with an enthralled and morbid dread. His reaction was beyond her ability to imagine, as were the measures he would take against his daughter. There was no telling what he might do.

"How dare you?" Lady Hafton said. "How dare you accuse me? When you know so little of all I have done for you. You and your brother have had everything!"

The hasty step of Lord Hafton's shoes on the boards in the passage cut her off. All of them turned towards the door as it opened abruptly and admitted the tall lean figure of Susannah's uncle. A few paces behind him the nonchalant form of Edward appeared and leant itself against the door frame to watch.

"What in God's name is going on here?" Lord Hafton demanded. "Shrieking, wailing, panicking servants. Somebody enlighten me." He stood with his hands on his hips, tapping an impatient foot against the rug. "Well?" When no one said anything, he turned to his wife and grasped her arm. "Wife? You summoned me here, now in God's name tell me what is going on."

Lady Hafton swallowed, ran a quick tongue across her lips, and for the first time Susannah realised that her aunt was afraid of her husband, uncertain of his anger.

"Your daughter ..." she began. "Eleanor ..."

"I know my daughter's name, wife. Now for the love of God tell me or do I have to beat it out of you?!"

Lady Hafton took a step back as her husband clenched a fist. Looking towards her daughter, away from her husband, she blurted, "Eleanor is with child."

The silence in the room vibrated. Susannah heard the blood

whoosh inside her ears and held her breath for what seemed an age. Lord Hafton's face grew pale, knuckles whitening as his fists tightened with his rage. When finally he spoke, his voice was quiet and controlled but the menace in its tone was unmistakeable and even Susannah was afraid.

"Look at me, girl."

Eleanor breathed deeply, shaking, and lifted a tear-stained face to face her father.

"Is this true?"

She nodded.

He stepped forward, opened his hand and struck her full force across the face, sending her sprawling off the bed and to the floor. Susannah sprang down to aid her, but her uncle's voice stayed her in her tracks.

"Leave her be. Eleanor, get up."

Eleanor pushed herself up, stood before her father, swaying slightly, trembling.

"Come closer," Lord Hafton commanded. "You whore."

She took a small step towards him, her head still bowed.

"Who is the father?"

Eleanor shook her head.

"I said, who is the father?"

She shook her head again, and with her gaze still lowered she did not see the hand coming that felled her once more to the floor. She raised herself slowly, gingerly, wiping blood from her lip with the heel of her hand, painfully unfolding to stand again before him. Her head was lowered, and her hand still pressed against her lip.

"Who is the father?" he hissed again.

Eleanor raised her head, eyes almost level with her father's. He was trembling with rage, cheeks florid, knuckles white. He started forward and Eleanor flinched for the expected blow. "Tell me, you little whore!"

She swallowed. Then, drawing herself up to her full height, chin tilted in a faint semblance of defiance, she said in a toneless voice, "Gifford. The father is Sir Daniel Gifford."

The name was so unexpected that even Lord Hafton gasped. A

moment of silence pulsed through the room and Susannah stared in disbelief, frozen, unable to react.

"Is this true?" Hafton turned to his wife.

Lady Hafton looked uncertain. "It is possible," she replied.

No, Susannah thought. It cannot be possible. It cannot. Daniel was hers, and he loved her. She was sure of it – she had seen it in his eyes, known it in the tenderness of his touch. For him to be the father was impossible. It had to be. She shuffled back silently towards the bed, finding the edge of it with her hand, easing herself down before her legs buckled under her. Weakened by her illness, she was afraid the shock would prove too much, and she had no wish to faint in front of everyone.

Lord Hafton was pacing, immersed in thought, cheek muscles twitching wildly beneath the grey whiskers of his beard. Eleanor stood as he had left her, head bowed once more, apparently submissive and patient. Edward still lounged at the door, surveying the scene with detached and supercilious interest until his eyes lit on Susannah, discovered her distress, and smiled. She looked away, the triumph in his face unbearable. Unsteadiness crept through her body, threatening to overcome her, and she breathed deeply, searching for the strength to stay upright, to keep calm. She had never felt pain so intense.

Lord Hafton halted in front of his daughter. Her head remained bowed, humbled, fearful, a different Eleanor from the girl Susannah had come to know. "You are sure of this?" he demanded.

Eleanor nodded. "Yes, sir," she murmured. "Quite sure."

In the silence that followed Susannah recalled every time she had seen them together; Eleanor's coy smile and the laughter, a familiarity between them she had apparently misjudged. How could she have missed it? How could she have been so misled? He must have played with them both, she realised, and Eleanor had proved to be an easier prey. How could she have been so fooled by him?

Anger at her own stupidity, her naiveté, spiralled through her body. Tears stung behind her eyes, nausea lifting from her belly. She blinked, set her lips, struggling to control the turmoil of emotions within her. She could feel the heat of Edward's gaze from across the room and she recoiled beneath it. They were all of them hateful, and all she wanted was the chance to go home.

Lord Hafton sighed, then squared his shoulders, a decision made. He turned to his son. "Come Edward. Bring your sword. We are going to pay a visit to Gifford Court."

Susannah said, surprising herself, "You won't find him there. He's in London." Her voice sounded strange, unlike her own, as if the sound had come from a great distance away.

All eyes turned to her. "What's that you say?"

"He is in London," she repeated. "At the behest of the Earl of Leicester. To defend against the Spanish."

Lord Hafton advanced towards her. She raised her face to look at him but she was too weary and sad to be afraid. "And how came you to know of this?" he said.

She shook her head and shrugged, and Lettice, curtseying by the door, said, "Beg your pardon, my Lord, but I told her. I have a brother is a groom for Sir Daniel ..."

Lord Hafton turned on her. "What are you doing in here?" he spat. "Who asked for your thoughts on anything? Get out! You're dismissed! And if you ever breathe a word of this to anyone, I will hunt you down and beat you myself, do you understand?"

Lettice dipped again, stricken, then spun round and almost ran into Edward who was deliberately taking his time to move out of the door. Even then, he moved only enough that she must squeeze through, her shoulders brushing against his chest. Susannah thought he would have been the kind of boy to enjoy torturing animals, and the memory of his body and mouth against hers brought an involuntary shudder.

Her uncle turned again to address his son. "London, eh? Well, make yourself ready, boy. We've a long ride ahead of us."

Edward shoved himself from the wall, flashed a grin at Susannah, and disappeared, Lord Hafton following with rapid strides in his wake. She could hear them pacing down the passage, shouting instructions for horses and baggage at servants, their voices loud and peremptory, ringing through the house.

Lady Hafton took her daughter's arm in a steely grip and led her to the bed. Eleanor offered no resistance. "Sit there," she ordered. Eleanor sat obediently, eyes still lowered to the floor. Then, turning to Susannah, Lady Hafton said, in hostile accents, "Leave us."

Susannah rose silently, carefully, testing the strength of her limbs with each movement before she crossed the room to the door and, closing it gently behind her, she made her way unsteadily in search of Lettice.

She found her in the main kitchen where preparation for dinner was under way. The heat in the huge room was stifling, sweat breaking out along her spine as soon as she entered. A spit was being turned by a kitchen boy over a blazing fire, and stockpots were bubbling; the air was heavy with the scent of meat and herbs. She remembered she had barely eaten for more than three days, pangs of hunger biting at her gut, but the sight of Lettice in tears on a stool near a doorway into the yard swept all thought of food from her mind.

"Lettice?" She crossed the busy kitchen to her maid, who stood up hurriedly at her approach, dragging at her tears with an apron and dropping into a clumsy curtsey.

"Never mind that," Susannah said, taking Lettice's arm, "Let us get some air."

She led her into the courtyard, from where the various rooms of the kitchen could be reached. Beyond, through a narrow passage, she could see the stables, and in the other direction another lane led between the buttery and the boiling house towards the kitchen garden where so much of the food they ate was grown. A kitchen boy ran past them on an errand, slowing for a stride or two and ducking his head in deference. Susannah gave him a small smile in return, but he was gone before he could notice it. They found two barrels in the shade of a wall and leaned themselves against them. Susannah found herself swaying with weakness and hunger: it was an effort to stay upright.

"We must talk," she managed to say, but Lettice silenced her with a hand on her wrist.

"Not till you've eaten something, Mistress. You look as though you're about to drop."

Susannah nodded her assent, and Lettice took off back to the kitchen where she could raid one of the larders. Susannah watched her go, the lively young step across the cobbles, her own misery forgotten as she tended to her mistress. When the maid had disappeared from sight she rested herself on the barrel, trying to decide what she should do, her world crumbling around her, everything she had been certain of an hour before now as fragile as a piece of charred paper turning to ashes in her hand.

She was still numbed by the news, the truth too appalling to fully comprehend, though this much she was sure of – she had been a fool to trust him. An image of the night at Gifford Court flickered through her mind – the moment she had almost fallen, her seduction almost won. He had lost her trust that night, her instinct cautioning her against him: she should have taken warning then. But he had searched her out again with sadness in his eyes and won her back with honeyed promises he must have known she wished to hear. And how she had desired to hear them, how she had desired him to be true. So she had believed what she had wanted to believe, and closed her eyes to all the evidence against it.

Now, she felt like such a fool to have thought that he had loved her when all the time he was taking Eleanor to bed. She should have known. She should have guessed. He was a virile man, after all, a soldier, a knight who would be used to having his way, taking his pleasure where he could. And Eleanor had thrown herself before him, young and pretty and eager. She remembered seeing them together in the churchyard, her cousin's coyness in his presence. Why should it surprise her if he had taken what was offered when she herself refused him?

Yet he had handfasted himself to her and made her promises of marriage. Why had he done so? She guessed she would never now know his reasons, because the contract had been nullified – his bedding of her cousin had made sure of that. She would see him no more. He was no longer hers, and the promise between them had been broken.

She had lost him.

The final realisation took her breath away and she buried her face in her hands, eyes tight shut against the tears, forcing them down. There was no time for grief now; a plan had to be made.

When finally she raised her head, Lettice was returning across the yard with a tray of food: game pie, cheese, bread, and mugs of ale for them both. Placing the tray on one of the barrels, she invited her mistress to eat with an anxious smile and a gesture of her hand. Susannah ate, small bites at first, worried that her stomach might reject it after so long without, but when she discovered her body welcomed the food she ate rapidly, strength returning and her mind beginning to clear. When she had eaten her fill, she turned to Lettice, who had drawn up a pail to sit on while she waited.

"Thank you," she said. "I feel almost well again now."

The maid smiled. "Your colour has returned, thank the Lord."

She reached down and took Lettice's hands in her own, drew her up to stand level with herself so that their faces were close. "Listen, Lettice," Susannah began, her voice lowered to an undertone, though there was no one in the yard to overhear them. "I must leave Hafton Hall before my uncle and cousin return. There is no future for me here. I must go home to Abbey Leigh. Come with me. You'll be happy there, I promise you. I have three sisters and it is a good home, a happy home." She paused. "We will both be happy there."

"But what of Sir Daniel?"

She shook her head, shrugging. "You heard what Eleanor said. Sir Daniel is lost to me. Whatever there has been between us is no more and I must think now for myself."

"He will marry her?" Lettice looked doubtful.

Her throat tightened at the thought of it, tears burning behind her eyes once more. She swallowed them down, squaring her shoulders.

"That is not my concern," she said. "But Master Edward is my concern. The business with Eleanor won't put him off his plan to marry me, merely delay it a little. He will fetch the special licence somehow or other and he will return to force me into marriage. I must leave before that happens. Come with me, Lettice. I would rather not go alone."

"Two women on the road and no man to protect them, Mistress? It's a long way. How will we go?"

"We'll hire horses from the inn. You can ride, can you not?"

"As well as any farm girl, bareback and astride with my skirts hitched up."

Susannah's lips twitched in a smile: they were not so very different, she and Lettice.

"That will suffice. We will go dressed as boys. I thought at first your brother might escort us, but the summer barley's almost in and I know his hands are needed. Perhaps though he might spare some clothes for us to borrow?"

Lettice looked doubtful. "It's still an awful risk, Mistress. What if we are discovered? We'll be in all sorts of trouble."

"Then we'll just have to take care not to be discovered, won't we?"

"But ...?"

"No buts. I am going whether you come with me or no. I cannot stay and marry Edward. So I ask you, will you come with me?"

"Of course I will. I just wish there was another way."

"As do I. But there is no other way."

The clatter of hooves on the cobbles in the stable yard beyond the kitchen buildings startled them from their plans and, instinctively, Susannah shrank back against the wall. But it was too late. Edward was already approaching, dressed handsomely for riding, his sword at his hip.

"Cousin." He bowed before her. "I have been searching for you to take my leave."

"Well. It appears you have found me."

"Indeed it does and thus I say my farewell." He took her fingers in his hand, bowed lower and lifted her fingers to his lips where he held them, lingering for a moment. Inside her, everything recoiled, and it took every last speck of willpower she possessed not to wrench her hand from his grasp. Finally, he let it go and stood up straight. "I will return as soon as I may to claim your hand for my own. Farewell."

"Farewell," she said, and watched him walk away.

With God's good grace, she thought, she might never have to see him again.

CHAPTER 18

They left with the dawn, creeping from the house at first light before most of the servants were awake, a bundle each containing a set of women's clothes that they could wear at the journey's end. Susannah had left behind all the fine dresses the Haftons had given her, taking only the wool gowns she had brought from Abbey Leigh. She was glad to be rid of them, tainted as they were with the poison of the Haftons, and as she half-walked, half-ran across the park, she felt strange and slightly naked in the boy's breeches, used as she was to the feel of heavy skirts around her legs, the swish of movement as she walked. They said nothing to each other, anxiety to escape Hafton Hall unnoticed touching their every thought. Once on the road they slowed a little, catching their breath, small smiles of triumph at the first hurdle cleared.

Their horses were waiting as Lettice had arranged. It had taken the last of Susannah's small purse of money to pay for their hire – a servant from Abbey Leigh would be charged with their return. But that was still far in the future. They had the best part of two days' ride ahead of them and the road was a dangerous place.

They stayed off the highway wherever they could. Lettice knew the Hafton Valley well and once they had passed through the village, they cut off the road straight away, following a footpath that skirted the edge of a neighbouring estate and led them in a westerly direction. They rode side by side and conversed in lowered voices. Lettice was full of questions about Abbey Leigh, about Susannah's sisters. But through all their conversations both were vigilant, observing every passer-by, every traveller for signs of danger, and as the day wore on, the problem of the night's rest ahead began to tug at Susannah's thoughts.

Two young men, to outward appearances farmers' sons, riding alone, could not expect a room of their own in an inn. And even if they could they had not coin enough to pay for one. But they could hardly share with other lads and expect to maintain their disguise. They would have to make camp somewhere off the road and hope to remain unseen. Susannah knew it carried risks of its own, but they had no other choice: they would just have to find a sheltered spot that was well hidden from the road and hope for the best. They rode on, eyes scanning now for a likely site to camp, and as the sun fell lower in the sky, clouds began drawing in above them. Both of them surveyed the skies ahead with anxious eyes.

"Let us pray it stays dry at least until the morrow," Susannah said. "I don't mind riding tomorrow in the rain, but I would hope to spend a dry night first."

Lettice smiled her agreement. "It grows late, Mistress. Perhaps we should be starting to think of making camp."

Within a mile they had come off the road. A small coppice of oaks offered shelter on a gentle hill where they could light a small fire that would be hidden from the road. Susannah tended the horses, making sure they were tethered securely while Lettice gathered wood and made a fire. When that was done, they collected piles of leaves and moss to lie on as their beds then sat in the fire's warm glow to eat the bread and cheese and ale that Lettice's mother had given them for the journey.

Without the danger of the road it would have been a most wonderful evening. The rain held off, the clouds passing high overhead to drop their load elsewhere, and the two friends talked late into the night though neither dared to mention what was uppermost in both their minds, frightened to break the spell of safety that had brought them this far unhindered. So they talked instead of their childhoods and their families, Lettice the only girl amongst seven boys.

"Your father must count himself very blessed," Susannah murmured, thinking of her own father's dearest wish for a son.

"He does," Lettice agreed. "But I am the apple of his eye."

Susannah laughed, and in the dying light of the fire, they took to their beds, cloaks spread as blankets, bundles of clothes as pillows. She lay on her side and watched the flickering embers, hoping sleep would quickly claim her but her mind refused to let her rest so easily.

All through the day's ride she had schooled her mind away from thoughts of Daniel, knowing that once she gave into them her sorrow would consume her and she would be useless for the journey. Instead she had pressed herself to notice every tree and bush and bird that they passed, and for every passer-by and every village she had written a tale in her mind – long-winded, far-fetched stories she would have been embarrassed to share. But they occupied her thoughts and helped to chase away the images of Daniel that hovered always at the corners of her mind.

Now, with nothing to distract her, her thoughts were not as biddable and every moment she had spent with him, every lie he had told her, rehearsed itself again and again in her mind. She recalled once more how close she had come to seduction the night at Gifford Court and his coldness in the morning after she refused. How had he regained her trust after that? How had he convinced her? She had come so near to falling, almost giving up her virtue in a church for the lure of a promise it now seemed he had never planned to keep.

Tears rose and she let them fall, warm against her cheeks. He was worse than Edward in a way, she thought, more duplicitous, more treacherous. At least Edward had been honest – no promises of love or tenderness, just the desire to take what he believed would soon be his by right. Somehow the thought of him repulsed her less than when she had believed Daniel loved her. Perhaps there was not so much to choose between them after all.

The last thing she told herself before she fell asleep was that she hated all of them, but in her dreams her heart betrayed her, and when she woke just before first light, sore and aching from the hardness of the ground, the pain of heartbreak almost bent her double: love had not yet turned to hate, and her heart was still Daniel's to command.

CHAPTER 19

The rain held off till mid-morning the next day, but by the time they arrived at Abbey Leigh late in the afternoon they were cold and drenched and miserable. She had never been so glad to be home, the horses clattering beneath the familiar stone entrance arch, the lion's head above it roaring down at them unnoticed as servants appeared from the stables, wary at this unexpected arrival of two unknown young men.

Susannah slid down from her horse, grateful to be at her journey's end at last. On the ground she removed her hat and shook out the wet black hair so that it fell about her shoulders. The groom stared, eyes wide and blinking in the rain. "Do you not recognise me, Simmons?" she said.

The young man blinked again against the rain in his eyes, took a moment to recover, then said, "Of course, Mistress Archer," and bowed. She handed him the reins of the horses, bid him have their bundles brought inside, and then beckoned for Lettice to follow her into the house.

Her sister Olivia was the first of the family to find them, and despite the fact her sister was dripping, she threw her arms around her, delighted. "Su!" she cried. "What brings you home again so soon?"

"It's a long tale and we are wet and cold and hungry. Let us wash

173

and dress and then we can talk. Can you tell our lady mother that I am arrived?"

Her sister nodded and turned to hurry away, while Susannah led Lettice up the stairs towards the chamber she had used to share with Olivia. In the familiar room that was warmed against the storm by a low-burning fire in the wide stone hearth, Lettice helped her mistress out of the soaking clothes, rubbing her dry and wrapping her snugly in a towel while they waited for their bundles to be brought up. Before long both were dry and dressed, and one of the maids took Lettice away to show her the house and her place within it. Susannah stood at the door of the chamber a moment, composing herself, the enormity of what she had done coming home to her now that she was about to explain herself to her mother.

She found the family in the main hall, assembled at the long table in the centre, candles lit already in the darkness of the rainy after-noon, a fire smouldering in the great stone fireplace. She stood in the doorway and took in the room before her, the tapestries hanging either side of the hearth, the swords that were hung above it and the woven rush mats beneath her slippers. A sense of comfort and belonging assailed her senses, a connection to this house she loved. Everything was known and loved, every object in the room familiar, every turn in the wood, every imperfection, every facet, a part of who she was.

It was good to be home.

She breathed deeply, inhaling the scent of the house she had grown up in, gathering courage. Then she approached her mother who sat at the table, a hesitant smile on a face that was troubled by this sudden unorthodox arrival of her eldest daughter.

"Madam," Susannah said, curtseying before her. "I hope I find you well?"

"I am quite well, thank you, Susannah," her mother answered, holding out a hand to bring her daughter closer. "Just a little uneasy to see you here, and to have you arrive in such a manner." She looked around. "Where is Sir Daniel?"

Susannah ran a tongue across her lips. All the words she had rehearsed on the ride through the morning fled from her mind with her mother's question, and she could not think where to begin. Confused, and overcome at last, the tears she had kept in check for so long began to flow and despite her best efforts she could do nothing to stem them. "Forgive me, madam," she sobbed.

Her mother held out her arms and Susannah went to her, kneeling at her feet, her face buried in the warm dark gown, the familiar scent of wool and soap giving her comfort as it had done as a child. Quietly, with a gesture of her hand and her head, Mistress Archer dismissed the other girls, and when the door had latched gently to behind them, she bent down to lift her daughter's tearful face.

"Dear child," she said, "what can have happened to upset you so? I haven't seen you cry like this since you were just a girl."

Susannah pushed herself to her feet and wiped her tears away from her face with an impatient hand. Her mother motioned for her to sit on the nearest stool and when she was settled, she said softly. "Tell me what has happened. Tell me all."

The words spun in Susannah's head, and all she could think to say was, "I have lost him."

Her mother waited for her daughter to go on but when Susannah fell silent, her gaze taken by the flames in the hearth and her thoughts elsewhere, Mistress Archer gently coaxed her back. "What has happened to bring you home like this, Susannah?" she asked again. "Tell me."

Susannah turned her gaze from the fire and wiped the last of the tears from the corners of her eyes. She gave her mother a small sad smile. "It is a long story," she said.

"I have time," her mother replied, squeezing her fingers again.

Susannah began at the beginning, repeating what her mother already knew from the letters, but it was easier to tell it that way, without breaks, each thing following on from the last though she made no mention of either man's attempts on her virtue, too ashamed to speak of such things to her mother. Eleanor's confession she related in a whisper, tears on her cheeks and the words hard to form. Her heart still rebelled against the truth of it and it was painful even just to say his name.

When the tale was told, her mother sighed, patted her daughter's hand as she let it go. Then she sat back in her chair, thoughtful. After a moment, she said, "So you are betrothed to Sir Daniel?"

"I am. He persuaded me against my better judgment. I wanted to wait for your blessing. I wanted to be sure. But he said it would keep me safe from the Haftons ..." She stopped, remembering, the pleasure of the memory turned now to regret. "But I believe his ... intimacy ..." The word barely left her lips, the image it evoked slicing pain across her thoughts. She turned her head away as if that way she might avoid it. " ... his intimacy with my cousin, may render it void?"

She lifted hopeful eyes to her mother: however much she still loved him, to marry him now would be torture, knowing how he had deceived her, that she had shared him with her cousin, that Eleanor's child was his.

"I believe it will," her mother replied. "Though if he is unwilling to marry your cousin, he may try to use it as a way to escape her."

She lifted eyes to her mother. "Forgive me, madam."

"What for?"

"If only I had liked Edward more."

Her mother smiled but the sigh that lay behind it betrayed her anxious thoughts. She said, "We won't think of it for now. But when your heart has healed a little from its wounds, we will think of him again and perhaps you can find your way to some rapprochement."

"And Sir Daniel?"

"Sir Daniel? You must write to him to release him from the contract and to end any understanding between you, on the grounds of his fornication with your cousin."

Her mother's blunt words turned a leaden weight inside her – the thought of him with Eleanor provoked a real and physical pain and she flinched, steeling herself against it.

"And then," her mother went on, "you must set your mind to forget him so we can turn our thoughts to the business of the future. Abbey Leigh still requires an heir and if it is not to be Sir Daniel Gifford then we must look again to the possibility of Edward Hafton."

She said, "I have no address for Sir Daniel in London."

"Then you shall write to him at Gifford Court," her mother, always practical, replied. "I'm sure his staff will know where to send it."

She nodded her agreement, accepting that there was no other way. But she could barely imagine herself composing such a letter, wondering how she would even begin to write the words she would need to tell him.

～

It was the hardest letter she had ever had to write, putting to rest all her hopes for happiness with each new stroke of the quill, and though she knew the letter itself was but the final word in a much longer story, still she was reluctant to utter it and sever herself from him completely.

In the end, she had made it brief and cold, the only way she could prevent herself from crying out her heart to him in all her sorrow, and as soon as it was done she took it to her mother who would see it sent to the post with a servant at the first opportunity.

"It is for the best," her mother said. "You cannot marry such a man."

She nodded but said nothing. It was done then, and she would never be in Sir Daniel Gifford's arms again.

CHAPTER 20

*N*ight was closing in when news finally reached the assembled troops that the Spanish Armada was on its way. Along the coastline the beacons flickered into life, readying the defenders against the near arrival of their enemies.

In the camp at Tilbury, six thousand men lounged at ease, well trained and ready under the leadership of the Earl of Leicester, Robert Dudley. Behind the lines of sharpened stakes that were planted strong and deep to repel the invader, low fires burned between small groups of men, flames crackling amid a low murmur of conversation. Steel whistled against sharpening stones, and the hammers of blacksmiths plied their trade late into the darkness. Above the tents, flags whipped lightly in the breeze and the horses of the cavalry stamped and snorted from their lines, bridles jangling.

Not long after sunset, the captains were summoned to the Earl of Leicester's tent. Daniel and Sam walked together, silent. They had fought together too long and knew each other too well for a need for words, both of them tense with readiness for the battle, the familiar heat of nerves and excitement: still, they exchanged a brief smile before they ducked beneath the flap that led into Leicester's tent. Other men acknowledged their arrival with nods and small bows, and the atmosphere hummed in the small space as they waited for the Earl to speak.

Daniel looked around him. He could have been back in the Netherlands, he thought. The same flags and banners hung from the walls in the familiar Tudor green and white, the same rich furnishings that befitted the status of an Earl. The Earl himself stood at a great oak table that was spread with a map of the eastern coast of the realm.

Leicester had aged, Daniel thought, in the year since he had seen him last, and grown portlier, his complexion more florid. But he had retained the confident charm that had held the Queen's heart for so many years, and the men arrayed before him still looked up to him as their leader. Though he had led them astray in the Netherlands, his charisma still held their respect. Besides, Daniel thought wryly, he was the only leader they had – what other choice had they but to follow him?

When the captains were all assembled at last, waiting silently, the Earl cast his eyes around the gathering. There were many faces he knew from the campaign in the Netherlands and he took the time to nod a greeting to each man that he recognised, a personal acknowledgement, before he addressed them all.

"Good morrow, gentlemen. I thank you for your attention." The atmosphere stiffened; the silence grew tense. "We have news that the hour is almost at hand. The English fleet now sails on the tide from Plymouth Sound and the Armada fast approaches. We all of us know our duty. Ready your men, stand firm and may God protect us all."

The camp bristled with tension, expectant and ready. Horses stamped and tossed their heads, and men stood or paced, restless with anticipation, impatient for news. Daniel sat with his friend in the tent they shared, a hundred horse each under their command. All was prepared and there was nothing more to do but wait. They spoke little beyond the commonplaces of a shared, close-lived life, but when a messenger arrived with a letter for Daniel, the interruption stirred Sam from the silence into sudden interest. He sat forward in his chair.

"Who is it from?"

Daniel gestured with a hand for his friend to be patient though he knew at once that the writing was Susannah's. It was a single sheet, folded neatly, tied and sealed, and he broke the seal with a slight sense of apprehension. Some vague sense warned him that it was not good news and his heartbeat quickened as he folded out the page and ran his eyes across the words it held.

Sir Daniel,

Forgive me for writing at such a time, when you have matters of great import to the realm to consider, but I regret to say I am writing to release you from your contract with me and to bring an end to any understanding between us, on the grounds of your intimate relations with Eleanor Hafton.

I wish you well in your endeavours against the Spanish and ask that you pass on my good wishes to Sir Samuel.

Your obedient servant, Susannah.

The letter was brief, no more than a few short lines, but their meaning stopped his breath, and all thought of the Spanish was wiped from his mind.

"What news?" Sam asked.

Though there was less than a few feet between, it seemed as though the voice came from a great distance away.

"It's from Susannah," he managed to murmur, his eyes still running over the lines she had written, searching to find some mistake, or some clue that might explain.

"Well?" Sam said, lips curved in a smile of curiosity. "What does she say?"

Daniel lowered the page and regarded his friend, barely able to order his thoughts. Confusion filled him – it was impossible to make sense of the message before him, to understand its significance.

"She ..." he began, waving the letter as if to shake a different meaning out of it, "She has broken off our contract." He met his friend's eyes, his own gaze dark with incomprehension and hurt.

Sam's smile faded and a frown of perplexity took its place. "But why?" he asked. "What reason does she give?"

Daniel lowered his eyes again to the page as though to remind himself, although the words had burned themselves across his mind already: they were words he would never forget.

"*In view*," he read out, "*of my intimate relations with Eleanor Hafton.*" He looked across at Sam again, shaking his head in disbelief. "What does she mean? Sam, tell me, what can she mean? I have had no intimate relations with Eleanor Hafton." He spat the offending words through teeth clenched tight with fury. "Is she toying with me? I had not thought her capable of such a thing."

"Nor is she, Dan."

"Then why? God help me, why?"

Sam shrugged. "I can only think she must have been misled, lied to."

"Edward Hafton. It has to be. It can be no other. But why would she believe him over me? She has the measure of his character, the measure of mine. How could he persuade her against me? What could have happened to sway her?"

"Does she say anything else?"

Daniel shook his head, hopeless, and handed the letter across to his friend. Sam cast his eyes over the few lines. There was no clue, no hint of Susannah's state of mind behind the cold curtness of the words.

"When this is over …" Sam began.

"When this is over," Daniel took up the sentence, "I shall ride with all haste to Hafton and discover the truth of the matter." He swung abruptly away to face the walls of the tent, fingers clenching into fists then flexing, trying to keep his rage and frustration in check. He wanted to hit out at something, someone, fury burning through his veins, scalding and corrosive. Every fibre in him was taut to breaking point, ready to snap. God help the first Spaniard that came across him. He took a deep breath, then another, forcing himself to calm, mastering the torrent of emotion. When he thought he could get words past lips still drawn tight with rage, he turned back towards his friend.

"Without her pre-contract to me," he said softly, "she is free to marry Hafton. I am afraid for her, Sam, and that I may be too late to save her from him."

"You think Hafton may have forced her to write this?" Sir Samuel held up the offending note.

"Does it not seem possible to you?"

"Possible, yes … but …"

"You think she wrote it of her own free will?" He could not believe it of her, knowing how she loved him: he refused to believe she would give him up so easily. He stepped towards his friend, challenging.

"I think it more likely," Sam said carefully, "that she has been persuaded against you by some lie she has been brought to believe."

"But how could she believe that of me? How?"

"She is alone amongst them, Dan, and dependent on the Haftons. They are a family with much influence and few morals. She is friends with Eleanor, is she not? And in her company daily? It would come as no surprise to me to learn that Eleanor had some skill in the art of deception." He shook his head. "And have you forgotten that Eleanor had eyes for you herself, Dan? You surely must have noticed? All that giggling and coyness? Perhaps she is trying to clear the way for her own ambitions."

He said nothing, weighing Sam's words, fury turning to uncertainty. Doubt began to settle in his mind. He ran his thoughts back across all that had happened: the night at Gifford Court, the morning in the church. Perhaps he had used her unfairly, he thought, persuading her to intimacy too quickly, rushing her. She was a maid after all, and he was not proud of the way he had treated her, driven by his need and the knowledge that only she could save him from his darkness. And he knew for sure he had pressed her both times, taking her far beyond where she wanted to go. He had knowingly ridden roughshod across her reluctance, using the desire he awoke in her, his fingers skilled in giving pleasure. The scene played across his thoughts again, his own frustrated desire stirring, warm in his gut. Had he gone too far that day and pressed her too hard? Perhaps he had. And if she believed he had done so she might more easily be persuaded he had done the same with Eleanor.

He cursed his own impatience, his eagerness. He should have trodden more gently, he railed at himself, and allowed her to wait as she wanted. But he had been too impatient to prove his love, to make sure of her and keep her safe from Hafton.

"I would the Haftons were damned to Hell!" he breathed. "I hate them all."

He turned away again, pacing, feeling caged and impotent, his instinct to go to her now, to ride all night if need be, to bring Susannah the truth. But the Spanish were at the gates of the realm and England's survival was at stake. He could not go. Sam stepped forward and laid a hand on his friend's broad, armoured shoulder. "There is still time, Dan. Write to her – the messenger still waits. Write her the truth and all will be well."

"All will be well?" Daniel flashed him a small wry smile. "I said the same words to Susannah before I left. The very same. And look at us now."

"Write to her and have faith, my friend. Have faith."

Shaking his head, trying to clear the doubts, Daniel took a seat at the table and, reaching for paper and a quill, set about turning his mind to winning back the woman that he loved.

Susannah was dreaming: she was walking along a path with a child that wasn't hers, though his eyes were dark as night, his face the image of his father. The boy kept smiling up at her, but she was crying because she was taking him somewhere she'd forgotten, a place they could never reach now because they'd taken so many wrong turns and they were lost.

A sense of desperation filled her, a longing to be home. Daniel appeared, sad and searching for something in a forest, a sword in his hand, armour on his back. There were shouts and Spanish soldiers and though she tried to call out, to warn him, she could make no sound with her voice, and so he passed on through the trees and then out of sight amongst them. She tried to follow, still calling out his name in silence, but the child refused to go with her, and it was beyond her power to leave him behind.

She woke up trembling as the images still lingered across her thoughts, and she lay for a moment, following the dream again in her mind to try to make sense of it. She would never forget him, she thought. She would never love anyone else. And if she cared about the Spanish at all it was only so that he might stay safe against them, whatever she tried to tell herself in the daylight hours when her heart was more firmly trammelled.

Restless, she rolled out of bed. Despite the early hour she knew she would sleep no more tonight. She padded barefoot to the window and wriggled between the curtains to look out over her beloved Abbey Leigh. The moon was almost full, low in the sky now and on its way down, but its light still shed a silver glow and under it the gardens led away from the house in a silent ghostly procession.

So many times she had imagined Daniel here, showing him the house and grounds, knowing he would love it just as she did, taking picnics by the river, riding through the park. His eyes would never see it now and she must take some other husband for Abbey Leigh to pass to.

If she could not have Daniel, she decided, it might as well be Edward. No other man would ever win her heart, so her choice of husband made no matter anymore. Let her father have his dying wish and let Edward take her for his own. She sighed at the thought of it. Then she shook her shoulders with a self-reproach. England stood on the brink of war, she told herself, the sovereignty of the realm at stake. The man she loved now stood shoulder to shoulder with other men of England to keep her shores defended, and all she herself could do was pine like a lovesick milkmaid.

A movement beyond the garden caught her gaze. A fox stood frozen in the moonlight, brush raised, nose turned into the wind. She knew he was a menace, a constant threat to the chickens, but she could not help but admire his sleekness and the confident way he commanded the night. He turned his head towards the house, seeming to look straight at her for a moment, self-assured, before he trotted lightly away and out of sight. Behind her, in the bed, Olivia groaned and shifted, turning her face away from the window and the shaft of moonlight that crossed the room where Susannah had opened the curtain.

Somewhere, she thought, out at sea beyond England's eastern shore, English men were fighting, the small and speedy English ships pitted against the powerful galleons of the Spanish. There were twice as many Spanish ships as English, she had heard – it would be a most unequal battle. But it was impossible to imagine a Spaniard on the English throne, the nation hauled back once more to the authority of the Pope. She was too young to remember the reign of Bloody Queen Mary, but her father had talked of it sometimes, a reign of terror as the Sovereign had attempted to force the people back to the Catholic faith by force. Would it be like that again if the Spaniards won, she wondered? Would hundreds of protestants burn at the stake as they had done under Mary? God forbid they should return to such a world.

Beyond the window, the silver shimmer that covered the grounds began to fade as the moon dropped lower in the sky and the sky began to lighten with the coming of the day. Turning from the view, she silently began to dress herself, a simpler procedure at Abbey Leigh than at Hafton Hall. She drew on her favourite blue wool bodice, which laced at the front and nicely matched the darker blue brocade of her skirt and sleeves. Then, finding her boots in the greying dawn light, she pulled them on and crept past the bed and out of the room, down the stairs and out into the garden.

The air was cool despite the season, a light dew touching the grass and a low fine mist that would lift with the coming of the sun. She stood for a moment, breathing in the freshness and the scent of summer wetness before deciding which way to go. Then she turned her steps around to the front of the house and headed across the grass towards the village. The sun was just peeping over the horizon when she reached the village green and she stopped, the light magical, rainbows in the mist. She passed workers on their way towards the fields and wished good morrow to the blacksmith, whose fire was already burning hot, his arms and forehead slick with sweat.

Instinctively her steps were drawn towards the church, a low and ancient edifice that was sacred with the prayers of generations. Inside was cool and hushed, the stones beneath her feet worn smooth by four hundred years of worship. She walked slowly to the family pew, soothed by its familiarity. Then she bowed her head and prayed to God for Daniel's safety and the safe deliverance of the realm.

~

For ten days the whole nation hovered on a knife-edge, news moving swiftly from town to town with each development in the battle that would decide the sovereignty of England. It was all that anyone talked of – false rumours flew of Spanish troops along the South Coast, of babies butchered and women raped, but in the porch of every church in the land official notices were posted every day, bearing more truthful accounts and keeping Queen Elizabeth's people abreast of the fate of their nation.

The second week in August, news of the triumph finally came. Susannah heard the bells from the garden at Abbey Leigh where she was gathering herbs for her mother. Her heartbeat quickened in relief: the danger was over. The Spanish would never set foot on English soil and Daniel would not have to go to war against them. Cutting the final stalk of rosemary and dropping it into the basket, she rose from her knees, brushed the dirt from her skirts, and ran inside to tell the rest of the household the news.

~

"I wish to talk with you, Susannah."

Later that day, her mother stopped her as she descended the stairs on her way towards the supper table. She halted, halfway down, one hand resting on the banister. Her mother's expression was hard to read but there was a set to the line of her mouth that boded ill. A sense of dread coursed through her. "Right away, madam?"

"Now is as good a time as any."

She nodded and followed her mother away from the stairs to the room her father had used as his office. It still served as the hub of the house, where all the business of the estate was transacted. She had spent many hours in this room since her return, conferring with her mother and the steward and the bailiff, taking on the duties of running the estate.

A map of the boundaries lay open on the desk from a meeting that had taken place earlier in the day. Susannah furled it neatly and placed it in the large oak chest beneath the window, then moved to stand before the desk. Her mother had taken her place by the chair her father had used to occupy, fingering the heavy oak back of it but reluctant still to sit in it and make it hers.

"I cannot bring myself to sit there, either," Susannah said.

Mistress Archer looked up quickly with a slight brief smile, but it was gone in an instant. She took a deep breath before she spoke.

"I am sorry to broach this again so soon, but I am afraid that now the danger of war is past it can no longer wait." She paused and forced a stray strand of hair back into place beneath the linen cap with impatient fingers. "I've received another letter from Lord Hafton."

Susannah paled. She knew what was coming – she had only hoped it might be delayed a while longer. Her mother unfolded the letter she was holding in her hand and passed her eyes across the page. "He writes … that though he was somewhat upset at your precipitate departure from Hafton, he understands there were certain circumstances that upset you. And that because of the unfortunate circumstance of his not being there himself to comfort you, it was quite natural you should have sought the solace of your family." Her mother looked up briefly before she lowered her eyes again and went on.

"And although the irregular manner of your going is not to be easily overlooked, he is quite willing to forgive your behaviour and to resume the negotiations pertaining to your marriage to his son."

Susannah stared at the ground, hands clasped in front of her, fingers twisting round one another. She said nothing.

"I understand, Susannah," her mother said, her voice more gentle, "your feelings for Edward Hafton are not warm, but he was your father's choice for you and the only way of keeping Abbey Leigh in the family. Both of us would have accepted Sir Daniel in his stead but he has proved himself unworthy, and in the absence of other suitors, well, Edward Hafton must be considered a very ..." she turned her hand in the air, searching for the word "... suitable match. In time you will become a viscountess. You will be Lady Hafton, and your children will bear titles also. This is a good match for our family, Susannah, for your sisters' prospects also. It is a good future for you and for your children. I won't force you into it, but I would remind you of your promise to your father."

She swallowed, forcing away the image of the dining chamber at Gifford Court, the warmth before the fire, Daniel's smile as they talked across the hearth. It was a future she had almost held within her grasp, a future she had lost. Though he had replied to her letter with protestations of his innocence, she had steeled her heart against them – she had believed his lies for too long. The life she had dreamed of had been no more than an illusion, and with her next words she would seal its loss forever.

She said, "I will do my duty. You may write to my uncle and tell him I accept. You and he can work out the business of it between you. I have no interest any more. May I go?"

Her mother regarded her across the desk she still thought of as her father's, an expression that was almost tender in the aging eyes. "You may go," her mother replied.

Susannah dropped into a curtsey, then turned and fled the room.

CHAPTER 21

It was several days more before the troops amassed at Tilbury were decommissioned and allowed to go home. Daniel spent those days in an agony of waiting, each day tempted to take the risk and go – the Spanish were no longer a threat and there was no good reason to remain but the fact of orders from the Queen. When, finally, the word came to disband, he was prepared and waiting, and Sam ready to go with him.

"We shall see you at Court in the days to come, Sir Daniel, Sir Samuel?" the Earl enquired of them as they readied their horses to depart.

"Another time, perhaps, my Lord," Daniel replied. "I have urgent business in Somerset to attend to."

"Then God go with you," the Earl said, "and I pray He keeps you safe on your journey."

"Thank you, my Lord." Daniel swung himself into the saddle and took his leave of their commander, mud kicking up under the horses' hooves as the two men sped on their way.

They rode hard, the roads good in the dry summer air, their animals fit and hardy, and their own strength driven by Daniel's impatience. The distance to Hafton took them three long days and they drew into the village in the shadows of the late evening dusk.

"Where first?" Sam asked.

Daniel hesitated. His first instinct was to go straight to Hafton Hall. He could hardly bear to pass another night without seeing her, without telling her the truth. His whole body craved to find her without any more delay. But he knew that he was filthy from the ride, his clothes black and reeking and the hour was growing late. He would present a better picture in the morning, clean and washed, sweeter smelling.

He sighed. "It had better be Gifford Court, I suppose. Though it grieves me to spend another night of waiting."

"I think it's wise, Dan," Sam agreed. "You don't present a very agreeable aspect as you are. You'll be far more handsome in the morning."

Daniel smiled, and the two men settled their horses into a gentle jog towards the house at Gifford Court.

In the morning he rose with the dawn, having slept only little – restless, dream-filled sleep that had left him weary and unrefreshed. He should have gone to her last night, he reflected wryly, when he had still had the momentum of the journey to sustain him. Servants hurried to lay breakfast as he descended the stairs and he sat at the table as meat and bread and ale was brought to him. He ate it absently, his mind on the task ahead, and looked up in surprise when Sam took his place at the table across from him.

"You're up early," Daniel said.

"Military habit," his friend replied. "Shall I go with you?"

"I need no escort." The reply was testy.

"As you wish. I just thought if the Haftons turn ugly … they may object to you taking her."

Daniel shrugged. He cared nothing for the Haftons, his only thought to bring Susannah back and persuade her of the truth. He would be damned if he would let the Haftons prevent him. "As you like."

"My pleasure," Sam said, and the smile in his tone drew Daniel's eyes to meet his friend's gaze. He held it for a moment before returning the smile.

"Thank you, Sam. You're a good friend. Let's away."

They saddled their own horses, too impatient to wait for the groom and, riding as they usually did without the encumbrance of attendants, they left the court at a gallop. The keen air was good against his face, dispelling any lingering tiredness, and the horses raced willingly across the grass and into the lane towards the village. He was on his way to claim his bride and there was nothing in the world could stop him now.

The clatter of their horses' hooves brought servants running to the main entrance of the house. Throwing the reins to one of them, Daniel strode towards the door and once inside he shouted out for attention.

"Hafton?! Are you here, Hafton?"

His voice drew people from all parts of the house, servants afraid to have kept their master's visitor waiting. Daniel paced the entrance hall, face flushed from the gallop and his anger, riding cloak slung back across one shoulder. Sam stood close by, arms folded, as a portly middle-aged servant in the Hafton livery blue hurried down the stairs towards them, stopped abruptly, and bowed.

"Lord Hafton wishes you to wait on him in the hall, if you please," the man informed them. "He will be down directly."

They said nothing but followed the man into the hall. Inside, Daniel closed the door and approached the servant closely. "Tell me something," he said. "Where is Mistress Archer?"

The servant's eyes widened in surprise. Fear flickered behind them at the anger in Sir Daniel's face. "M-m-mistress Archer?" he stammered.

"Yes, you fool. Susannah Archer. Cousin to Edward and Eleanor. Niece to Lord and Lady Hafton."

"She has left, sir, and gone back to her family."

Daniel exchanged a glance with his friend before looking back to the servant who was staring from one to the other, evidently made nervous by the questions, and the apparent ill-temper of the questioner. "When?" he demanded. "When did she go?"

"Perhaps a month or so," the servant ventured.

"Then we're wasting our time, Sam," he said. "We must leave for Abbey Leigh with all haste."

He swept round on his heel and strode for the door and the servant half ran across the room behind him, one hand held out in supplication. "My master begs that you will stay and speak with him."

Daniel rounded on him so fast the servant staggered back and almost fell. "He told you to keep me here?"

The servant regained his steadiness and nodded, with a nervous glance at the door.

"Why?"

"I cannot say, sir."

Daniel grabbed the man's doublet in both his hands, pushed him backwards across the room. The servant shot an appeal to Sam for help, but Sam flicked his eyes away, towards the door, keeping watch.

"Cannot or will not?" The words were low and dangerous, and uttered through teeth that were clenched in fury. "Why does he want me detained?"

"Mistress Eleanor, sir." the servant mumbled.

"What of it?"

"The master went to London to find you, sir. And Master Edward. To hold you to account."

Daniel loosed his hold on the man's clothes, patted his chest where a moment before he had held him fast. The man backed hurriedly away, out of arm's reach.

"Hold me to account?" Daniel breathed. "For what?"

"Mistress Eleanor's ... condition, sir."

Abruptly he understood. "Eleanor is with child?" he asked softly.

The servant nodded. "But I am not supposed to know, sir."

"Of course you are not." He wheeled away from the servant and strode to the door, standing close to his friend, mind reeling. No wonder Susannah had broken off the betrothment if that's what she thought. No wonder she had run away to Abbey Leigh.

"But why?" he murmured. "Why would Eleanor accuse me of such a thing?"

"To force a marriage?" Samuel suggested. "And to turn Susannah towards her brother?"

Daniel nodded. "We must go," he said, yanking open the door. But as he stepped out into the lobby, he was met by Lord Hafton with several servants at his back and a sword at his hip. The sight of it almost made him smile, but he was in no mood for humour, impatient to be gone.

"Inside," Hafton ordered with a gesture of his head back towards the hall they had just left.

Daniel considered the options, Lord Hafton's men arrayed across the hall blocking the way. They would not make it. With a slight nod to his friend, he backed into the hall to await the right moment, but he kept his eyes on Lord Hafton: he would not have put anything past him.

"Sir Daniel, at last," Lord Hafton said when the door was closed behind them, two of his men standing guard just inside it. "You have led me a merry chase, indeed."

"My whereabouts have been no secret, sir. I've been at Tilbury, my Lord, with the Earl of Leicester and six thousand troops. I'm sure you're aware the realm has lately been at war?"

"Don't patronise me, Gifford. You well know the road to Tilbury was closed to all but fighting men."

Daniel smiled. Lord Hafton was a man used to being obeyed and putting fear into those beneath him, but Daniel was not a man to be bullied and Lord Hafton had no power to frighten him. "Was there something in particular you wished to discuss?" he asked.

"Enough!" Hafton commanded, cheeks reddening above the wisps of grey beard. The two men eyed each other across the length of the rich Turkey rug. In spite of Hafton's age and leanness there was a cruelty in him that kept Daniel wary. There was still strength in the old man's sinews, and the will to hurt.

"Enough of playing games, Gifford," Hafton snarled. "I've chased you the breadth of the country and now you will answer for it."

"And tell me, pray, what I have done to so offend you, my Lord."

"You do not know?"

"I do not."

"Can you make no guess?"

There was a silence. Samuel stood at the empty hearth, apparently unconcerned, but his eyes never left the scene and for all his apparent nonchalance, he stood ready for whatever might happen next. Lord Hafton stepped in near to Daniel, their faces close, and Sam tensed, prepared and vigilant.

"My daughter," Hafton breathed, "is with child."

"I am sorry to hear of it." Daniel stepped away, putting distance between them. He was wasting precious time, a two-day ride ahead of them and the morning ticking by.

"She tells me that you …" the viscount broke off, pointing a finger that was trembling with rage at his enemy, the presence of the servants forgotten in his fury. "She tells me that you, sir, are the father."

"Then your daughter, my Lord, is a liar." The calmness of his words belied the hatred beneath them, and the effort such apparent serenity was costing him. He could barely breathe for anger.

Lord Hafton regarded him a moment as if considering, and Daniel wondered if it had even crossed his mind that his daughter might be lying. After a moment, Hafton said, "Then let us ask her."

"As you wish." He hoped she might buckle in his presence, that she possessed some kind of conscience he might attempt to stir. Otherwise she must have a heart that was hewn from rock.

Hafton sent one of his men to fetch her and she came quickly, waiting nearby, Daniel assumed, for her summons. She came into the room as wary as a hare before the hounds, frightened eyes, blood draining from her cheeks, and it occurred to him she had been schooled to make this lie, that either brother or father had forced her into it. Poor girl, he thought, to be born into such a family. Then she turned her eyes towards him and under the fear a coldness lurked that made a mockery of his sympathy: he would find no moral conscience in her to help him, he was sure. She had told her story and he had no doubt she would stick to it. God help him.

"Mistress Eleanor." He gave a small bow, though the courtesies seemed absurd in the situation.

"Sir Daniel." She curtseyed.

Lord Hafton raised his hand to point at the man she had accused. "Is this man," he demanded, "the father of your child?"

She dropped her eyes and nodded.

"Speak up girl, we cannot hear you."

She raised her face, but she looked at her father and not at him as she answered. "Yes, father. He is."

"You lie," Sir Daniel said softly, moving towards her. "Why so? Who is it you wish to protect?"

For an instant a flicker of doubt crossed the hardness of her expression, but she subdued it in a heartbeat and turned cold eyes on him again. "I am protecting no one, sir, just claiming what is mine by right."

"You will marry her, by God. You will marry her." Hafton strode closer, his breath hard and rasping in the silent room.

"And if I refuse?"

"You cannot. She has named you as father. You cannot refuse."

"I am not the father."

"Have you no shame, man?" Hafton was almost beside himself with rage and frustration. It was unthinkable to him that his daughter might ever bear a bastard, and he was seemed completely unprepared for Gifford's flat denial of his part in it. Daniel guessed that he had just assumed his quarry would accept the facts and then his punishment, and whisk his daughter away to church. Eleanor was a good enough match for a knight after all: she was the daughter of a viscount. Daniel watched as the older man's conviction began to waver.

"You might ask your daughter the same question, my Lord," he said. "It is she who is with child, the father unknown."

"Eleanor?" Hafton gripped his daughter's arm so hard she winced, dragging her forward across the floor towards the man she accused. "Do you still claim Sir Daniel as the father? It is your word against his."

She lifted her chin, but kept her eyes averted, the coldness still within them despite the pain of her father's grasp. "He is the father. I swear it."

"She swears." Hafton turned back to Gifford, his hand remaining vice-like on his daughter's arm. "What say you now?"

"I say she lies. As you say, it is her word against mine and there is an end of it."

Another silence fell, an impasse reached. A sense of the day wasting began to agitate Daniel's thoughts. He wanted to be gone from here, on his way to Susannah, the Haftons' business their own and nothing to do with him, whatever Eleanor claimed. He was losing precious time for the journey and resentment began to simmer beneath the still-calm surface. He flashed a glance to his friend who understood straight away, standing away from the hearth, poised and ready for movement.

"We will call a justice of the peace," Hafton said.

"You may call whomever you wish," Daniel returned. "But I have no more time for this." And so saying, he strode towards the door where the two servants still stood guard, looking uncertainly towards their master. In a moment, Samuel was by his side. Between them they easily shoved the servants aside: in the absence of orders from their master they offered no resistance.

With Sam beside him, Daniel flung open the door, and the two men paced across the entrance hall, out and away from the house, but neither man spoke until they had cleared the gates of Hafton Hall and were once more in the lane to the village.

CHAPTER 22

Susannah dressed for church on Sunday morning with a heavy heart, Lettice quiet and morose behind her as she laced her mistress's sleeves. She stood impassively, arms held out, accepting her maid's ministrations with neither comment nor complaint. There was none of the usual friendly chatter and even Olivia, dressed and ready, sat patient and silent on the bed.

When she was ready with her hair neatly brushed and pinned, she stood before the glass and examined her reflection, not caring for what she saw even though she was wearing her favourite green wool. But it no longer mattered – the deal with the Haftons had been struck, the details of the business nutted out in letters from her mother to Lord Hafton. On the morrow she would go from Abbey Leigh as a maid for the final time to become Edward Hafton's wife.

They rode to church in silence. Her mood cast a shadow over all the girls until her mother, growing cross, finally snapped at her. "Will you leave off all your moping. It is a marriage that you're going to not a funeral."

Susannah forced a smile. "Forgive me, madam. But I am sad to be leaving Abbey Leigh once again."

Her mother softened. "It is not the end of the world, Susannah, and you must make the best of it. Please. For the sake of your sisters?"

She nodded, looking round and noticing for the first time the solemn faces of the other girls. She had no right to disturb their happiness when she would be gone so soon. She wanted to remember them laughing and joyful, memories to hold and comfort her in the loveless days ahead at Hafton Hall.

She dug deep to find her last reserve of will and called out to her youngest sister, Charity, riding behind on the ancient roan pony that had once belonged to her. She reined in her own horse and waited for her sister to catch up. When the pony drew level and they were riding side by side, she began to ask questions about the doll that Charity had been sewing, making suggestions for names and clothes, discussing the best method to give her eyes.

By the time they reached the village church, the whole party had become enlivened, the laughter between the oldest sister and the youngest spreading through them all. They dismounted merrily and Susannah's mother waited at the door of the church for the household to go in before her as had always been the family custom. Susannah came last, and as she went by her mother squeezed her hand. "Thank you, Susannah," the older woman whispered. "Look at them now."

Susannah cast an eye across her family, nodded with another forced smile, and stepped inside the church.

She maintained an outward peace but inside she was desperate, her last days at Abbey Leigh darkened by the shade of her coming fate – the rest of her life as Edward Hafton's wife. Back at home after church, she chatted with the others over dinner as though it were any normal day, but her voice seemed to her as someone else's, the words coming from thoughts that did not seem to be her own.

Dinner was almost finished when the unexpected sound of hoof-beats roused them from the table. Excited, the younger girls crowded to the window and Susannah stood behind her sisters, following their gaze towards the drive with little curiosity. But she recognised one of the horses at once. The chestnut gelding, Regent, stamped and shook his head on the path beyond the door. And even though the rider's face was hidden by the angle of his head as he dismounted, she knew that it was him. And with him was Sir Samuel, looking up to cast his eyes across the house, admiring.

Heat flooded through her, her head spinning, limbs light and throbbing. She threw a glance towards the door, wondering if there was time to make it out and up the stairs before he reached the house but even as she thought it, he was almost at the step and it was too late for her to go anywhere. All she could do was wait and pray for strength.

"Who are they?" Olivia was asking. "And why have they come?"

"Is one of them the man you're going to marry?" Charity asked, looking up into her sister's face.

"No, Char," she managed to whisper but the question brought tears to her eyes, and hastily she wiped them away, hoping they would leave no trace.

"Why are you crying?" Charity said with the open curiosity of the very young.

"I'm not crying," Susannah replied, wiping at her eyes more savagely.

"Yes, you are," her sister argued, but by then the men had entered the hall with her mother and all the girls dropped into curtseys. When they rose, a gesture of their mother's head sent them hurrying from the room, all except Susannah, who remained at the window, maintaining a distance, fighting to control her breath.

"Madam," Sir Samuel spoke to her mother. "Let us give them some time to talk alone."

She saw her mother vacillate for a moment, for once undecided, before she gave a curt nod of agreement. "I will be just outside," she said to her daughter as she stood at the door, "if you should want anything."

"Thank you," Susannah said, but the words left her lips as a whisper and she was unsure that her mother even heard them. The door clicked shut and then she was alone with him. Panic threatened to rise, and she forced herself to breathe, looking away from him, struggling to master the conflict within her. He was everything she remembered, the curls of dusky hair, a little longer than before, the same deep dark eyes that were searching her now as he moved across the hall towards her. He was as she had seen him that first time in the church in the dark wool breeches and riding boots that were dusty from the road, his cloak carelessly about his shoulders.

"Susannah." He spoke softly, and there was a gentle intensity in his eyes that sought to reassure her. "I am glad to have found you at last."

"You should not have come," she whispered, seeking to avoid his gaze, afraid of the power he could wield over her.

"I know what you think," he said, coming closer. "But it isn't true. None of it is true."

She watched him warily, said nothing.

"I have ridden half the night to come for you. Your letter came to me at Tilbury and I was unable to leave. We were waiting for the Spanish …. I wanted to come right away, but I could not." He stopped and waited for her to speak, but she could find no words to say to him, emotions roiling inside her.

"I went to Hafton first," he went on when she said nothing. "I thought that's where you would be. We made the ride in three days, Sam and I, to get to you."

"You should not have troubled yourselves," she managed to say. She kept her eyes lowered to the carpet underfoot, afraid to look at him, all her senses crying out against the words, and it was hard to keep the tremor from her voice. "Your letter came, and there is nothing more to be said."

He made as if to take a step towards her, then stopped himself. She could see the frustration in the tension of his body, his jaw tight, fists balled. "But I have had no intimate relations with Eleanor Hafton. And whoever told you different is a liar. I swear to you, Susannah, I was never intimate with Eleanor …" He lifted his hands in a gesture that was somewhere between despair and bewilderment. "You must believe me – I have never so much as laid a finger on her."

Her heart twisted, desperate for it to be the truth, but still distrustful. She could not bear the pain a second time. She said, "Why should I believe you?"

"Because you must know that I love you. And that loving you, I would not lie to you. Surely you know how much I love you?"

"I know that you wanted me," she answered. "That much was clear enough. In your bedchamber, in the church. I thought you loved me then, but now ..." She shrugged. "It seems I was mistaken." She looked at him then and for the first time she saw fear in his eyes, the dawning understanding he had lost his power to sway her.

"Why would you believe such lies?" he said, "I asked you to marry me. I would have wed you then and there if only you would have agreed. And I would marry you here and now, if you would have me. You must know this."

"And what promises did you make to Eleanor?" she demanded. She stared at him, breathing hard, and a strand of hair fell forward across her face. She flicked it back with an impatient movement of her hand.

"I made none," he said. "As God is my witness, I swear it – I have never known Eleanor's body. I have wanted no one else since the day I first laid eyes on you. Why will you not believe me?"

She turned away from him, gazing out of the window across the flat expanse of grass that stretched away. A wind had risen and stray petals and leaves blew across her field of vision. She did not know how to answer him, her heart crying out to take his word, her head warning her against him. He had turned her from her better judgement twice before, using her passion and her love for him to win her round, the power of his charm, the touch of his hand. And he was here now to finish the game he had begun with her, to possess her utterly before he turned and walked away. Her mother had warned her about such men, men who could charm the birds from the trees to leave them where they fell without a backward glance. How many others had fallen under his spell? How many others had he ruined?

"I was mistaken in you," she said, shaking her head, and when at last she turned again from the window to face him, he had moved to stand so near behind her she could feel the warmth of his breath against her face. She jumped, startled to find him so close, disconcerted.

His eyes searched hers, and she averted her head to avoid the penetrating gaze, the passion in his eyes that had so nearly undone her twice before. But his proximity made her breathless, the desire to have him touch her almost overwhelming. Gently he took her hand in his, lifted it to his lips. Her breath stopped completely, passion stirring, warm and liquid inside her. With a strength of will she had been unaware she possessed, she withdrew her hand from his.

"Why will you not believe me?" he asked again, still searching to find her gaze, his face close to hers.

"Because I dare not," she managed to breathe. "You must marry Eleanor, and I must marry Edward, and we shall be brother and sister ..."

"And our whole lives will be a torture to us, to live so close but be parted. It is in your power to save us from such a fate."

She squeezed herself free of him, moving away towards the centre of the hall, finding space to breathe around her. It had been impossible to think with him so near, his lips so close to hers just waiting for their chance. She spun round to face him as he stood with his back against the window, the light of the storm colouring the sky rose and steel behind him.

"I have the power to save us?" she repeated. "How? By ignoring the truth? And what of Eleanor? What of her fate?"

"What do you care about Eleanor's fate? This is us I am talking about. You and me."

"You've grown tired of Eleanor now?" she said. "And when you have used me the same, will you grow tired of me and discard me too?"

His jaw set with anger, his fists clenched at his sides. He hesitated for a moment at the window before, abruptly, he pushed himself from the wall and strode towards her. She took a step back, chary, but he closed his hand around her arm and held her close to him. She turned her face away, reluctant to meet the passion that flared in his eyes.

"Look at me," he breathed. "Just look at me."

She turned her head slowly, raised her gaze to his and held it, forcing herself to face the desire and the anger she had roused in him, his eyes dark with conflicting emotion. Was it possible he was telling the truth, after all?

"Would I do all this just to get you to my bed?" he whispered, his face close to hers, his strong hand gripping her arm, holding her tight before him. "I have ridden hundreds of miles to come to you, to tell you the truth. I can have any woman I want in my bed, any woman, but you are the only one I want as my wife."

She lowered her eyes away from his, turned her head away. "Please let go of me, Sir Daniel," she whispered, tears forming, impossible to stop. "You're hurting my arm."

Immediately he loosened his hold and stepped back, hands raised palms outwards in a gesture of apology. "Forgive me, Susannah. I did not mean to hurt you. I just need to make you understand." He shook his head and walked two strides away from her, placed his hands on his hips and lifted his eyes to the ceiling, searching for a way to convince her.

"Perhaps you do love me," she said then. "But Eleanor is with child."

She faltered for a moment, the words hard to force past her lips. Then, "I saw you together, Daniel. I saw the way she looked at you and though I didn't realise it then, perhaps I should have."

He lowered his eyes to her once more, but she would no longer meet his gaze. He said, "Then you are decided?"

"I leave for Hafton tomorrow. Edward has procured a special licence and we will be married when I arrive."

"And what of the promises we made?"

She hesitated again, the words hard to find. "You broke your promise when you …" She stopped, unable to say the word.

"When I …?" Making her say it, forcing her to name the accusation.

She took a deep breath. "When you … fathered Eleanor's child."

A sudden squall of rain against the windows startled them both and drew their eyes outside beyond the glass. The day had darkened though it was still just past noon, and low, ponderous clouds hung across the sky. Rain gusted in against the house and the low fire crackled and hissed in the fireplace.

He was silent, breathing hard, and she watched him, this man she loved in spite of everything, this man she could not have. Sorrow swirled inside her and she drew in a deep breath, forcing down the impulse to take back all of what she had said, to forgive him everything and take him in her arms again. How could she bear a life without him? To live so close and have his company forbidden her? She backed away from him, half the hall between them now, a gulf that seemed unbridgeable. He turned his head away from the storm beyond the window and regarded her again.

"Susannah," he said softly. "Please … As you love me and I love you … I beg you, don't do this …"

For an instant she wavered. Her last chance. Her heart turned with regret for all the love they would not now share, all the lonely days ahead of them. "I am decided," she said.

She saw his muscles tauten. He would not beg her again and there was nothing more to be said. He bowed stiffly. "Then I bid you good day, madam," he said through tightened lips. "I had hoped this meeting would end otherwise."

"Good day, Sir Daniel," she replied, lowering into a curtsey. "I am sorry you've had a wasted journey."

He nodded, and they took one last long look at each other, before he walked past her to the door. She stood and watched him go.

Then she hid her face in her hands and wept.

CHAPTER 23

*B*eyond the gate he kept going, neither knowing nor caring his direction, his only wish to put distance between himself and the source of his pain. Sam followed on behind, knowing better than to ask any questions, and they stopped finally in a tiny village, the chestnut snorting beneath him outside the inn, the road deserted. Only then did he notice the rain.

Samuel squinted through the downpour. "Where now?"

He made no answer. Gifford Court was too close to Hafton, too close to where she would soon be Edward's wife. Sam saw the hesitation.

"We could go to Riverwood," he said. "It is too long since you saw my parents, and you would receive a warm welcome there."

Briefly, he thought of the Earl of Leicester's invitation to court. The pleasures of London would offer him more distraction than a Devon country manor, but he had lost all taste for such games.

"I have a fine new pair of greyhounds," Samuel said, smiling, tempting. His horse stamped under him and swung itself round to place its hindquarters into the rain, shaking its head.

He had to go somewhere, Daniel thought, and the pretty estate of Riverwood with a good friend and fine hunting was not unattractive. He had spent many happy weeks there over the years as both man and boy. "Very well," he answered. "We shall go to Riverwood." Then, turning the gelding's head back into the rain, he touched his heels to its sides, and the horse sprang forward, eager to be gone.

The ride was slow, the dry dust of the roads quickly turning to squelching mud under the onslaught of the storm. They halted early, the day growing dark, the horses weary from the softness of the ground, and the men beginning to feel the effects of sleepless nights and too many days hard riding. But there was no urgency to their journey anymore, no need to drive themselves on, so they stopped at an inn just beyond the wool-trading town of Frome, settling their horses in the stables before taking a chamber for themselves.

Washed and dried and changed, they lounged in front of the fire in silence a while, nursing pewter goblets of wine before Samuel apparently decided he had waited long enough. He said, "I take it she refused to believe you."

Daniel nodded, still not trusting himself to speak of it.

"But why? Why would she believe the Haftons before you? She loves you, I am sure of it."

"I am sure of it too." He recalled the moment of struggle in her eyes, the desire he had sensed in her when he held her fingers in his. But he only had himself to blame: he had pushed her too hard, in his chamber, in the church, and now he was paying the price. He should have trod more gently, gained her trust with time. "Yet," he shrugged, "here we are, and by the weekend she will be Hafton's."

His friend said nothing and took another mouthful of wine, staring into the small fire, shadows flickering against the walls in its light. Daniel drained his cup, leaned down and placed it by the hearth. "I have lost her, Sam. There is nothing more I can do."

Sam sighed and drank his own cup. "Shall we take supper at the common table? Distract ourselves with some company?" he asked.

"As you like," he answered. Though he had no interest in where they ate or who they spoke to, he could see the sense in searching for some distraction. He gave a half-shrug of acquiescence.

The two men got up from the fire, locked the door of their room, and found their way downstairs.

~

The table was rowdy, the inn filling fast with merchants gathering in readiness for market on the morrow, and gentlemen travellers like themselves seeking early shelter from the storm. In the corner of the room a pair of young musicians with a pipe and lute were entertaining the guests. A young gentleman was adding lewd lyrics to the music to the general appreciation of the crowd who were laughing and stamping in approval.

Daniel slid his friend a brief half-smile as they entered the room. The evening's entertainment looked to be hopeful as some kind of diversion from his thoughts. They found two seats at the board and ordered wine from the staff who instantly attended them. He would eat later, he thought, when the wine had given him an appetite.

The musicians stopped playing to raucous applause and offers of refreshment as they took their places at the table. Daniel glanced around him at the other diners: the young gentleman beside him nodded a greeting, lifted his goblet in salute. He looked familiar, a face Daniel had seen somewhere in the crowd before. He scanned his memory, searching through the men he had known in the Netherlands, men at Court, but no recollection came to mind. He regarded him again in profile as the man traded conversation with the merchant across the table.

He was of a very fair complexion and pleasant looking, his cheeks ruddy now with the warmth of the room and the wine, and a mobile mouth that readily wore a smile. He was wearing the garb of minor gentry: good quality wool, well cut and expensively trimmed, and there was an easy confidence about him that was attractive.

Daniel turned to his friend at his side. "D'you see the man next to me?"

Sam leaned forward to look for a moment, then sat back and nodded.

"Do you recognise him?"

His friend half shook his head. "Perhaps. But he has the kind of face you see a lot at Court. Young and callow and hopeful. Just waiting to be corrupted."

Daniel gave a wry smile to his friend's cynicism. Neither of them had ever enjoyed the world of Court, the glittering battle of preferment and advantage, a dangerous game of alliances and enmities. He slanted another glance towards the young man. "I am sure I do, from somewhere, but God alone knows where ..."

The gentleman noticed his neighbour's attention upon him and turned towards his observer.

"Do we know each other, sir?" the young man asked. The question was polite but carried a hint of amusement. A slight smile played at one corner of his lips.

"I think we might," Daniel returned.

The two men observed each other for a moment, the young man's open countenance against the darker more hard-bitten visage of the older man. Daniel waited, saw the sudden recognition in the other man's eyes, and the quick extinction of the friendly light that had been there.

"Yes," the man said. "I know who you are, sir. You are Sir Daniel Gifford."

Daniel nodded, curiosity piqued by the young man's reaction to the realisation. "Indeed I am. And you are ...?"

"Francis Aston, sir. Lately Gentleman of the Horse to Lord Hafton. We were neighbours, sir."

A memory of the young man's face outside the church in Hafton, attending the Viscount, the horse's stirrup in his hand, slid through Daniel's mind. "Yes," he said, "that's where I've seen you. I've a good memory for faces, but I couldn't place you."

There was a pause. Gratified to have solved the riddle, he recalled the young man's discomfiture. He turned his head towards him again, sensing his uneasiness, the easy smile no longer in place. "We *were* neighbours?" he repeated.

Aston inclined his head in assent. "I am ..." he began, reluctantly. "I am no longer in Lord Hafton's service."

Sir Daniel regarded him with interest, a masterless man, unusual to come across. The gentlemen in a noble's service were not easily let go, too much invested on both sides. His interest was aroused. "How so?"

The young man swallowed and pinched his lips together, eyes grazing across the table in front of him, apparently uncertain how best to answer.

"Come, Aston," Sir Daniel coaxed. "You can tell me."

Aston looked up and searched the older man's face, as if still undecided what to say. Then he dropped his eyes away and said, "It was a personal matter, sir. Nothing of importance."

"Personal? Perhaps. Unimportant? I doubt it. Gentlemen do not leave their master's service without good reason." He smiled, encouraging, but he saw at once he had overstepped the mark. The open face shut down, tension twitching in the muscle of his cheek as he stared into the empty goblet he held in his hands before him.

"Forgive me," Sir Daniel said with the easy charm he had used so well with the men in his years as a soldier, an instinctive feel for the tone that would best win their confidence. "I mean not to pry. I am merely curious. Lord Hafton and I have had our differences over the years ... And too, I have no gentleman of my horse at present ..."

Aston gave him a tight reluctant smile, eyes flicking away. "I thank you for your interest, Sir Daniel, but I am on my way elsewhere. If you will excuse me, I must go to the stables and check on my horse." So saying, he rose from the table and moved away, casting an anxious backward glance across his shoulder before he slid through the door and out into the passage.

Daniel watched him go, then turned immediately to his friend. "Sam."

Sam turned to him with a broad smile on his face, obviously enjoying the conversation of his neighbours. "What?"

"The man who just left. The man I recognised ..."

Sam sobered instantly at the tone in his friend's voice.

"His name is Francis Aston. He has just left Lord Hafton's service and he would give me no reason beyond that it was personal."

"You think ...?"

"I think he knows more than he's saying, that's for sure. He paled like a corpse when he realised who I was."

"Where is he now?"

"Gone to check on his horse, he said."

Sam smiled and nodded, delighted by the challenge. "Leave it with me and I'll discover what I can." Climbing out from his place on the bench, he picked up a jug of wine and two goblets and went on his way to find Francis Aston.

As soon as he returned Daniel knew from his expression that he had no good news to tell.

"He has already left," Sam said. "Ridden off into the rain and dark. Your questions must have frightened him away."

"Then he does know more," Daniel replied. "We must find him. Do we know which way he went?"

"The ostler said he thought he turned west. He heard him mention something about heading to Bristol."

"Then we have no time to lose. Get the horses ready. I'll settle with the innkeeper."

"There is barely a moon to see by, Dan, with the rain and all."

His friend was right – the road would be dark and dangerous, the moon obscured by the rain, but he dared not lose this chance, this one possibility to find the truth and bring it to Susannah. "There is enough," he replied.

Sam smiled, acquiescing, knowing his friend well enough to make no more argument. They parted quickly for their tasks and within a few minutes Daniel was heading through the main entrance of the inn. On the road, Sam was mounted and ready, holding with difficulty the reins of the chestnut who was dragging against him, unwilling to be led into the rain. Daniel swung himself easily into the saddle and the gelding settled quickly under his master. Turning west, the two men bowed their heads into the downpour and urged their horses forward on the westward road to Bristol.

CHAPTER 24

Susannah's mother could offer little comfort.

"Dry your eyes – Edward Hafton is not going to want you with red-rimmed eyes and puffy cheeks."

Good, she thought. That would be fine. But she dragged the back of her hand across her face, sniffed and blinked, choking back the urge to weep more. She stood at the window, watching the space where Daniel had ridden away, her thoughts charged with doubts. What if he had been telling her the truth? How could she be so sure that he was lying?

"I suppose he came to tell you you were mistaken?" Her mother's blunt question forced her mind away from such imaginings.

"He did," she admitted.

"But you sent him on his way?"

"As you see," she answered, a little testily.

"It was well done, my love," her mother said, approaching, a softer tone in her voice. "I can see how he might have charmed you. He is a handsome man and he has great … presence. A man like that can be hard to refuse."

Susannah nodded, still sniffing.

"Be thankful you discovered the truth before you married him. Be thankful it is Eleanor with child instead of you." She patted her daughter's arm. "You have had a lucky escape, my girl. You should thank God in your prayers tonight."

She nodded again, but the certainty she felt before had left her, his words trailing through her mind, the frustration she had sensed in them at her refusal to believe him. She knew his reputation – he had told her as much himself.

I can have any woman I want in my bed, he had said, *any woman*.

But perhaps he was telling the truth when he said he had promised Eleanor nothing. Perhaps there had been no need – it was easy to believe her cousin might have given up her virtue without it.

She turned her head away from the image the thought of it carried. Daniel's hands on Eleanor's flesh as they had once been on hers, caressing, kneading, stroking. His mouth against her cousin's. Had he roused the same desire in Eleanor, the same swelling of love that had driven her? Yet he swore he had never known Eleanor's body. Swore his soul to damnation if he were lying. Her guts twisted inside with the pain of uncertainty, the fear she had sent him away innocent, dooming them both.

"Anyway," her mother was saying. "You've made your decision now and there is no remedy: the marriage is set, and you could do a lot worse than Edward Hafton. One day you will be a viscountess. Think of that!"

It was the wrong thing to have said.

"I don't want to be a viscountess!" she cried and, gathering her skirts, tears flowing again, she hurried from the hall and up the stairs to her chamber, where she gave way to her tears, unchecked.

By morning she had conquered her emotions. A fitful night of sleeping had left her feeling dull and unrefreshed, but in the sleepless hours of the night she had unearthed a sense of resolution, and a resignation to her fate. As her mother had said, she had made her decision and now she must bend her will to live by it. She would do her duty to her family and marry Edward Hafton, bearing his children as the heirs to Abbey Leigh.

She stood quietly as Lettice laced her into her gown, the rain still gusting at the windows, though the clouds had lightened a little with the promise of fairer weather to come.

"It is an evil day for a journey, Mistress Susannah," Lettice said. "But I still wish I was coming with you."

"You'll be far happier here at Abbey Leigh, Lettice," she replied. "And I think my uncle would not welcome you back at Hafton."

Lettice nodded, her tears held back with silence and bitten lips as she finished dressing her mistress, sat her down and began to arrange her hair.

"I shouldn't take too much trouble with it," Susannah said, casting a glance to the window. "It will be in rats' tails in no time."

"Who is going to attend you on the journey?"

Susannah smiled. Her maid's sorrow was a buffer against her own, a stir to keep her own emotions in check.

"Don't fret about me, Lettice. Master Edward will meet us half-way, at the inn at Brewham, with servants to attend us from there. And Olivia and my lady mother are accompanying me to Hafton for the wedding. Olivia is quite able to dress me and arrange my hair – she has been doing so for years."

"You should wait until the weather clears. You'll catch your deaths in this."

Susannah lifted her eyes to the window once again. The rain was easing off to a fine and heavy drizzle. By noon, she was sure it would be clear, and she was anxious to be on her way before her resolve began to fail her and her courage to weaken. "We'll be fine," she said brightly. "See? It is clearing up already."

The maid's eyes followed her mistress's gesture doubtfully. Susannah ignored the unspoken protest.

Standing up before the glass, Susannah twisted this way and that, assessing the reflection. Then, satisfied with what she saw, the mask in place, she said, "I am ready."

Lettice nodded and curtseyed, then followed her mistress out of the room and down the stairs. Susannah paused for a fraction of an instant on the threshold, tempted to look back to the room where she had grown up, but she checked herself, setting her face instead

firmly forward to the future, and stepped out into the passage with a
determined tread.

CHAPTER 25

The two men rode for most of the night, the going slow in the dark and the rain, the way missed more than once so that they had to turn back, losing precious hours, their quarry gaining ground ahead of them. They had searched every inn on the road for any sign of Francis Aston but they had found no hint of him, and by the time the morning had begun to lighten with the dawn they started to wonder if they had taken the wrong road.

"We must rest the horses, Dan," Sam said as they slid off their mounts to stand in the churned-up mud at yet another hostelry. A dull leaden grey began to creep across the sky, signalling the morning behind the clouds of rain. "And get a couple of hours sleep ourselves. I'm done in."

Reluctantly, Daniel agreed, leading the weary chestnut through the stable arch to find the ostler, standing to oversee the horse's care before he would tend to his own.

"Busy night?" Daniel asked in the guise of idle chatter. "Many travellers come in?"

The ostler looked up from his rubbing down of the chestnut. "Ah, we had one young gentleman passing through. Took a couple of hours rest in the straw with his horse and he was on his way again. Looked about ready to drop, both he and the horse, but he insisted he had to get on. Not long gone in fact – went with the first sign of the day. I didn't dare to ask his reasons." The ostler raised his eyebrows at Daniel with a knowing look and Daniel smiled.

"Heading to Bristol, no doubt?"

"Aye," the ostler agreed. "That's where the road goes."

Satisfied, both with the horse's care and the answers he had got, he left the ostler to his work and went to find Samuel, who had secured them a room for a few hours' rest.

"We're stopping only an hour," he said, slumping onto one of the beds, kicking off his boots. "He is just ahead of us. He left at first light."

"He knows we're behind him," Samuel replied. "You must have put the fear of God into him, Dan. What was it you said to him?"

"He was afraid of me before I said a word. It was my name that rattled him. We have to catch him and find out what he knows."

"But first," Samuel said, giving in to a yawn, dragging off his own boots, lying down fully clothed on the bed. "I must sleep."

"I've asked to be woken in an hour with bread and meat," he said, but Samuel's eyes were already closed, his breath deepening and regular, sleep coming quickly.

"Sweet dreams." Daniel smiled. It had ever been thus. On the road through all the years in the Netherlands, in camp at Tilbury, Sam could sleep at a moment's notice, anywhere, at any time of day. It was a rare gift and there had been many a sleepless night that Daniel had envied him.

Lying back on the soft bed himself he thought about Francis Aston, wondering what he knew that had made him ride alone through the night on a dangerous road to escape their questions, but the thoughts troubled him only briefly, exhaustion taking over and sleep at its heels close behind.

~

He woke with a groggy mind to the insistent knocking at the door. Sam was still sleeping, innocent like a child. Going past his friend to open the door, he swiped at a stockinged foot with his hand, but the foot merely moved out of range and its owner did not stir. Taking

216

the tray from the servant who had brought it, he came back inside the room and put the meal down before shaking Sam's shoulder. "Hey! Wake up. Breakfast."

Sam blinked his eyes open, took just a moment to orientate himself and remember where he was before he sat up fully awake, eyes bright, a hand sweeping back through the sandy hair. "I would swear I've only been asleep a minute," he said.

"Have some meat," Daniel answered.

They ate quickly, wrapped the remains in a cloth and took it with them as they left. The ostler was evidently surprised to see them so soon but he was too good at his job to be put off: the horses were quickly saddled and ready, and they were once more on their way.

Sam lifted his face to the morning sky, damp with a fine mist of drizzle, trees dripping with their load of rain as they passed underneath. "At least the rain is clearing," he said. "That's something."

Daniel said nothing. He couldn't care less about the rain; all he cared about was finding Francis Aston and getting closer to the truth, time running out with each hour that passed. She would have left Abbey Leigh by now, he thought, and be on her way to Hafton. With each hour that took him down the Bristol road, she was moving further away from him, and closer to her marriage to Edward Hafton. Easing the chestnut into a slow loping canter along a stretch of grass by the side of the mud-filled road, he prayed to God he would not be too late. Aston's knowledge might yet be the saving of them all, but it had to come in time, and time was a luxury he no longer had.

Finally, late in the evening, they caught up with their prey at an inn just outside of Bristol. He must have ridden as though the devil was on his heels, but discreetly greased enquiries to the staff discovered the location of his room, and when Aston opened the door to their insistent knocking, the shock registered as terror on his face.

"You found me!" he breathed, backing into the room, aware that to try and elude them now would be futile.

"Apparently so," Daniel growled.

The two men followed him into the small and dimly lit chamber, a narrow window giving on to the street, the grey daylight barely penetrating the glass.

"Sit down, Aston," Daniel commanded, and the young man sank obediently on to the edge of the bed. Daniel drew up the single wooden chair and placed it so that when he sat he was near enough to touch his quarry with ease. "Now," he said. "I have had little sleep and there is little time left to me for my purpose, so be warned you will find me an impatient man."

Aston nodded to show he understood.

"Why did you leave Hafton Hall? What happened there?"

"I'll be a dead man if I tell," Aston said, but though the words betrayed his fear, he kept his countenance and the semblance of outward calm.

"You'll be a dead man much sooner if you don't." Daniel leaned forward, took the collar of his victim's doublet in his fist. Aston was silent. Daniel thrust him roughly away and stood up, pacing the small square of floor between the bed and the window. "I have no time for this, Aston. I swear to God."

The young man watched him, still silent, until Daniel swung towards him in a swift movement of his body that sent the young man reeling back in surprise.

"They sent me away," he said quickly.

"Who did?"

"Eleanor and her brother. They gave me money to go, to disappear and stay quiet."

Daniel lowered himself again to the chair, his eyes never leaving the young man's face. "Why?"

Aston swallowed, eyes darting nervously between Daniel close before him, and Sam, leaning against the window frame, arms folded, observing.

"She said ... she said ... you wouldn't offer for her if it came to light about me ..."

"About you?"

"We have known each other since we were children, Sir Daniel …"

"In plain terms, if you please. I am losing my patience."

"In plain terms?" Aston swallowed, forming the words in his mouth before he uttered them, testing. "In plain terms then," he said slowly, eyes still moving between the two older men, "you are not the first man to have known Eleanor Hafton, Sir Daniel."

Daniel flicked a quick glance towards Sam, a mystery answered, time ticking on. He turned back to Aston. "You would swear to this?"

Aston stared, bewildered. "But …"

"There is little time, Aston. Will you swear?"

The young man nodded, but the incomprehension was clear in his face.

"Then come," he said, grabbing the man's doublet once more, hauling him to his feet. "We have a long ride ahead of us."

"We will need fresh horses," Sam said.

Sir Daniel shoved Aston back to the bed. "Go and arrange it, Sam. I'll take our young friend to our chamber where we can keep an eye on him." Then turning again to Aston, he said, roughly, "Get your things."

Aston obeyed, gathering his few belongings, stowing them back in their bundle before Daniel took his arm and directed him to the door, along the passage and to the chamber they had taken. There were two beds and he ordered Aston to one of them while he sat in a chair, dragging it close to the door.

Sam returned. "No horses till morning," he said. Then, forestalling the question he saw rising on his friend's lips, "Not for love nor money. I tried."

Daniel leaped up, smacked a fist into his palm. "We don't have the time, Sam. We don't have the time."

She would already be in Brewham a day's ride ahead of them on the way back. If Hafton had met her there it might already be too late, though he hoped, prayed, they would wait to get home to tie the knot in the church at Hafton.

"She is halfway there already." He was tempted to take their own horses, to risk them as far as they would go, and find new horses when and where they could. The horseman in him hesitated, going against the grain to push good horses so close to breaking, but he had little choice. He dared not risk losing so much time, putting himself so far behind her. "We'll go at first light," he decided, give the horses and themselves a half-decent break. "First light."

"But the horses," Aston said. "They're exhausted."

"Yes. And we have you to thank for that," he snapped. "Now go to sleep."

Dragging the chair before the door, he stretched out his legs, his cloak rolled up as a pillow against his shoulder. It was hard and uncomfortable, and he greatly regretted giving Aston the bed, but it was the only way to make sure the young man could make no attempt at an escape. Just as he was falling into sleep, Aston's voice spoke through the darkness.

"Forgive me, Sir Daniel, but I don't understand. You seem almost pleased by what I've told you."

"Get some sleep, Aston," he said. "I'll explain on the way."

He barely slept, the discomfort of the chair and the worry of being too late stirring his mind into restlessness although his body was every bit as weary as lengthy marches and sleepless nights in wartime had ever left it. He was getting older, he reflected, and the long rides and lack of rest were taking their toll. In fitful sleep he dreamed, always arriving too late, the same image over and over until he felt Sam's hand on his shoulder, waking him.

"Take the bed," his friend said. "You need to rest."

He obeyed, too weary to argue, his body aching, his mind exhausted, and fell finally into a dreamless dark that ended with the cock's first crow and the beginning of the new day.

CHAPTER 26

By the time she arrived at the inn at Brewham, Susannah had schooled her emotions into submission. Though the pain inside was real and her thoughts were still haunted by his betrayal, images of Daniel with Eleanor always flicking at the corners of her mind, outwardly she had trained herself to harden her composure, a rigid coldness in her bearing that kept the hurt in check. She would cry no more about it and accept her fate with good grace, but to do so required a distancing, a placing of herself aloof from the life before her.

She greeted her uncle and cousin with curtseys that were cool and polite, and Edward observed her carefully, noticing a difference but unsure of what had changed precisely. She guessed he would soon lose interest: once he had made her his, her attitude and emotions would no longer count for anything. Lord Hafton made the introductions, barely casting a look her way. Edward greeted her mother and sister with his most courteous bow – it was interesting to note how charming he could be when he tried. Olivia was won immediately by the self-assured confidence and handsome face. Her mother was less easily convinced but the circumstances inclined her to see the good and, when all the introductions had been made, Edward turned to her, bowed deeply and took her hand.

"Cousin," he said. "I am most pleased to see you again."

Once more restraining the temptation to wrench her fingers from his grasp, she curved her mouth into a smile and let him lead her inside the inn and up the narrow staircase, her mother and Olivia following close behind.

At the door to their chambers he gave her the key and bowed again. "My father requests that you join us for supper. He has taken a private room downstairs for the purpose. But now I'm sure you would like some time to rest and refresh yourselves."

She took the key and opened the door. "Thank you," she said, forcing a smile as she stepped into the room, away from him. "Till supper."

He nodded and turned away and she heard his heavy footsteps tread along the passage towards the stairs.

Supper passed quietly. She sat next to Edward, but they barely exchanged a word, preferring to allow their elders to talk. The conversation remained determinedly light, turning on the day to day issues of running an estate, the effect of the rain on the harvest, the changing price of wool. In other times she would have been happy to contribute, her own knowledge of the estate equal to or greater than her mother's, her understanding of the business based on years spent at her father's side. But tonight the topic held no interest, aware as she was of the presence of the man at her side, the desire in every sidelong glance he cast her way, a tension in his body that betrayed his impatience to make her his.

Inside she recoiled at the thought of it, every detail of the morning in the woods still perfectly remembered, the revulsion at his hands beneath her skirts, the weight of his body as he forced himself against her. She suppressed a shudder and remained outwardly composed, her physical body divorcing from her spirit, which huddled hidden in a place inside her that Edward could not touch.

Olivia looked on, her untutored eye puzzled by the silence

between them as she endeavoured to give her attention to her mother's conversation, aware of an atmosphere she could not understand.

"How is Eleanor?" Susannah asked her cousin at last, when she judged her mother and uncle were too engrossed in their own talk to notice theirs.

"She is well."

"Really?" She turned in surprise. "She was not so well when I left."

He tilted his head to show he understood, then risked a glance towards his father, so that she would understand that now was not the time to talk of it.

"We can talk more freely on the road on the morrow," he said. "But not now. Not here."

"I understand," she replied, and thought it was probably the most straightforward conversation she had ever shared with him – no hidden meaning, no overtones of sexual predatoriness.

When supper was over, she escaped by pleading tiredness from the journey, and Edward escorted the women back to their chamber. He bowed at the door, still the courteous suitor, before he returned downstairs to the private dining room and the rest of an uncomfortable evening in the company of his father.

They left early next day, the road bogged and treacherous from the rain in the night, the going slow. Edward rode beside her, solicitous and polite.

"I trust you slept well, coz?"

She smiled at him, faintly amused by this display of courtesy she knew was foreign to his nature. "I slept very well, thank you, Edward," she lied. "How about yourself?"

"The bed was a little hard," he replied. "But quite well, yes."

They went on a few strides in silence. Then he turned to her again. "You wanted to know about Eleanor?"

"Yes," she replied. "If we are to be sisters, we must be friends. And," she hesitated, unsure if it was wise to say so much, but deciding in the end it made no difference. "And ... I am sorry for her condition. It cannot be easy for her now."

Edward turned his smile on her, the smile she had come to know well, the sardonic twist of his mouth, no humour in his eyes. "Yes. Her condition is to be pitied. Especially since the father has refused to own the child."

She steeled herself against any reaction, aware of her cousin's scrutiny, his search for any sign of weakness. "Indeed?" she managed to say, surprising herself by the coolness of her tone, the apparent disinterest in the subject.

"He claims it is none of his," he said, still observing her, waiting.

"That is indeed unfortunate for Eleanor," she answered carefully before she turned her head to face him. "What will happen to her now?"

"She is to be sent away before the servants get to hear of it. The child will be given up and no one will be any the wiser when she returns. Not an ideal solution, certainly, but she is too far gone to dupe any other man into having her."

Daniel's child, she thought bitterly, turning her eyes away from Edward towards the road ahead of them. A bright sun peeped from behind the scattered clouds, reflecting on the puddles in the mud as they passed. Daniel's child neglected, unloved. How could he be so callous to abandon his own flesh and blood? She had been sorely mistaken in his character: there seemed now to be little to choose between Edward and Sir Daniel. As Edward's wife, she decided, she would look to the baby's welfare – it was the least she could do, a small kindness to atone for her own near miss.

"You seem very calm, cousin," Edward said then. "Considering all that has occurred. I thought you would have put up more of a struggle before you consented to marry me."

She forced up the corners of her mouth in a smile and turned to him again. "Would you have enjoyed that, cousin?"

"Very much," he replied, a genuine smile on his lips. "I've enjoyed the chase immensely and I am very much looking forward to bringing it to its conclusion tomorrow. I'm sure I will find great pleasure in our marriage bed."

He ran his eyes across her body, lingering over her breasts. Even cold and aloof as she had made herself, such naked lust was hard to stand. She took a deep breath, training herself to put distance between him and the spirit inside her she had determined he would never break, though she had no doubt he would try. Domination was in his nature.

"But," he went on, "I'm also a little sorry the hunt is over. Now that you have come to heel, I shall have to find a new diversion to occupy my time."

His arrogance almost took her breath away. "You have never even tried to make me like you, or want to marry you," she said, her detachment failing. "Does it not matter to you at all whether I care for you or not?"

He shrugged. "Not really. I guessed you would marry me out of duty to your father. And at least I've practised no deception. Unlike some others. What you see is what you get – I've never pretended to be anything but what I am." He smiled, sensing that his comment had found its mark.

She turned her head away from him, staring into the trees that bordered the road, shafts of sunlight cutting between them. On another day she would have thought them beautiful and stopped to look. But now she breathed deeply, oblivious to the sunbeams. She would have to hide her feelings better, she realised, or he would torture her all through their life together, needling for the weak points, finding ways to hurt her. Squaring her shoulders, she turned back to face him.

"Yes," she agreed, with a bright smile that challenged the smug arrogance, enjoying the slight dent her unexpected response made in his self-assurance. "And that is something to be grateful for, I'm sure."

Irritated, he made no reply but lapsed into the familiar sullen silence, and she was left alone once again with her thoughts.

Daniel rode hard through the morning, grim-faced, silent, aware of the chestnut growing tired underneath him, but still willing and eager. The weather held for them, the sun warm behind the scudding clouds, but the road was swampy and flooded in places, and often they had to dismount to lead their horses through the worst of the mire, the difficult chestnut always reluctant to be led, rearing up, refusing to go forward. Each delay cost precious time. Every time they had to dismount, every minute they spent coaxing Regent onward was time they did not have to spare.

They reached Wells in the mid-afternoon, the horses lathered and spent, Daniel's patience hanging by a thread. He saw the animals tended and made arrangements for fresh mounts while Sam took Aston inside and saw about getting them victuals. He joined them in the dining room for a meal of chicken pie and ale, and all of them ate with relish, their stomachs unfilled since a hurried breakfast with the dawn, and hours of hard riding since.

Even Sam was silent, all his energies reserved for the journey, no spirit for conversation. Daniel passed him more of the pie and caught his eye. The two friends exchanged a weary smile. He was glad Sam was with him – it would have been much harder alone.

He let them rest a short while after eating, his own muscles sore, an ache in his bones, and he saw the question in Aston's eyes as they remained at the table, too weary to seek out more comfortable places to sit. He was in no mood for talking but he judged Aston had a right to know and he had held his peace till now. "You want to know why I'm taking you to Hafton?" he said, turning his eyes to the young man beside him.

Having resigned himself to ignorance, the question took Aston by surprise. He nodded quickly.

"I have no interest in Eleanor Hafton," Daniel said. "Whatever she told you, whatever she and her brother have made you believe, I can tell you now I have never so much as laid a finger on her. I have no intention of ever making an offer for her, nor have I ever harboured any such intention."

"But …"

"Listen." Daniel cut him off. "Eleanor Hafton is with child. That much you know?"

"She is with child?" The shock in the young man's face was plain. "I did not know."

Daniel lifted a quick glance to his friend, who nodded in agreement. It was clear that Aston had been cruelly used.

"Is it your child?" Daniel said.

Aston's eyes searched the table, unseeing, trying to recall. "Yes," he said at last, looking up. "Well, it could be, I suppose. Unless there were others."

"She has claimed that I am the father."

"But why? Why would she do that?" Aston's eyes were wide with incredulity, his innocence unable to comprehend such duplicity.

"It is complicated," Daniel said. "But briefly, I believe it was to force me into marriage with her instead of with the woman I love, who even as we speak is on her way to marriage with Edward Hafton."

"Mistress Susannah." Aston slumped in his seat, overwhelmed by the deception he had unwittingly been part of, shaking his head in disbelief. Three times he raised his head and opened his mouth as if to speak and said nothing, but on the fourth time he found the words he needed.

"Eleanor and I have known each other many years, since we were but children. And we have lain together countless times across those years. I tried not to think about the future. We made some kind of promises to each other, promises to be together always, but I am not a complete fool. I may be gentle-born, but she is the daughter of a viscount …" He lifted his gaze from his hands on the table before him and met Daniel's rapt attention. Then he flicked a glance to Sam, who also followed each of his words with interest.

He lowered his head and went on. "So when she told me you had offered your suit it came as no surprise. I thought she would marry and we could go on meeting as we had been doing. We would still be neighbours, after all."

He looked up at his listeners for understanding, hoping they would excuse his naiveté. Shame was written in his eyes and Daniel shook his head at such guilelessness. Aston lowered his eyes again, watching his fingers as he picked at a nail that was broken.

"But then she said I must leave," he continued without raising his head. "Because if you found out about my … our … relationship, you would refuse to marry her." He swallowed, glanced up quickly at Daniel, then looked away again, embarrassed. "I loved her too much to refuse, to question. But it seems she played me for a fool."

"Indeed she did," Daniel said gently, laying a hand on Aston's shoulder, reassuring. "But now you have a chance to make things right, and a chance to win her back." He rubbed the young man's shoulder, then raised himself to standing. "Come," he said. "We still have many miles ahead, and time grows short."

Aston nodded and pushed himself to his feet. Sir Samuel followed, and the three men left the inn for the stables, where fresh mounts were waiting for them.

~

The hired grey gelding was lazy and the constant need to press him forward put an extra burden onto weary muscles. In the end Sam went ahead, the grey going better behind the others, but it was hard going nonetheless, the road south of Wells worsening through the late afternoon, and a carriage stuck in the ooze and blocking their way – some foolish nobleman who should have had more sense than to use a carriage after such rain – it was all Daniel could do to keep his temper. They had no choice but to stop and assist, and more precious time passed, evening drawing on, Hafton still some miles distant as the sun lowered in the western sky, the shadows growing long. He could only hope the road from Brewham was as bad and Susannah's journey as slow as his own.

It took the strength of all of them – even the nobleman himself had his shoulder to the wheel, his fine silk hose slick with mud before the horses could pull the carriage free, but he held little hope they would travel far before it bogged again. Mounting their own horses quickly they sped on their way, leaving the earl and his ridiculous carriage far behind them.

But it remained slow going. The road was a quagmire, the horses slipping in the squelch, their feet getting bogged, and as the day began to give way to a moonless night, he started to despair. The road was too treacherous to ride in the darkness with no moon for light – they could barely make their way in the daylight. They would have to stop overnight and make the last few miles in the dawning day tomorrow.

They found a down-at-heel inn at Stapleton but none of them cared, torn between relief to be off the road, a chance to rest, and dread that tomorrow they would be too late. Daniel lay awake a long time, listening to the deep regular breaths of Sam and Aston, oblivious in sleep. Why should they not, he thought. It was not their future happiness that depended on the morrow. He thought of Susannah, guessing she would be at Hafton now – was she lying sleepless in these dark hours as he was? And did she think of him?

He turned on to his side, holding the thought of her close to him, letting his thoughts get lost in the memory of having her in his arms, but the last thing he thought of before he fell asleep was the words of their last conversation and her refusal to believe that he loved her.

CHAPTER 28

Susannah rose from her bed with reluctance, the bright light of the morning creeping in through a chink in the curtains. She blinked against the brightness after a fitful night of sleep and thought that rain would have better suited the day, or at least a cloudy sky.

Their party had arrived at the Hall late in the evening as the first bright stars had begun to show their light in the sky. It had been hard going through the mud, the road bogged and the journey broken many times. But it had been no hardship – each delay had seemed a blessing, another hour's freedom before the walls of Hafton Hall would close around her.

She had slept in a proper bedchamber of her own last night, one of the grand rooms with a view across the park for the night before her marriage to a Hafton. Her mother and sister shared the chamber next to hers and they talked together late into the night, though they had skirted the subject of the wedding, talking instead of Abbey Leigh and the neighbours there, the imminent arrival of a new gentle family in the derelict house to their north.

"Perhaps they will have a son, just your age," she had teased Olivia, whose blush couldn't hide the hopeful smile.

She had excused her sister from helping her dress this morning despite Olivia's pleas, not trusting herself to maintain the lie at such a time to the sister who knew her best. A maid had lit the fire already; although the day promised to be warm, much of the house never lost its chill, sunlight struggling to find its way in through the narrow windows. The room they had given her faced to the north and never knew the sun at all. Briefly she wondered if this would be her chamber after her marriage, but the thought didn't interest her long.

The maid smiled as she sat up, bobbed a curtsey. She was younger than Lettice and shy of her new duties as a lady's maid. She waited for Susannah to tell her what to do.

"Come, Sarah," Susannah said. "Help me to wash and dress. We have a big day ahead of us – we may as well get on with it."

It was less the day ahead though than the night to come after it she wanted to get behind her, the thought of the marriage bed filling her with dread. Perhaps once she had done it once, she reasoned, it might not be so bad the second time and the third and the fourth.

She stood placidly to let Sarah wash her with a cloth, the water warm against her skin, leaving goose bumps in its wake. They were silent as she dressed, the layers of the rich gown that they had ordered in Bristol slowly building, the deep blue brocade of the skirts, the lighter blue of the bodice and velvet sleeves that were trimmed with gold: if the dress had come from anywhere but the Haftons she would have loved it, but everything they touched felt tainted, and though the dress was gorgeous she still preferred the fine wool gowns she had worn at Abbey Leigh.

Finally dressed, she sat before the glass to let Sarah arrange her hair, trusting to the maid's skill and judgement, her own interest minimal. She watched the girl work, weaving delicate braids through a head-dress of finely wrought gold wire that was dotted with pearls. When it was done, she had to admit it was beautiful, and she smiled her thanks to the maid.

Then she rose, ready for the day ahead, squaring her shoulders, resolve tucked deep inside, the outward shell slowly hardening around it. Swallowing, she refused to let the images of her dreams haunt her daytime thoughts: Daniel could be nothing to her now – he was merely a memory that she needed to forget.

She rode the dappled mare to church and forced away all thoughts of the chestnut gelding she had so hoped would one day be hers. She wondered where Daniel was now, if he had forgotten her already, if he had found another woman to seduce.

Beside her Olivia chatted on, happy and oblivious to her sister's mood, remarking on the clothes and horses that surrounded them, asking about all the people in the household, and Susannah answered with a studied lightness that passed unnoticed. She had forgotten the sense of awe she had felt in her first days at Hafton Hall, the richness and splendour of it all, and her sister's excitement brought it back. If only she had known then where it would lead her, she thought with a rueful smile. What would have been her feelings then?

At the head of the column rode Lord and Lady Hafton, stately and serene, a groom at the head of Lady Hafton's horse, leading it carefully around the worst of the puddles and the ruts. Next came her mother with a lady's maid in attendance. She could see them exchanging brief comments and smiles; it seemed that her mother was well pleased with the progress of the day. She tried not to think what her father might have thought – he was not one to be easily impressed by grandeur, a more discerning eye at work.

Her cousins rode behind: she could hear the lilt but not the words of Edward's voice as it carried on the breeze towards her, though Eleanor's replies were inaudible. They had greeted her as a united pair this morning, Eleanor pale and drawn, and only a cold polite smile for her cousin as they exchanged a formal greeting, the first time they had met since Eleanor's confession. For his part, Edward had been courteous, resplendent in sumptuous gold brocade, a deep green cloak across one shoulder, a single feather in his hat. He had taken her fingers and made a deep bow above her hand, but behind the courtesy she had seen the sardonic amusement, and the confidence of becoming her master.

The steeple rose into view too quickly and within a few minutes they had reached the village, the party drawing to a halt at the gate of the church. Susannah hurried to dismount but Edward was too quick for her, his large hands about her torso, supporting her weight as she slid from the saddle. He stood before her for a moment longer than he needed, trapping her between his body and the horse but she turned her face away, refusing to give him the pleasure of her question.

"Thank you, Edward," she said as the moment dragged. "May we get to church now?"

His lips twisted into the semblance of a smile. "Of course," he replied. "It would hardly do to keep the bride waiting, now, would it?"

He stepped back to let her pass then took her hand, every bit the gentleman, escorting his bride to the altar. One of the maids from the Hall stepped forward with a bouquet for her to carry, white roses and rosemary. She wondered who had thought to make it, who at the Hall might have cared enough to think of it. A memory of the rosemary in the churchyard at Daniel's parents' grave touched her thoughts and she shrugged it away, refusing to let her eyes wander across the yard towards it, setting her strength against such thoughts.

Not here, she told herself. Not now.

She took the bouquet and smiled to the maid who curtseyed before moving back into the group of servants who were attending. The others stood aside to let them pass. She caught a smile from her mother and her sister, but only a cold look of disdain from her cousin. She swept past her, indifferent now, her fate sealed and upon her. This was not the wedding she had imagined for herself.

Villagers stopped in the road to look, surprised by the sight of the wedding. A Hafton marriage had always been a big affair in the past, with revels and feasting for all at the Hall, two days of celebrations. But this time no banns had been called and no invitations issued. Out of curiosity, in dribs and drabs they followed the wedding party into the churchyard, wondering at the suddenness of it, the rumours already beginning.

At the door of the church she halted, heartbeat hard with dread, and the sudden unbidden suspicion that Daniel might have been telling her the truth. Edward was still holding up her hand beside her and when she stopped, he turned his head towards her.

"Hold hard, coz," he murmured. "It will soon be over."

She smiled at the unexpected kindness, straightened herself, gave a small nod and together they stepped into the cool dim hush of the church. The vicar hurried down the aisle to greet them, inviting them towards the altar rail, gesturing towards the various pews for the guests. The uninvited villagers slid into the rows at the back. She could hear the murmur of their conversations at her back as she moved slowly through the church toward the altar.

Unwillingly, automatically, Susannah's eyes slid to the Gifford family pew as they passed it. She swallowed and forced her eyes to face forward, aware of the pressure of Edward's fingers on hers, the grip of ownership. Lord Hafton approached and took her hand from his son, marking her as his to give away. His hand felt the same as his son's, the strong bony fingers, the unforgiving hold. Edward stood at her right side, and next to him was a servant, Edward's gentleman of the chamber, to serve as best man.

The vicar, an elderly man with a kindly face, moved to stand before them. He waited for a hush to settle over the church, the excited conversation amongst the villagers slowly dying down. Then, with a smile of encouragement to ease the nerves of the couple before him, he began the words of the ceremony.

"Dearly Beloved, we are gathered here today in the sight of God and in the face of this congregation to join together this man and this woman in holy matrimony ..."

The voice droned on, the introductory words familiar from all the weddings she had witnessed at the church in Abbey Leigh across the years, words she had once thought were wondrous and special, words she had assumed she would one day hear herself with a sense of hopeful joy. Now her heart was leaden within her and there was neither hope nor joy. She forced her attention back to the voice of the vicar, watching the pale lips as they moved, the wobble of the fleshy jowls around them.

"Therefore," the vicar was saying, "if any man can show just cause, why they may not lawfully be joined together, let him now speak, or else hereafter forever hold his peace."

There was the customary silence. Then the sudden scrape of the door on the flagstones turned every head in the church towards it. Daniel appeared, striding to the centre aisle, boots ringing loud on the flagstones.

"I can show just cause," he said, his voice loud and harsh after the vicar's measured singsong tones. His dark eyes glimmered, his jaw worked with tension, and his boots and cloak and breeches were slick and wet with the mud of the road.

The breath caught in Susannah's throat and the bouquet she held in her hands dropped, forgotten, onto the flagstones at her feet. Beside her, Edward stared, shock registering across his pale face. She could feel him almost trembling with some emotion she did not understand.

"Indeed?" The vicar looked interested. He moved down the steps to hear more, and a shout came from Lord Hafton at Susannah's side. She swung round, startled, to see him puce with rage, pointing a trembling finger at Daniel as though the Devil himself had appeared.

"Get this man out of here!" Hafton began screaming orders to his servants, who exchanged bewildered glances but remained where they were, reluctant. Sir Daniel's presence and bearing brooked no challenge, and there was no one in the church who was willing to pit himself against him. The villagers turned to each other with excited curiosity, whispers passing between them.

"Do as I say!" Lord Hafton bawled, impotent with fury, but nobody moved except Eleanor, who shrank against her mother, the slight movement catching the edge of Susannah's gaze in the stillness.

The vicar moved along the aisle towards the intruders. "You can show just cause, Sir Daniel?" he asked. The tone of his voice suggested that, as yet, he did not quite believe it.

"Aye. I can," Daniel answered. His eyes sought Susannah's and held them, passion and determination flaring in their depths, a certainty in him now that refused to be denied. She returned his gaze with a steadiness that belied her inward turmoil.

"The woman you see before you, standing ready to wed Edward Hafton ..." Daniel said, gesturing towards her. He let his eyes roam the congregation, gaining their attention before he settled his gaze on the vicar, who regarded him with a curious wary interest. " … is not free to wed him. She is already contracted to be married to another. She is contracted to me. We handfasted here in this very church more than a month since. There was a witness."

Susannah's heart was racing, her mouth dry. What game was he playing? The contract had been nullified – his infidelity had seen to that. They had spoken together, and she had made herself plain. Did he hope now to claim her in spite of it? Sam stepped forward and cast her a brief and encouraging smile. She looked from one man to the other, baffled and wary. But she was ready to hear him, the uncertainty coiling with a new-lit hope inside her that she might yet be delivered from her fate as Edward's wife.

The vicar turned to Sam. "You saw this?" The surprise was clear in his voice.

"I did," Sam replied, nodding. "And I will swear to it."

The vicar sighed lightly and turned back towards the bride, still standing immobile at the step beside the groom. Absently, she lifted a strand of hair to its proper place behind her shoulder, her gaze still fixed on Daniel, trying to read the light in his eyes, struggling to understand.

"Is this true, Miss Archer?" the vicar asked. "Did you contract with this man?"

Briefly she turned her eyes from Daniel towards the vicar. She was still barely breathing, still unable to believe what was happening. She nodded but the words to explain failed to come, and she was aware of Edward still next to her, the cruel curl of his mouth, the deep breathing of his hatred. She shifted her gaze back to Daniel, entranced by his presence. He met her look and his lips lifted in the briefest of smiles towards her before he once more addressed his words to the vicar.

"But she believed she was free of it. She broke off the contract," Daniel said, "because of a lie."

"What lie?" the vicar asked.

"It is no lie!" Eleanor cried out from her place in the pew. "It is true. It is true, I swear it!" Her words were swallowed in her tears, and everyone in the church turned to watch her as she buried her face in her hands, her whole body wracked with sobs.

"What lie?" the vicar repeated.

A heavy hush fell, broken only by Eleanor's sobs. All eyes swung back to Daniel, waiting, expectant.

"It is no lie." Eleanor's final tearful plea hung across the silent congregation.

"It is a lie," Sir Daniel answered softly. His words were addressed to all in the church, but his eyes were levelled at Susannah. "I am not the father of Eleanor Hafton's child," he said.

Susannah blinked and her head inclined a fraction, still unsure – he had already argued his case before her. Why should she believe him now? The young man who stood at Daniel's shoulder stepped to the fore. She had barely noticed him, her attention so intent on Daniel, her eyes only on him.

"Francis," she murmured, recognition starting to penetrate the turmoil of her thoughts, understanding beginning to dawn.

Aston paid the bride-to-be no attention: his focus rested only on Eleanor, his face filled with pain at her distress, but she was unaware of him, her head still in her hands, her shoulders juddering with her tears. Daniel touched a hand to Aston's shoulder and the young man took two steps forward, squaring his shoulders against the looks of all the congregation. His eyes wandered the church, meeting every gaze that was trained on his face, letting them look and see who he was.

Daniel said, "This man is the father. His name is Francis Aston, and he used to be Lord Hafton's Gentleman of the Horse. This man made promises with Eleanor Hafton. This man lay with her and begot the child that she carries."

Susannah let her breath go with a gasp – she hadn't realised she was holding it. A recollection of Eleanor crossing the stable yard, furtive, secret. A remembered piece of straw in her fine blonde hair, and suddenly it all made sense.

Daniel looked towards her again, tilted his head in his own silent question, hope bright in the near-black eyes. Would she believe him now? She nodded, lips twitching into the beginnings of a smile, relief running through her blood. Another moment and she would have run to him, but Edward shocked her from her thoughts by wrapping long hard fingers about her wrist and dragging her towards him. She fought against his grip but his hand was too strong. She remembered his grasp from before, shuddering with the memory, but she was not alone now and she was not afraid.

"It is a lie," Edward snarled, turning to the vicar, tightening his hold on her arm. "Now marry us."

"I cannot marry you, Edward," she said, drawing herself up as best she could to face him, "I am pre-contracted to Sir Daniel, and there is no reason now to break it."

Her cousin's grip closed tighter, painful, like a vice. Viciously, he twisted her arm, so that she half fell at his feet, crying out with the pain, struggling against his hold.

"You will marry me," he hissed at her, bending down to place his mouth beside her face. "I need Abbey Leigh. I need it! I have debts to pay ..."

Daniel heard her cry, and in three strides he was at the steps. Edward saw him coming just in time and he dropped Susannah's arm, backing away from her, falling over his own feet in his haste, sprawling across the cold stone. Daniel got to him as he fell and grabbed the front of the golden doublet, bending over him, fist clenched, battling against the instinct to hurt him, to make him pay for all he had done, all he had intended to do.

Edward stared up in horror at the dark face above him, cringing, waiting for the blow.

"I am sorely tempted," Daniel breathed, "to beat you within an inch of your life ... it is no more than you deserve ..."

"Daniel?" Susannah's hand on his arm, her voice at his side, recalled him from his rage. "Daniel. I'm so sorry, Daniel."

He turned his head towards her and in the moment his attention was distracted, Edward squirmed away, scrambling to his feet, hurrying to join his family in the nave of the church. Daniel let him go and turned to face the woman at his side.

"Are you hurt?" He touched his fingers to her shoulders, resting them lightly, and his eyes searched her face. His own expression was taut with concern. "If he has hurt you, God help me he will pay."

"I'm fine," she said, her own eyes lifted to his, a small hopeful smile alight behind them. "I should have believed you … I'm so sorry …"

He said nothing but lifted his hand to touch her face, and she lowered her cheek against it, rubbing like a cat, her eyes still holding his as though the connection should never be allowed to break.

She had come so close to losing him. Too close.

She let him take her hand. Her wrist was red from Edward's grip and Sir Daniel lowered his gaze to look, running practised soldier's fingers across the weal that had already risen on the pale skin – she would have bruises there tomorrow. She flinched as he probed it with his thumb, and he looked up quickly.

"Is it painful?" he said.

"A little," she replied. "But it'll be fine. It is no more than a bruise."

He nodded, her slender arm still in his fingers, their faces close as they bent together above the injured limb. He slid his hand along her wrist to take her fingers in between his and lifted her hand to his mouth. The warmth of his lips against the cool skin of her fingers lit the familiar heat, and as his other hand slid beneath her hair to cup the back of her head, her lips parted in a smile of delight. Then he bent his head to kiss her, his lips brushing hers, lightly, briefly, with a promise of all that was to come.

A cough at her shoulder dragged her thoughts unwillingly from the pleasure of the kiss and they drew apart easily, naturally, though her hand stayed in his as they turned to face the interruption. It was Sam, hands raised, palms out in apology for disturbing them. "You need to listen to this," he said.

Daniel nodded. Then, with a light touch of reassurance to her cheek and a smile, he took her hand and led her with his friend towards the huddle that had formed around the Hafton pew. They said nothing, their attention drawn by the ugliness of the argument before them.

Lord Hafton was berating his daughter. "You lying whore!"

His arm was lifted in threat, her wails fighting to be heard above his ranting, and Aston's pleas for calm going unheard. Edward was watching with the same sardonic detachment he brought to everything until Eleanor, with a sudden surge of spirit, pointed a finger at her brother.

"This is his fault!" she screamed. "His idea. Not mine. I would have married Francis … I would have, but he made me lie!"

Lord Hafton fell silent, and all eyes shifted to the tall form of his son. In the pause, Aston stepped forward to put a comforting hand on Eleanor's shoulder and she turned in towards him, giving herself to the comfort of his arms.

"What does she mean?" Lord Hafton demanded. There was no sign of the uncontrolled fury of before – his voice was soft and low, the same tone of menace Susannah remembered from Eleanor's bedchamber. She shivered with the memory and wound her fingers more tightly through Daniel's. He glanced to her quickly in surprise and returned the pressure of her hand.

Edward shrugged. "She's just making things up. Trying to save herself."

Eleanor turned from her lover, calmer now, her decision made to no more bear her brother's guilt.

"Tell him, brother," she spat. "Or I will. I am not going to protect you anymore. You do not deserve it."

Her brother swallowed, looking round at the hostile waiting faces, Daniel among them, a darkness in his stare that threatened violence. Edward faced his father, but his eyes were averted and his mouth bore the familiar curve of distaste. Even in disgrace he bore himself with nonchalance and his voice carried no trace of remorse or of shame.

"I am … in debt, sir," he began. "Again. And this time for a far greater sum than I knew you would be willing to pay. Probably more than you could pay, even if you were willing. The card tables at Court are expensive, sir, and winners show losers no mercy." He gave a mirthless laugh. "Why d'you think I left Court? Did you think I liked the company at Hafton?"

His father stared; his son's arrogance even greater than his own.

"I needed Abbey Leigh," Edward said with a tilt of his head and a smile to Susannah. "I needed it to sell to keep myself out of Newgate."

Susannah could not suppress a quick gasp of breath. Daniel turned to her briefly and gave her an understanding glance.

"But Susannah seemed to have other plans," Edward went on. "And so, it seemed, had Gifford. I had to think of something to get rid of him." He shrugged, apparently unrepentant.

"Eleanor's condition fell rather conveniently ..." He flashed his sister a smile. "You played your part to perfection, Nell. My congratulations."

She returned him a stare of loathing.

"It almost worked," he said. "I was that close." He held up his thumb and forefinger with a hair's breadth between them.

Lord Hafton staggered back against the pew and sank down, struggling to take in what Edward had told him: his son soon to be in debtor's prison, his daughter either to bear a bastard or marry far below her. His world was crumbling round him, and he seemed to be the only one who cared.

In the silence that followed, Daniel's fingers tightened on Susannah's. "This is no concern of ours," he said. "Let us leave and get away from all of this. Come. We'll go to Gifford Court. I can send a man to Hafton for your things."

She nodded her agreement and looked up at him with a smile. He was right. The Haftons no longer mattered, their affairs were their own. Her life was with Daniel now, a life at Gifford Court, a life of shared evenings before the hearth as she had once imagined and hoped for, her dream coming true at last.

He slid his arm about her waist, drawing her towards him. Then, with a word to her family that they were leaving, she faced towards the door, tightened her own hold around him and together, side by side, they walked out from the church and into the warm summer morning.

PLEASE HELP OUT AND LEAVE A REVIEW!

Reviews are critical to getting books out there. So, if you enjoyed this book, please leave a review! Just a few words about what you liked will help other readers like you (and me) find and enjoy books like this one.

I do read every review.

I thank you in advance from the bottom of my heart!

ALSO BY SAMANTHA GROSSER

ANOTHER TIME AND PLACE

England 1944. In a tea room young American pilot Tom Blake watches a woman who is waiting for a friend. He isn't looking for love, but seeing Anna Pilgrim changes everything.

So begins a passionate affair.

Their happiness does not last. When Tom is shot down, he has no way of telling Anna that he is alive and struggling to return to her, while the pregnant Anna must face gossip and the wrath of her mother.

As the months pass, Anna begins to lose hope. How can she know that the thought of her is all that keeps Tom going on the long and arduous journey home?

"Gripping. A good story, well-told." Historical Novels Review

Available from all good online bookstores.

ABOUT THE AUTHOR

Historical fiction author Samantha Grosser has an Honours Degree in English Literature and spent many years teaching English both in Asia and Australia. Although she originally hails from England, she now lives on the sunny beaches of Sydney, Australia, with her husband, son, and a very small dog called Livvy.

For news and updates visit www.samgrosserbooks.com